The Kosher Delhi

IVAN WAINEWRIGHT

RedDoor

Published by RedDoor
www.reddoorpublishing.com

© 2019 Ivan Wainewright

The right of Ivan Wainewright to be identified as author of this
Work has been asserted by him in accordance with sections
77 and 78 of the Copyright, Designs and Patents Act 1988

ISBN 978-1-910453-78-0

Lyrics taken from 'Peggy Sang The Blues' by Frank Turner,
published by Pure Groove / Universal Ltd., 2011.
Published with permission

A CIP catalogue record for this book is available
from the British Library

Cover design: Rawshock Design

Typesetting: Tutis Innovative E-Solutions Pte. Ltd

Printed and bound in Denmark by Nørhaven

And she said
It doesn't matter where you come from
It matters where you go
No one gets remembered
For the things they didn't do

'Peggy Sang The Blues',
Frank Turner

London

1992

It's the height of a busy lunch serving at the restaurant. The kitchen is raucous, the volume turned up high, plates are flying out of the door.

I am at my station, preparing fish. I start to gut a sea bass. My fingers show a few knife scars from previous weeks' work, but I ignore them.

The sweat is pouring off us all.

'Cohen.'

I look up. The Head Chef is beckoning me with his finger. I put my knife down and wipe my hands on my whites.

'Now, Cohen,' Chef barks, and I hear him mutter under his breath, 'stupid Paki.'

'You're for it now, Cohen,' one of the other commis chefs says to me quietly.

I walk towards the Head Chef, who spins on his heels and leads me towards his office. I can hear Yvonne's voice in my head telling me to stand up to whatever bigoted or abusive remarks I receive from him. 'He's just a racist prick,' she's saying, 'Don't give in to him, Vik. Tell him he's a bully.'

She may be right, but she doesn't understand my position here. It's true I have been on the end of Chef's castigation since

I've been in the kitchen, but I'm not walking out. Not quitting. By not rising to his bait, by refusing to cower to him, that's how I'm not giving in.

But I am starting to wonder if there is a limit. Is there a point where I should hold up my hands and say enough is enough? Walk away from the restaurant? I consider this as I follow the Head Chef.

No. Not yet. I'm not capitulating. I've worked too hard to get here. I can handle his vitriol.

After all, they're just words.

Part 1

Leeds to Weston-Super-Mare

One

Considering all the things we did during our brief spell in Somerset that should have got us into trouble – smoking weed, pinching bottles of gin from the hotel, setting free the chickens from the farm – it's ironic that the act which did cause the police to come looking for us was an accident.

We had finished our shifts at the hotel early that evening and Yvonne had nicked a half-full bottle of London Dry from the bar. It was a bitter February night, and we drank the gin huddled in our usual corner at the end of the pier. Unsurprisingly, we were both pissed in no time. I had a few coins in my pocket, and once we had finished the bottle, Yvonne suggested we go to the offie and buy another. But the cash was all I had until my next pay cheque, and I didn't want to blow it on more alcohol. I tried to argue with her, but my protestations ended with Yvonne hugging me tightly and sliding her hand inside my jeans, and before I knew it she had grabbed the money out of my pocket and was running back up the pier towards the off-licence.

In the end, all we could afford were a couple of bottles of Holstein, and we slunk off towards a covered bus stop on the seafront to drink them. An old man was already hunched in the far corner of the shelter. Not that the dilapidated wooden structure provided much protection against the wind racing in off the channel.

I must have been more drunk than usual because I carried on arguing with Yvonne even as we were drinking the beer, something I would never normally have done because of my fear of upsetting her.

'What's your problem with me gaining experience in the hotel kitchen?' I demanded.

Yvonne took a swig of beer. 'You still dreaming of being a chef, Vik?'

'Why not?'

'There's more chance of me becoming prime minister.'

'There's more chance of that than you becoming a singer,' I yelled back.

Yvonne glared at me. 'Youse saying I cannae sing?'

'Margaret Thatcher can sing better than you.'

My words came out before I could stop them. Of course Yvonne could sing, she had a strong voice. I had heard her perform many times in Leeds pubs. But I was pissed off with her, wanted to get a reaction.

Yvonne didn't pause, and with a furious shriek, she hurled her bottle of Holstein at me. I saw it coming and ducked, but as I swerved out of the way, I watched the flight of its trajectory as it sailed through the air and hit the old man square on the forehead. It knocked him sideways and he fell, his head bouncing off the shelter and then against the concrete floor as he crumpled to the ground.

We stared in horror at his prone figure, expecting him to moan and try to get up, before I realised it was more serious. I edged up to where he lay and peered at his face. He wasn't moving. I leaned over him – his eyes were closed but he was still breathing.

'Jesus, Yvonne.'

'Wha'?' She looked at me uncertainly.

'You could have killed him. Look.'

'Ye must be joking. Stop pissing me aboot.'

Yvonne's Scottish accent always became more pronounced when she was angry. Or scared.

'I don't know –'

'Vik, he's not unconscious. The guy was already drunk.'

'Are you sure? Look at him. Maybe he's in a coma.' I hesitated. 'Christ, what are we going to do?'

'Well, feel for his pulse or something. '

'What do you think I am, a medic? I don't know how to do that.'

I looked around to see if anyone had witnessed us. Luckily there was nobody else on the windswept front, it was just a typical, dismal Wesson scene: all the shops had their shutters pulled down, the pier was dark and uninviting, damp fag-ends littered the floor of our bus shelter.

I knelt beside the old man, my fingers hovering above his face. I noticed what could have been the first shades of a bruise colouring the side of his head.

Yvonne reached down to grab my hand.

'Come on, Vik. Let's get out of here. Now.'

'But –' I looked up again. On the other side of the road was a man walking a dog, but apart from him there were only one or two people hurrying along with their scarves wrapped tight against the wind, and they didn't seem to have noticed us. The old man wasn't visible from that side of the street. 'We can't just leave him. Shouldn't we do something?'

Yvonne snatched her woollen hat from her pocket and pulled it down tightly over her short hair.

'He'll be fine. He's probably just fainted. I'm sure someone else will come along in a minute and check on him.'

'You think?'

'Look, let's just go, all right?'

We abandoned him. We ran back towards the hotel, praying noone would see us fleeing the scene, not even daring to pause at a phone box to call an ambulance, my fear outweighing my guilt. By the time the Hotel Neptune's façade loomed up ahead, I was having second thoughts: I should have called for an ambulance. Why hadn't I? But at least we had got away with it. As we reached the back entrance of the hotel, Yvonne turned and winked at me. We hadn't really killed some poor old duffer, we couldn't have. That sort of thing didn't happen to us.

When we were lying in bed that night, Yvonne was uncharacteristically quiet. I assumed she was thinking about what might have happened. She lay in my arms and occasionally rubbed her cheek against my chest, but barely said a word. I didn't know if I should break the silence or let her lie undisturbed; all that happened was that I got increasingly more tense. Pins and needles kicked in. Eventually, I heard Yvonne's breathing change and I knew she was falling asleep. I started to ease her body off my arm, but as I did so, she stirred and looked up at me sleepily.

'Still thinking about that old man, Vik?'

'I can't help it. We should have called an ambulance.'

'And then we'd have been questioned by the police and both lost our jobs here. He'll be fine, don't worry.'

'Are you sure?'

'We didn't kill him, Vik. Trust me.'

We didn't… Not I, we. Even though Yvonne had thrown the bottle.

'Vik, I have to ask you something.' Yvonne shifted her weight.

'OK…'

'I can…rely on you, can't I? If it comes down to it?'

'What do you mean?'

For a few seconds, Yvonne's eyes fluttered shut again, but then she turned her face towards me. 'Would you kill someone for me, Vik?'

'Are you serious?!' I let go of her for an instant. 'Right now?'

'No, not now,' Yvonne murmured. 'Not at this moment. But sometime in the future, if I asked.'

'Um…'

'I'm deadly serious, Vik. I need to know if you would do that for me. If I can rely on you.'

'Well, I…'

I didn't say anything. Was she serious?

Yvonne waited for a moment. 'Well, Vik, would you?'

I squeezed her more tightly. 'I would never let anyone hurt you, Yvonne. I promise.'

We lapsed back into silence. After a few minutes, I heard a gentle snore, and I let out a long breath as Yvonne drifted back to sleep.

Her question remained unanswered.

But I had thought about it. I had thought about it for over thirty seconds, and for all that time I wondered whether I could say no. It took me that long to come to a conclusion. Yvonne had that kind of power over me.

'I would do anything else for you,' I whispered in the dark.

I forgot all about her question for three and a half years.

Leeds, March 1990

I met Yvonne at an Original Landlords' gig in The Fox and Firkin, a short walk from my shared-house in Burley. I was waiting for one of my house-mates to get me a beer, half-thinking that Dave would come back any second and tell me they wouldn't serve him because he looked under-age, even wearing his faded Wedding Present T-shirt. We were both twenty, but whereas I never got challenged about my legal status, Dave still had to carry his ID.

The last thing I expected was for a mesmeric young woman to chat me up. In fact, when Yvonne did approach me with her short, punky peroxide hair, multiple rings in each ear, as well as her nose, I assumed she was trying to take Dave's chair. She sat down beside me in her ripped, black T-shirt and short skirt without even asking, and gave me a wicked smile.

'So, your nose. I noticed it was big but is that because you are Jewish, Punjabi or just because you have a big hooter?'

Other men might have laughed at that or told her to fuck off, but I did neither. I sat there somewhat stupefied, unable to take my eyes off her.

'Or is that too personal a question?' Yvonne added.

Well, yes! Of course it is.

'No, no. It's fine,' I stammered.

'Good. So?' Yvonne asked again. 'Oh and by the way, can I bum a cigarette?'

And that was that. She had got me. I managed to croak a few lines about my family history – Jewish father, Indian mother, mixed up heritage – to which Yvonne nodded sagely and blew rings of smoke. Then she asked me my name, told me hers, enquired where I lived, and finally told me to wait there and not to move. Jumping up, she pushed her way through the throng at the bar and disappeared from view for a few seconds. Then she was back at my table and reaching out towards me. I looked at her blankly.

'Your hand, dummy,' she said kindly and held up a biro. 'Give me yer hand.'

I held out my left hand and she pulled it towards her, twisting my arm around and scribbled some numbers on the back of my wrist.

'Call me,' she said succinctly, 'we'll go out sometime.'

I watched her walk back to her friends, but she didn't look back once.

I didn't call Yvonne after the Landlords' gig. I woke up the next morning back in Burley, still with her phone number tattooed on my arm, but I knew she hadn't been serious about me calling her; why would someone like her want to go out with someone like me?

Two weeks later, however, there was a knock on our front door, and there stood Yvonne, arms crossed with a pissed off look on her face.

'I thought you were going to call me?' she said.

I didn't know what to say, as per our first encounter; I just stood there with the door open. Not getting any response, Yvonne tutted and strode past me into the house.

'Were you at the Poll Tax protest last week?' she called as she marched into our shared lounge. 'You must have been there, right? No?' I shook my head as she spun round. 'Jesus, Vik, we could have done with yer support. We need to show Thatcher that she cannae just push us around with something which is so fundamentally unfair. Look at me – I'm twenty-one fer Chrissake, and I can't afford to pay it. Imagine what it would be like for a pensioner.'

We went out that evening to the pub and by closing time I was captivated. And for some reason, she still appeared interested in me. In no time, I was getting the induction course in the ways of Yvonne Anderson. This involved discovering her favourite haunts, starting with the more disreputable pubs and clubs of Leeds and, after a couple of nights in my room, moving on to her preferred, more extreme places for having sex, whether that was indoors, outdoors or on moving transport.

I was renting a room in a shared house when I met Yvonne. My income was a pittance, gleaned from a combination of cold calling for a 'marketing firm' and a few lunchtime shifts at our local fish n chip shop on the Kirkstall Road; but at least that meant I got a free meal if there were any leftovers.

Yvonne, after she graduated from Leeds University, lived in a squat west of Hyde Park. She spent most of her days distributing protest leaflets, in deep political discussions with other squatters, or volunteering with a local women's charity. She was always circumspect about where she got her money, but somehow she always seemed to have enough cash for a couple of pints or a few grams of weed.

Yvonne did make a few quid playing guitar in Leeds pubs and she had an occasional spot as guest vocalist for a local band called The Young Bilkos, who played in some of the more ignominious pubs in the city. On one occasion when she was singing with the band, one young lad came right up in front of her, and winked and waggled his tongue. I was sure she was going to clock him, but Yvonne just smiled and beckoned him towards her with a finger. The lad grinned, and as he got closer to her, Yvonne pulled him provocatively towards her by his shirt collar and then abruptly pulled her neck back and headbutted him. Hard. The guy fell backwards, screaming while Yvonne just flicked her earring and carried on singing. The audience gave her a standing ovation at the end of the song.

At least the aftermath of that event gave me the opportunity to confront Yvonne about something which had been on my mind. We were back in my bedroom after the gig and we were discussing what had happened.

'Didn't it hurt?' I asked her.

'Of course it fuckin hurt,' Yvonne spat, 'it hurt like fucking crazy, but I wasn't going to let him see that. The prick deserved it.' She stubbed her cigarette out. 'Now hand me the Rizlas, will you. Maybe a spliff will stop my head pounding.'

She rolled a joint, and we lay on our backs on my bedroom floor and smoked it. Then she rolled on top of me, pulled off my T-shirt and we had long and slow, weed-enhanced sex for the next hour.

'Jeez, Vik,' Yvonne said happily after our session, lying naked with her back across my legs, 'I am so glad I met you. You are so good for me after a day like today.'

I eased myself up on to my elbows, trying not to disturb Yvonne's position and reached for my cigarettes. When Yvonne came out with statements like that, all I really wanted to do was to press pause on my life and not move on. But it also worried me that one day she wouldn't say such things; after all, I was nothing like her, I didn't come from the same background as her, and I was sure she could have anyone else if she wanted to. I took a deep breath. There was something I had to do.

'Yvonne, can I ask you a question?'

'As long as the question is, do you want to have sex again.'

For a split-second I almost said it was but then I shook my head and steadied myself, and the words tumbled out of my mouth. 'When you first met me in the Firkin, why did you come and talk to me?'

Yvonne frowned and I thought she looked disappointed. I tensed. I had wanted to ask this for months, but I had been afraid that if I did, then she would suddenly realise that she shouldn't be with me, and just walk away. Now I had asked it, maybe I was right – perhaps she would jump up and disappear from my life. But she stayed where she was and pursed her lips.

'Well, the truth is that one of my friends dared me to say hello to you. I did it for a bet.'

I felt my stomach lurch. 'Really?'

'No, of course not dummy.' Yvonne sat up and smacked one of my feet. 'I wouldn't do that to anyone.'

'Oh. Right.'

'Look. You weren't to know of course, but I had seen you in the Firkin before, with your mate and I...I wanted to come over and say hello. We clearly shared the same taste in music as we were at the same gigs and you looked...interesting.'

'Interesting? Interesting good?'

'Oh, Vik, for fuck's sake. Yes, interesting good. If you want me to say it, then yes, I quite fancied you. In case you hadn't noticed, you're not like many boys who live round here. OK?'

'OK.' I grinned. I couldn't help it. 'Great.'

'And what I also found,' Yvonne continued more evenly, 'was a guy who is calm and modest, and articulate, and nothing like the sort of boys I had been with before. You intrigued me. Oh, and you're damn good in bed.'

'Oh, that's all...good, I guess.'

'Yes, it's very good! Christ, Vik, where has all this come from? Are you not happy with me? Is that what you're saying?'

'No! No.' I leaned forwards and grabbed Yvonne's hands. 'Of course not. I love being with you. I couldn't be happier. But I, I'm not always sure why you're with me.'

Yvonne slid across the floor and wrapped her legs around my waist, so our faces were inches apart. 'Vik. I am so happy I am with you. I want to be with you, and I am not about to run off with someone else if that's what you're worried about. OK?'

'OK. Great.'

'Good. Now. What about that other question…?'

I grew up in Harrogate, and being the late seventies, my older brother, Ajay and I were the only mixed-race children at our school. This, of course, meant that Ajay and I were on the end of some bullying, but the racism was more about words (Paki, Yid, darkie), and I brushed off the taunts, put up with the odd shove, ignored the real trouble-makers and kept to myself. But being called Ajay and Vikram Cohen made us stand out and even gave one or two of our teachers the chance to have some bigoted fun at our expense.

Ajay was two years older than me and studied much harder than I did, and he went on to Middlesex Polytechnic in London. I ended up with four O levels and a couple of CSEs, didn't bother with A levels and instead looked for work immediately after leaving school.

After a couple of short, dead-end jobs, I got a position as a waiter in a Harrogate café, where the head chef was as renowned for his tantrums as much as he was for his outstanding cooking. One Saturday evening after the third assistant chef had walked out mid-service, I talked the café manager into allowing me to work in the kitchen. There followed four of the most intense hours of my entire teenage life as I tried to follow chef's instructions without cutting myself, leaving out a key ingredient or poisoning any of the customers. I loved every minute. I had to work hard to persuade the head chef to keep me on, but he agreed, and although he continued to shout at me for the next three years, I let most of his tirades go in one ear and out the other, concentrating instead on learning how to cook. It may not have been gourmet cuisine, but it gave me a solid apprenticeship in cooking and the ways of a commercial kitchen.

By my nineteenth birthday, however, there was very little keeping me in Harrogate. Ajay was graduating poly and seemed intent on staying in London; and although I was comfortable working at the café, I was very aware that I wasn't making any new friends or broadening my horizons. Leeds seemed exciting with many more people my age, and compared to its northern cousin, positively cosmopolitan with its many restaurants. So I upped sticks and left for Yorkshire's largest city. Where I met Yvonne.

Weston-Super-Mare, August 1990

We moved to Weston-Super-Mare because of a stray copy of the *Western Gazette* Yvonne told me she had picked up on the bus. She had noticed the job ads and the Hotel Neptune's 'Positions Available' column had leaped out at her.

'I'd love to live by the coast again and I've always wanted to work in a hotel,' Yvonne told me when she showed me the advert that evening. 'It's perfect. We should definitely do this.'

'OK…' I said, less certain. 'But why should we go to… Weston-Super-Mare of all places, that's hundreds of miles away. Why can't we get a job in a hotel here in Leeds?'

'Come on, Vik. Do you really want to waste yer life away up here? There's so many other places to see. So much else we can do! And what better way than going away altogether?' She stood close to me and ran her fingernail up the inside of my thigh. 'Think about it. You and me, working together, in a hotel – with all those beds. Doesn't that sound enticing?'

We hitched from Leeds to Weston-Super-Mare with all our possessions stuffed into two battered old rucksacks, a five hour, four ride ordeal; God knows what we smelt like when we arrived. We grabbed a burger in a seafront café, splashed water on our faces from their toilets, and then went for the interviews. Yvonne got a job as a chambermaid and I as a porter. The best thing about it was that it was a live-in job and so we got a room included. We would barely earn any real money, but that didn't bother us too much. We made enough for a weekend joint and a six-pack of Holstein – what else did we need?

The Hotel Neptune was a sprawling Victorian property on the seafront with classically decorated bedrooms. By the time we left our jobs there, Yvonne had persuaded me to have sex with her in thirty-four of them. I was always nervous we would get caught, but that was, of course, half the thrill.

I grew to enjoy my time at the Hotel Neptune. Not because I liked carrying around luggage, but because I was working in a fairly classy hotel (at least by British seaside resort standards) with a comparatively refined restaurant. Whereas the kitchen at the Harrogate café had been compact and simple, the Hotel Neptune kitchen was the height of ambition for any local chefs. I loved everything about it: from the exquisite aromas to the enormous iron saucepans which could hold enough soup for a banquet. I loved the pans and skillets, the baking trays and fish kettles, the vast array of knives, the funnels, rollers, graters, peelers, whisks. I could scan the high shelves of jars, boxes, bags, the lines of herbs and the racks of vegetables, and find excitement in them all. I was fascinated by the walk-in fridge (despite the stories of people being shut in there for hours for initiation rites) and the piles of raw meat which the chefs got through. I even found stacks of plates and cutlery interesting.

But what I adored most was watching the chefs prep the food. Their chopping and dicing skills, their apparently casual, sweeping choice of herbs and seasonings, their shouts and cries to each other, and the ultimate, meticulous tastings. I would watch the head chef wander over to a sauce one of his sous chefs was preparing, and as he dipped a spoon in and held it to his nose and lips, it was as if I was watching a film in slow motion. At such moments, all other sounds subsided, and the world seemed to stop as he would cast judgement over the dish in question. Then with a nod or a shake of his head, the whole bustle of the kitchen would rush back up at me double-time, and the sounds of new orders and doors slamming would crash into my ears again.

I was eager to see if I could learn from the cooks at the Hotel Neptune, but the chefs were very protective of their hard-won territory, even after I stressed my culinary experience in Harrogate. But I persisted, with a combination of flattery, ceaseless questions and constant badgering. I even helped out with the washing-up for two days when one of the regular plongeurs didn't come in. Finally, one quiet day, the new sous chef agreed to show me some modern techniques I hadn't heard of, including sous-vide cooking and blackening fish, and introduced me to fresh ingredients and dishes I had never seen before; the sesame-crusted tuna was a revelation to me. He told me I was a quick learner, 'maybe because you are left-handed like me,' he said with a wink.

The kitchen staff comprised of many temporary staff like us, employed for the summer season. Some, like us, were kept on over the winter. Consequently, we didn't make many friends during our seven months at the Hotel Neptune, but we did strike up a relationship with the concierge, Gary.

Gary was openly gay and most of the time didn't give a hoot about what other people thought or said about him It annoyed Yvonne more than Gary or me when the occasional guest called him a poof within hearing distance or referred to me as a Paki, without caring that I was standing right behind them with their bags. I just let it wash over me, which frustrated Yvonne even more. But I was more concerned about keeping my job, and Gary just laughed at them behind their back.

While I was trying to improve my cheffing skills in the hotel's kitchen, Yvonne was busy trying to score weed. She was always on the lookout for dealers. In Leeds, she had known all the right people, and her squat smelt like a continuous pot party. But in Weston-Super-Mare she didn't have any contacts, and although the odd staff member in the Hotel Neptune gave her an occasional joint, she needed a regular supply. It seemed to me that she couldn't go more than a day without a spliff or the hit from a bong. She had been all in favour of growing our own on the hotel premises until it was pointed out to her that someone else had done that the previous year. They had been kicked out of the Hotel Neptune in five seconds flat when they were discovered with their plants in a sheltered corner of the hotel roof.

One late Saturday afternoon we were between shifts, and drifted down to the pier. Just outside the entrance, a busker was playing the guitar. He was tall, a bit gangly, dressed in Lennon glasses and a multi-coloured, three-piece dress suit. His guitar case in front of him, where the public could throw their coins seemed sadly meagre in its contents. He played Dylan, Fleetwood Mac, one or two obscure Beatles songs. I was surprised that Yvonne wanted to stay, but then she tapped her nose, and I knew that she had smelt marijuana in the air.

After a particularly melancholy version of 'I Am the Walrus', the busker put down his guitar and produced three fire-sticks. These he proceeded to set alight and began a fire-juggling act instead. This drew a few pedestrians, and several children who cajoled their parents into waiting with them. His patter was sound, and he got continuous laughs during his short set. He finished off with a classic bit of fire eating and then gave a bow.

'Thank you, ladies and gentlemen. My name is Miles High, and if you have enjoyed what you saw then please throw a few bits of paper at me, preferably those with the Queen's head on, or if you haven't got any of those, coins will do fine.'

He received a few claps and did get some coins thrown in his guitar case, and I think I saw a five-pound note. Yvonne approached him as he was gathering up his proceeds.

'Good act,' she said with a big smile.

'Thanks.' Miles studied Yvonne. She was wearing her T-shirt with a photo of the Unknown Protester from Tiananmen Square. 'Nice,' he said, nodding at her top. 'He was a brave man.'

'He was. It's hard to believe noone knows who he was.'

'Maybe the Chinese made him disappear.'

'Aye, could be.'

The conversation ceased. Miles looked at me for the first time. 'Is there something I can do for you?' he asked somewhat warily.

'I was just wondering,' Yvonne said sweetly, 'whether you could help us. We're looking for something a bit special to smoke this evening and, well, I wondered if you might know where we could buy some.'

Miles crossed his arms. 'I might do. Or I might have no idea what you're talking about. I've been tapped up by the police before, you know. How do I know you're not –'

'Oh come on,' Yvonne interrupted. 'How many coppers do you know in Weston-Super-Mare disguised as a Scot and an Indian Jew? Now, do you know where we can score some weed or not? Cos if not then we'll just fuck off and find someone who does.'

For a moment, I wondered if Yvonne had gone too far, before a big smile broke out on Miles' face.

'Miles Twelvetrees,' he said and held out his hand.

'Not Miles High?' Yvonne enquired.

'Surprising that, eh,' Miles replied and laughed. 'Come on, I think I can help you.' Then he turned to me. 'I assume you know her well or you wouldn't dare be with her. So can I ask you, is she always this cocky?'

'Just when it comes to sex and drugs,' Yvonne cut in.

Miles laughed again. And that is how we became friends. That evening, he took us to a back-street pub which we didn't even know existed, and introduced us to a couple of men who could sell Yvonne what she wanted, and then we got drunk together at the pub before going back to Miles' flat to get stoned. It was a pattern we were to repeat over many weekends while we lived in Somerset.

Miles lived in his own converted basement flat in a Victorian terrace, below his grandmother. She was almost stone deaf so we could play records way into the night, and Yvonne and Miles could jam together on Miles' guitars without worrying about the volume. I loved his home, partly because he always kept it so warm with the gas fire pumping out heat and semi-toxic fumes the whole time, and also because of the huge bean bags he owned, which we lounged around on all night, smoking his weed and doing poor impressions of Keith Richards or Axl Rose. He also had a second bedroom with a crappy old futon where he let Yvonne and me crash if we were too gone to make it back to the hotel.

Miles would get very deep when he was stoned. 'What you doing here, man?' he asked me several times, and I would repeat how we had left Leeds to get a job at the Hotel Neptune, after Yvonne had seen their ad.

'Yeah, but what are you doing here?' he'd slur. 'Not Yvonne. You said you want to be a chef.'

Well, obviously I am running around after this weird Scottish girl who I am so intoxicated with that I am sitting in a basement flat, hundreds of miles from my family, smoking weed and hoping she will give me a smile once in a while. I didn't say.

'What do you want to do with the rest of your life, Vik?' he'd ask gravely as he took a long drag of his joint.

I would shrug. 'I love food and I love being with Yvonne. I want to learn to cook. I don't know how to make that happen, though.'

'You need to find out, man, you need to,' Miles would say.

'Do I?'

'Yeah, man, you've gotta, gotta, um…' and then his eyes would glaze over and he'd half close them for a few moments before appearing to wake up again – then he'd have another puff and begin a completely new conversation about the importance of music or how he wanted to visit Thailand because that was 'the only place where you could truly find yourself'.

Gary occasionally joined us at Miles' flat on an evening, although he would mainly drink vodka or rum rather than share a J with the rest of us. 'Weed gives me terrible headaches,' he explained.

One evening, when Yvonne had a late shift at the Hotel Neptune, the rest of us decamped to Miles' basement and started drinking/smoking without her. Miles was soon high and happily strumming old Rolling Stones numbers on his guitar, and while I watched him, Gary plumped himself down beside me on a bean bag.

'So, Vik. I've been meaning to ask. Why did you decide to leave Leeds and come down to this stinking hole in Somerset?'

'It's not a hole, Gary, I quite like it.'

'I think you're taking the piss, mate. But that's beside the point. Why d'yer come?'

I shrugged. 'Like I told Miles, there were jobs here, and it's by the sea.'

'Really.' Gary took a slug of Smirnoff. 'Vik, I like you. I don't want to see you get hurt. That's why I'm asking you this.'

'OK, but…Why would I get hurt?'

'You're crazy about Yvonne, aren't you?' I nodded. 'But why did you actually leave Leeds?'

I cast my mind back. 'Because Yvonne saw an ad for jobs in the *Western Gazette*.'

'That was quite convenient, wasn't it?'

'What do you mean? Yvonne saw the hotel openings, and we just went for them.'

Gary leaned closer and rattled the ice cubes in his glass. 'And you don't think it was strange that Yvonne found these jobs in the *Western Gazette*, a newspaper that wasn't even your local rag?'

'She found a copy on the bus.'

'And so far from where you were living.'

'Wait a minute.' I sat upright and stubbed out my cigarette. 'What are you saying? She told me she wanted to live by the coast, try working in a hotel.'

'So she wasn't working in a hotel in Leeds?'

'No. She helped out at a local charity.'

We fell silent for a moment. Miles carried on playing along to the Stones' 'Wild Horses'.

'Let me ask you,' Gary began again. 'Where do you think Yvonne got her money when you were both living in Leeds?'

'Her singing? Working in the pub?'

'And that would be enough for all her drink and drugs 'n stuff?'

'Well, she was living in a squat, she didn't need much cash.' I paused and then shrugged. 'Yvonne could always look after herself. I never thought about it.'

'I know. Why would you? You wanted to believe in her.' Gary put his hand on my arm.

'Are you trying to tell me that she was lying to me?'

Gary shook his head. 'I've met people like Yvonne before,' is all he would say. 'Other people might wear rose-tinted specs but...' His voice trailed off.

I nodded self-consciously and stared at the floor. Did Gary know about the gin she'd stolen from the bar? Could we trust him to keep this to himself? I thought about it for days, and less than a week later, I very nearly did ask Yvonne what she thought Gary might have meant. We were sitting on the pier, huddled together having a smoke and sharing a can of Heineken, and I was just about to raise the subject when Yvonne leaned across and kissed me. And the moment was gone. I never did talk to her about my conversation with Gary.

Two

That winter, I continued to receive my crash course in the politics of Yvonne Anderson – there was a lot for her to pontificate about. Margaret Thatcher had been in power for eleven years by the end of 1990, and Yvonne and many others had spent much of that time hating all that she stood for. So when it looked like her time was coming to an end, first with Geoffrey Howe resigning as deputy prime minister and then with Michael Heseltine challenging her as leader of the Conservative party, Yvonne couldn't contain her glee. 'It's everything she fucking deserves,' she told me happily.

At the turn of the New Year, the coalition forces led by the United States entered Kuwait in Operation Desert Storm. Supposedly to liberate the Kuwaitis from Saddam Hussein's invasion of the tiny country. Not that Yvonne was having any of that. 'They wouldn't be rushing into some small African country if a foreign force invaded their neighbour. No, it's all about the oil and protecting the West's oil supply. That's all that Bush and Major care about.'

In February, we celebrated my twenty-first birthday with a heavy evening of drinking at Miles' and getting stoned late into the night. Miles had a bootleg tape he had been given of a new Mancunian band called Oasis, which blew us all away. Apart from sex, drugs and politics, Yvonne's other main love was music. The

'Bristol Sound' was breaking through at that time, and bands like Massive Attack and Smith & Mighty were playing small music venues and underground clubs in the nearby city.

There was also a new movement in Bristol led by a street artist who called himself Banksy and Yvonne loved it whenever we found a new graffiti image which he had sprayed on the walls of the town. The combination of art, politics and Banksy's anti-establishmentarian approach ticked all her boxes.

One Sunday evening in February when Yvonne, Gary and I all had the evening off, we went out together with Miles. We had decided on the Anchor for a few drinks, a relaxed boozer, mostly colonised by locals and resident workers. We knew the landlord, Geoff, pretty well and he didn't mind the odd bit of dealing as long as we didn't use it in the pub itself.

Miles, Gary and Yvonne started drinking quite heavily, and were in the middle of an argument about whether Neil Kinnock was the best person to be leading the Labour party now, when a group of seven or eight London lads walked in. My friends seemed oblivious to their entrance, but I remembered that they had been especially loud and obnoxious when they had checked into the Hotel Neptune for their stag weekend the day before. I saw them glance over at us, but after buying their drinks, they stayed by the bar and began knocking back their pints double-time. Maybe this was just pre-loading at the start of their pub crawl.

A few minutes later, Gary announced it was his round, but to get to the bar he had to pass through the London group. As soon as he reached their space, he must have recognised them as the well-dressed gang who were staying at our hotel. But by that time, they had noticed him. I watched one of the lads deliberately bump into him, nearly knocking our empty glasses out of his hands. He spat unpleasantly at Gary.

'Oi, watch where you're going, you idiot.'

'Sorry, mate,' Gary replied. 'You all right?'

The lad glared. 'Fuckin' faggot.'

All the other lads laughed. Gary, being Gary, ignored them and nodded at the barman. The atmosphere, however, was shifting. Yvonne looked over.

Two more lads came up on either side of Gary. 'You buying us a drink as well, mate?' one of them asked.

Gary glanced at him. 'I wasn't planning to.'

The lad poked Gary in the shoulder. 'Well seeing as you just spilt my friend's pint then maybe you should do, eh.'

'I didn't touch his drink,' Gary started, but he didn't get any further than that before the lad pushed him against the bar. A few other drinkers were watching now, but nobody made a move to intervene.

The London lad continued. 'Yeah? Well I said you did, you queer. So buy him a fucking drink now. And while you're about it, you can buy the rest of us a drink too. Right, lads?'

The rest of his group cheered. 'Go on, Spike,' one of the group called out, 'Let the shit-stabber have it.'

With hindsight, I suppose I could have run outside the pub and asked for help, or I could have grabbed Miles and stood up to defend Gary, but my gut instinct was to avoid escalating conflict. I knew Gary could talk his way out of anything, and these guys were probably just front. I turned to Yvonne to ask her what she thought, but it was at this point that I realised Yvonne was no longer sitting beside me; instead, she was marching purposefully towards the bar.

'Hey,' she called as she approached the lads at the bar, 'Have youse got a problem or something?' The conversations in the rest of the pub started to dwindle as Yvonne walked up to Gary. 'Take your fucking hands off my friend now,' she said vehemently to the one called Spike.

Without taking his hands off Gary, Spike looked Yvonne up and down. 'Well, what have we got here?' he grinned. 'You a dyke yourself, love? Or you just hang around poofs for fun?' More laughs from his friends.

'Don't worry about it, Yvonne,' Gary said quickly, 'it's fine.'

'It absolutely is not fine,' Yvonne countered. 'This prick needs to learn a lesson.'

It was a courageous thing to say. Spike tensed and several of his mates stepped forwards.

Miles nudged me. 'Vik, I think we had better go and help.' I nodded and we stood up, although I couldn't imagine what difference we would make.

Yvonne, however, didn't seem to care that she was outnumbered and stuck her face right into Spike's. For a moment I thought she was going to headbutt him. Instead, she just sneered at Spike.

'He's a better man than all of you,' she announced. 'And if you don't take yer hands off him now then you'll find out what kind of woman I am. And trust me,' she lowered her voice, 'you dinna want tae do that.'

Ignoring Gary, Spike moved closer to Yvonne. She didn't even flinch.

'Is that right? Well, I reckon I could show you what kind of woman I like and just what I like to do to women like you.' So saying, he grabbed Yvonne's right arm, but Yvonne immediately shrugged him off and pushed him hard in the jaw, not a punch, but enough to make him step back. Spike looked shocked, felt his face and then lurched back towards Yvonne. 'You're going to wish you hadn't done that,' he snarled.

'Oh, I don't think so,' Yvonne replied, and as Spike reached out to grab her, Yvonne ducked and then without pausing brought her knee up right into his groin. His howl made every man in the pub wince.

Geoff, the landlord, had seen enough. He stepped in and took control, addressing the prone Spike. 'Right. You and all your mates, get out. Go on. Out.' He stood over the still groaning Spike as his mates helped him up. 'And don't show your faces round here again, understand?'

Yvonne stood stock still as they left, and as I went up to put my arm around her, she held up her hand. 'Give me a moment, Vik, OK?'

I stopped and nodded, standing beside her, rubbing my hands together nervously. I was genuinely surprised by her anger and the fact that she had got involved, and so readily; I had never seen her confront a group of abusive men before.

Later in bed, I said this to Yvonne. She nodded slowly. 'Yeah, well, I had to do it, you know.'

'What you did was really brave,' I comforted her, 'supporting Gary like that. It was the right thing to do. But there are other ways to stand up to people like that without risking a punch in the face. You could have asked Geoff for help, or got him to call the police.'

Yvonne stayed quiet for a while after I had spoken. 'It could have been too late by then,' she said finally.

'Weren't you scared?' I asked.

'Of course I was scared. I was bricking it. But you have to stand up to divs like those guys, whether they're homophobes or racist dickheads.'

'I know.'

'There were eight of them for Christ's sake. All ganging up against ma friend.'

'Miles and I would have helped, we would have –'

'But I had to do it. I had to,' Yvonne carried on, ignoring my reassurance. 'Because, because…' And then, for the first time since I had known her, I thought I saw tears in Yvonne's eyes. 'You see,' she continued, 'something happened in Leeds, before you knew me, and I didn't do anything then, and I…I have always regretted that. And then also, also back home. Back in Inverness. With Kir…Kir…'

And then she did cry, burying her head in her pillow, her whole body shaking as she sobbed. I waited for several seconds before gently touching her shoulders, gradually trying to smooth her hair and stroke her arms. It was the first time I had ever seen her so vulnerable.

'Kir? Who's that?'

Yvonne shook her head. She stopped crying after a while and lay back in my arms. Before she went to sleep, she murmured one more thing which I never forgot. 'You think I'm strong, Vik. You think I'm tough. I'm just like everyone else. We're all scared really. We all want to be looked after.'

After Yvonne went to sleep I lay awake for a long time. Yvonne hadn't accused me of letting her down, but the unanswered question lay between us: why hadn't I stood up immediately to defend Gary or Yvonne?

Yvonne was invariably amazed at how apathetic I was towards racism and religious intolerance. Only a few weeks into our relationship, she had raised the subject of how bigotry was at the core of so much of the world's problems.

'Do you realise that until Mandela was released earlier this year, that your colour would mean that the two of us couldn't travel around together in South Africa.'

'Do you want to do that?' I asked.

'That's not the point!' Yvonne spluttered in exasperation. 'The point is that apartheid would have stopped us, but his actions are changing that. Don't you think that's important?'

Well, yes, of course I saw that that was important. But I couldn't relate to it.

Or Yvonne might say: 'I'm glad you don't believe in God, but it's so vital that those who do believe are allowed to do so without being spat at or kicked. And I can't believe with your background, that you don't feel the same.'

I would just shrug and murmur something about keeping myself to myself. Which would cause Yvonne to start up again about my parents and my heritage and why I should fucking well sort myself out.

My parents and heritage... Yes, OK, I can understand why Yvonne would think like that; after all, my father was Jewish and my mother, Indian. Both believed in their own religion and the culture surrounding it, but clearly, as they married each other, neither found it so critical that it meant they couldn't love someone from another background, someone else who might believe something entirely different when it came to God.

My father was the second youngest of six children, born in Yorkshire in 1937, thanks to his parents moving north from the East End of London. My mother was raised in Kenya but widowed when she was still a teenager, and she and her siblings left Kenya in 1963 to settle in Leicester. Only her brother, Neel left Britain and went to live somewhere in America. His 'defection' as it was seen by his family, was rarely discussed when

Ajay and I were growing up, but when we asked about him, we were left in no doubt that it had been an acrimonious departure and no one in the family approved of his decision.

My parents met when my father visited Leicester on business. By all accounts they experienced a crash-bang moment of love-at-first-sight, and married a few months later. My father was twenty-nine and my mother twenty-four. My mother moved up to Yorkshire and shocked all the locals with their mixed-race marriage. For Ajay and me, being brought up in an Indian-Jewish household meant that religion was always around us, and never around us. We couldn't escape either culture, there were so many things to remind us of our background: our skin colour, our mother's skin colour, that I was circumcised, religious festivals (even if we didn't observe them), and the fact that other people just weren't like us or didn't like us. And, of course, the food – both religions love their cooking and it's a central part of their festivities. We did 'celebrate' Hanukkah and Passover in so much that we went to one of my father's brothers for meals, and we enjoyed Diwali with my aunts and uncles on my mother's side.

My parents never forced either religion on us, never made us go to a synagogue or a temple, and answered the few questions I had about both faiths in a very matter-of-fact way.

Yvonne was probably right that I shouldn't have been so apathetic towards the racial intolerance which so many people had displayed in the 1980s, but until I met her, it just hadn't seemed a big deal to me. Yvonne set about trying to change my understanding.

Yvonne's other favourite pastime when we were in Weston-Super-Mare was going on Away Days. I couldn't imagine anyone else dreaming up some of our activities, let alone having the will or bravado to carry them out. It was Yvonne at her most daring and me at my most disciplic.

An Away Day would always start early, a rare occurrence for a night owl such as Yvonne, and would commence with taking a train (never paying of course) to somewhere an hour or so away from our seaside home. Yvonne always took her trusted old Adidas rucksack which she stuffed with 'essential tools' like her wrench and her wire cutter. We would then find a restaurant, eat, do a runner and then reconnoitre the town or area we had arrived in to set out the mission for the day. Very often that objective involved 'Setting Something Free.'

This was Yvonne's key phrase, and she meant it literally. Some of our successes included setting free an aviary of canaries from a back garden in Yatton, a shed load of pigs from a farm in Midsomer Norton, and a genuinely imprisoned cabin of cats being held on a farm for vivisectional purposes. They brought Yvonne close to tears.

Sometimes we achieved what she set out to do, sometimes we didn't, but if we didn't always manage it, then it wasn't for lack of trying. The nerve of it never failed to scare or excite me and the sex we had after the event (very often on the returning train) would be far better, far more intense than usual.

One 'setting free' stuck in my mind. It was late November, just a few weeks before Christmas, and it was absolutely freezing. We had decided to travel to Minehead, which turned out to be no more exciting than Weston-Super-Mare out of season, although the wind seemed to whistle through it even stronger. We ended up sitting in a pub for several hours over lunch, and then walking the streets, leaving the centre of town and heading out into the suburbs. Which is where Yvonne spotted the old metal sign, barely visible from the main road. It hung above our heads on a rusty pole planted behind a hedge, squeaking as it swung in the wind. Yvonne pointed at a farm down a country lane.

'There,' she grinned. 'There's today's target.'

I peered at the sign and tried to read the peeling paint. I could just make it out: 'Farringdon's Chicken Farm'. And below it, a faded picture of a sad but fat hen, its one eye gazing down and 'literally asking for liberation' as Yvonne put it.

'No way,' I said, once I had read the sign. 'You're joking.'

Yvonne jabbed me in the ribs. 'Yes way. Why not?'

I held out my arms in supplication. It was a familiar exchange. Yvonne suggesting something and me trying desperately to talk her out of it, but knowing I would always succumb to her proposal. I don't know why I bothered.

'Because there could be hundreds of them,' I said feebly.

'Even better!' Yvonne smiled.

'And the farmer could have a gun.'

Yvonne waved away my reasoning. 'Nah. Don't be stupid. This is the south-west, not the wild west.'

'Yes, but –'

'And it's so close to Christmas. We'd be saving hundreds of hens from ending up with their throats slit and their bodies rendered. It's our Christmas good deed for the year.'

'I hardly think, Yvonne,' I said dismissively, 'that we'd be saving any of them from the Christmas table. Not this close to the big day. Those birds have been packed and frozen months ago.'

'So? We'd still be saving some birds from being eaten later.'

'And you're not even a vegetarian. You love eating poultry.'

'That's not the point,' Yvonne retorted. 'Is it?'

'Isn't it?'

'No. It isn't.'

We glared at each other for a second or two.

'So what is the point?' I asked.

Yvonne winked at me. 'It's the act of Setting Free. Giving someone or something their liberation. Helping those who aren't able to help themselves.' She blew a ring of smoke from her cigarette and added in a passable American accent, 'Now let's case the joint.'

And that was that. Decision made, me outvoted, the game was afoot. As ever. With Yvonne already vaulting the fence to the adjoining field and running doubled up past the first few hedges, I had no choice but to follow. For thirty minutes we circled the farm, identifying where the hens were being kept, plotting a safe route in and an escape route out, and, as dusk approached, noting where the lights in the farmhouse were starting to come on, calculating where the owners might not see us approach from.

'Lot of dogs,' I said as we listened to a frenzy of barking.

'I love dogs,' Yvonne came back. 'And they love me. Don't worry.'

'And the lock on the barn holding the chickens looks tough,' I retorted.

'All the more of a challenge,' Yvonne said, grinning.

'And I'm fucking freezing and I want to go home,' I finished, pummelling my arms around my body. It was a clear night with the near-full moon lighting up the farm, but I was only wearing my Levi's, a flimsy Sonic Youth T-shirt and a thin fleece. Yvonne herself only had a ragged pullover on top of her T-shirt and leggings, but she didn't seem bothered by the wintry conditions so much. Her Scottish upbringing kicking in I guess. At least we had both brought woollen hats.

'So let's go focking do it and then ye can go home,' Yvonne hissed, and pulling her hat further over her head and swinging her rucksack round her shoulders, she started to edge towards the barn where the hens were stored. I followed her obediently.

Both of us sneaked across the farmyard, around to the large barn which held the hens. Yvonne put her finger to her lips and extracted her faithful secateurs which she always carried on such trips for this very requirement. We heard the snap of metal as she cut through the padlock on the barn entrance, and we eased the creaking door open as quietly as we could. As our eyes grew accustomed to the dim light, I saw that there were two layers of iron cages all around the edge of the barn, and a second balcony level at the back of the building which almost butted up to the roof, about eight feet off the floor. A dilapidated old ladder was propped up against the balcony edge.

There must have been hundreds of battery hens in the cages. I had expected a cacophony of clucking, but it was more like the hum of a theatre audience during the interval of a play. The chickens sat and watched us as if we were prop-hands who had just come on stage to move some furniture. It was only when Yvonne started to run around, opening cages and bodily lifting the birds out of their stalls that the chickens began to realise that something out of the ordinary was happening. A few seconds later, the volume did rise, and within no time there were screeches and cries of alarm from the birds, and the air started to fill with feathers and useless flapping of wings. I yanked open both the barn doors, and as Yvonne set the hens free from their cages, I ran around like a headless chicken myself urging the birds out of the barn and into the yard, encouraging them to stagger their way to freedom.

All the time, Yvonne and I were calling instructions to each other in overly loud whispers and trying not to get clawed by a loose hen. Then we heard another door slam, another raised voice and the sound of barking dogs split the night air.

I reacted first. 'Yvonne! Someone's coming.'

'What?' Yvonne was struggling with a rusted lock on a cage at the far end of the barn.

'I said someone's coming!' I called louder. 'We've got to get out.'

'All right, all right,' Yvonne spat. 'Just one more…'

'No, Yvonne, now!' I yelled this, and as I did so, I glanced over my shoulder. Not sixty yards away a man was running towards me. I say running, but it was more like a fast waddle as he was almost as fat as some of the hens. With his hair flying around and his legs pumping away as he careered towards the barn, I had a fleeting image in my mind that this was a giant chicken. I think I even laughed. Then I heard a voice beside me.

'Shit!'

Yvonne was also staring at our pursuer. She pointed at him. He was carrying a shotgun, trying to load it as he ran. With hindsight, it was probably only his inability to run and load the gun at the same time that saved us.

'This way,' Yvonne hissed and grabbed my arm, pulling me back into the barn.

'No, are you mad?' I cried back. 'We've got to get out of here.'

'We are getting out,' Yvonne snapped. 'Trust me.'

Still dragging me, she ran back inside the barn and up to the foot of the ladder at the other end of the building. She started to climb. I followed her blindly. When we reached the top, Yvonne dropped down on to her belly and crawled towards the edge of the balcony, sweeping aside strands of straw. Behind her, I tugged at the leg of her jeans. She kicked my hand away and twisted her neck towards me, putting her fingers to her lips. I cursed her silently and crawled behind her.

Down below, there was still chicken pandemonium with the birds scurrying around in all directions, not knowing what they were supposed to be doing, where they should be running, or if they should be running at all. From the corner of my eye, I could see the yard outside was also full of chickens and it was only this which was now stopping the farmer from reaching the barn's entrance as he tried to dance around them. When he finally did make it to the open door of the barn, he stopped and looked in cautiously.

'I knows you're in there,' he growled. 'But you're going to wish you wasn't.'

Then he started to inch his way ever so slowly inside, his gun held waist height like an extra out of *Dad's Army*. There were still a few hens inside but it was a lot quieter now, and I was sure he would be able to hear my heart thumping as he made his way down the barn. He stopped just below where we were lying, and raised his head, sniffing the air like a bloodhound. Which was when Yvonne rose up on to her haunches and jumped. Right on top of him. It was only seven or eight feet, but he must have felt as if a tonne of potatoes had fallen on his back.

There followed more screams and curses, more screeching from the chickens nearest to the writhing humans, and I could only just make out Yvonne's voice telling me to 'fuckin' hurry up and jump'. The next thing I knew, I too was rolling alongside the other two. Yvonne knocked the shotgun out of the farmer's hands and ran ahead telling me to 'get a fucking shift on', but as I got up, I slipped, and as I made to stand up again I felt the farmer's hand on my shoulder. Terrified, I yanked my neck, but not before he had managed to grab my hat. As I ran away bareheaded, shouting after Yvonne, I could hear the frenzied barking of dogs (fortunately still inside the farmhouse) and the farmer cursing behind me, and I imagined him waving my hat, a little piece of me, in defiance.

By the time I had caught up with her, Yvonne was halfway down the lane leading out of the farm, laughing and whooping, and only when I reached her did she cut away through a hedge and head back to the main road across the fields. I swore my head off once she stopped, but she just carried on laughing and gave me an ebullient bear-hug.

Just another great game for her, even though we could have been killed.

That was the only time when we nearly got caught on our Away Days, and the first of only two occasions that we made one of the local papers, even if it was anonymously. A few days later, Yvonne rushed into our room, waving the *Somerset Gazette*, squealing with delight.

'Look, Vik. We're famous. Look!'

And there it was. A report on what was apparently a whole squadron of vandals who had broken into Farringdon's farm, an interview with the irate farmer himself, and a photograph of him. The photo made me shiver. The farmer stood there, face like thunder, dogs gazing up at him and his shotgun crooked in his right elbow. But what scared me most was that in his left hand he held my hat. I automatically reached for my shoulder, where he had grabbed me, as I gazed at the picture. It could have been so much worse. From behind me, Yvonne ran her hand down the inside of my shirt.

February 1991

The day after Yvonne bottled the old man at the bus stop, we barely said a word to each other, just kept our heads down and got on with our chores at the Hotel Neptune; we didn't even go out drinking that evening. The following morning, Yvonne appeared in our room as I was taking a break from my shift, and threw a copy of the local paper at me.

'Vik. Look at this. Page five.'

I sat on our bed and opened the *Weston Recorder*. Right at the top of the page was a disturbing headline: MAN ATTACKED AT WESTON BUS STOP. Followed by the story: *James Peters, 78, is today fighting for his life following a vicious, unprovoked attack with a bottle on the esplanade.*

'Jesus, Yvonne…'

I started to read the rest of the story, but Yvonne leaned over me and jabbed her finger further down the page.

'Never mind that, look at the final paragraph. After the bit about his family.'

I scanned the article down to where she was pointing. 'OK. Ah, his family are worried…any information, please contact… Oh. You mean this bit… What, really?'

Yvonne nodded. 'Really. So what do we make of that?'

'I'm not sure.' I read it out loud. 'Police are treating the incident as GBH,' – I gasped – 'and they are looking for two youths who were seen running away from the incident shortly before the ambulance was called. They are searching for two black men, average height, short hair, probably in their twenties.' I looked up at my partner-in-crime. 'Why are they saying that? Is it a trick? Are they trying to lull us into a false sense of security?'

'Or maybe they really think that. The police always think that young black men are to blame. Remember the sus law?'

'But why? Why would they think that two black guys attacked that man?'

Yvonne snorted. 'Apart from their inherent racism, you mean. I've been thinking about that, and my guess is that someone did see us running away – wait, wait, don't worry,' she held her hands up as she saw my expression. 'It was dark, remember. Night time. I think that all they saw was two people, one being you, who might as well be black as any other colour to the locals here, and then they saw me wearing my black hat, and presumed I was a black man too!' She paused. 'It's almost funny.'

'Not to me.'

'No, no, I know, it's not funny, it's sad. In fact, it's tragic. But it does let us off the hook.'

'But what if they find out, Yvonne. What if the police work out it wasn't two black men, but it was actually us.'

'They won't. They have no reason to.'

'But what if someone else reads this and then goes to the police saying that they saw us and that we were there. I mean, how many black or Asian people live in Wesson?'

Yvonne sat down beside me. 'You might be right, there aren't many black people round here. Maybe we do need to be careful – especially you. Even if you're not black, the cops wouldn't worry about that little anomaly.' We lapsed into silence while we both contemplated if we could be identified.

'You know what?' Yvonne reached out for my hand. 'I think you are right, Vik. We do need to watch our backs. In fact, I think we need to do something new.'

'What?' I looked into Yvonne's eyes. The way she looked at me made me certain that, whatever she suggested, she was going to make everything all right again, and I was ready to believe in whatever she said next. I tried to forget about the startling question she had asked me that night – whether I would kill for her. 'What should we do?'

Yvonne smiled. 'I think it's time we left Weston. It's starting to bore me anyway. I think we need to stretch our wings and head off to the lights of the bright city.'

'But what about the hotel? The sous chef promised to give me a chance. If I could get work in the kitchen, it would be a real opportunity for me.'

Her smile faded. 'Do you really think he's going to do that?'

'He said –'

'He's just playing with you, Vik. It's never going to happen. Trust me, we need to move on.'

Her words hurt, but they resonated all the same. 'So you think we should head for Bristol?'

'No, dummy.' Yvonne punched me on the arm, and her eyes shone with excitement. 'London. I think we should move to London.'

The whole aftermath of our near capture at Farringdon's chicken farm, and the bottling of James Peters, summed up my first few months with Yvonne. Something dramatic happened, you moved on. You wanted something else, go and get it. At that point I was still in awe of her – the woman who had rescued me from a life of Yorkshire obscurity and was showing me what living was all about.

Part 2

London

Three

London might as well have been another world compared to where I had lived before. Yvonne was in her element from the moment we got off the coach in Victoria, but I felt daunted by the crowds, dazzled by the buildings and utterly bewildered by the labyrinth of the transport system.

Yvonne loved London. She loved the noise, the activity, the pace of the city. She even liked the smell and the arrogance of the capital. She made herself at home a long time before I began to feel comfortable; I barely breached Ajay's neighbourhood for the first week or so I was there.

The only thing we both enjoyed was the cosmopolitan, more accepting atmosphere of London, where in many pubs and restaurants and on most streets, I wasn't given a second look. I rarely went more than a few days in Leeds without hearing a remark about my colour, whether to my face or behind my back.

When we arrived in the capital, we lived with my brother and his Indian girlfriend, Ritika, in West London. Ajay had fallen on his feet when he met her as her family had helped finance the purchase of their flat. Having Yvonne and me stay with them wasn't a comfortable arrangement as Ritika and Yvonne didn't see eye to eye on many things, from smoking to sex. Plus Ritika was not happy at losing her spare bedroom, but Ajay played the family card and persuaded her that it was the right thing to do, telling her it was only temporary. That was true, but it was a more extended temporary than either of them had expected.

Ajay and Ritika's flat, a conversion on the top floor of an Edwardian house, was on the border of Shepherd's Bush, a decent size considering what they had paid for it in the late eighties. Stairs led up to their inside front door, with a bright lounge and galley kitchen at the front of the flat, and a spare bedroom, bathroom and master bedroom at the back. The bathroom split the two bedrooms, which all four of us were thankful for at night.

Ajay and Ritika had met in their second year at poly, and they had moved in together as soon as they graduated. Ritika had immediately found a junior position in Selfridges' buying department, but it took Ajay a few months before he was employed as a researcher and occasional writer for a fashion magazine, and during that time, Ritika had paid all their bills. I think he still felt a bit beholden to her, but fortunately she bit her lip when we moved in and said nothing more. At first.

Neither Yvonne nor I had jobs or any income when we first landed in their home and so, although we both continually looked for work, inevitably we spent more time indoors than any of us wanted. Ritika didn't smoke, and Ajay asked us not to light up in the flat; we survived two days by stepping out on to the street, but it didn't last. We opened windows when we smoked in the lounge but it was still apparent that we were disobeying their request. It came to a head two weeks in when we all had a blazing argument one Sunday evening, which culminated in Ritika storming out of the flat, Ajay screaming at us to sort ourselves out or leave, and the downstairs neighbours banging on their ceiling.

It was a wake-up call for Yvonne and me. Yvonne quickly found a job as a barmaid in a local pub, and I scoured the job ads in the local rag for similar casual work – anything that would give us a rental deposit for our own place.

'Just pick anywhere,' Yvonne urged me. 'Get a job in a warehouse if you have to. We've got to move out of here before you and your brother fall out permanently.'

'But I know I can get a job in a kitchen,' I insisted. 'Just give me a bit of time.'

'You've got two days,' Yvonne said. 'After that, you need a job doing anything.'

I redoubled my efforts, and the following day, while checking the vacancy columns in the local paper, I saw the tiny advertisement for a junior chef in the Dog and Dragon in Notting Hill. I had to ring the pub and sell myself over the phone, emphasising my experience in Harrogate. Despite that, they didn't want to see me at first, but I pushed so hard that they relented and invited me in.

In my interview, it was explained to me that their approach was part of a new vogue: something called a gastropub. Apparently, there was a pub in Clerkenwell called The Eagle which had moved away from the classic London boozer and started serving more contemporary food than the until-then traditional pub grub of ploughman's lunch and scotch eggs. It had caused quite a storm on the London food scene. The Dog and Dragon were keen to jump on the bandwagon and even had plans to turn one of their rooms into a dedicated dining area, which was unheard of in west London.

When I attended my interview, the main concern I had was that I clearly had to cook something and I had no idea if my limited repertoire would suit the pub's expectations.

After I had spent fifteen minutes telling Andy, the pub's owner, and his head chef, Graham why I wanted the role, detailed my previous experience at the Harrogate café (and even inserted a few embellished anecdotes about my cooking at the Hotel Neptune in Wesson), Andy asked me to make an omelette. Simple ingredients, simple to cook and very simple to fuck up. The two men watched me dispassionately as I whisked my eggs, added my ham and cheese, seasoned my mixture and delivered the result on a glistening white plate.

Graham pushed at my eggy mess with his fork and ate the tiniest slither from one edge before turning to Andy and shaking his head. Andy took a larger bite and grimaced.

'Vik, your whisking skills are amateur, your control of the frying pan questionable and the… thing you've produced looks more like a Spanish frittata. If you know what that is,' he added as he saw the blank look on my face.

Then Andy looked at Graham and grinned. 'On the other hand, the omelette is seasoned really well, and it tastes amazing, which is after all the name of the game, and you are clearly keen. You're the best we've seen so far. So if you want the job, it's yours. You need some serious training but Graham here is a top chef, so if you listen to him then you'll learn a lot. What do you say?'

I said yes without even taking a breath, before he could change his mind.

The Dog and Dragon did indeed take one of their rooms and converted it into a 'dining area'. They ripped up the sticky carpet and revealed bare, wooden floorboards which they sanded down and varnished. They removed the out-dated banquettes and cigarette-encrusted tables and brought in new wooden benches which were immediately scuffed up to deliberately make them look older, and tore down the yellowed curtains to replace them with blinds. Menus were chalked up on faux blackboards, and even the waitresses were directed to don a complementary appearance: black jeans and matching black T-shirts embossed with the Dog and Dragon logo. And, of course, the owners invested in a brand-new kitchen. It all cost a lot of money, which in the end was the undoing of the place.

Gone were the pork pies, pork scratchings and piss-poor ploughman's lunches, and in their place, new and fresh dishes arrived: bruschetta, foie gras toasties, tortellini, lamb shanks, salads with goat's cheese and sun-dried tomatoes, even spicy pork sausages served with thyme and olive-spiked gratin. White chocolate parfait and fruit crumbles for dessert. But customers could still drink beer with their meals. It meant that entire families now frequented the pub instead of just men.

I spent four months at the gastropub, and I learned more about cooking and food in that time than in my entire life before that. Andy was right – Graham was an incredible chef. He shouted a great deal and swore at everyone in his brigade, but he taught me new methods and helped my confidence in the kitchen to soar. Which, in turn, appeared to make me more confident at home too – sex was better and lasted longer. Although we were still living at Ajay's place while we saved up our deposit to rent somewhere else, I was working such long hours that I rarely saw my brother and his wife; Yvonne and I either stayed in our bedroom or collapsed in front of our landlords' telly when they were out.

Graham also encouraged me to experiment with my cooking. 'You have so much going for you Vik, yes? You are learning how to use all these beautiful ingredients, you have an excellent palate, and your family background means you should be able to take inspiration from two amazing culinary identities and create something new and fresh.'

I tried. My initial attempts at a gefilte fish curry were close to inedible, and my garlic and coriander matzo was rightly confined to the waste bin. It didn't deter Graham: 'Keep trying, yes? Just because you fuck up a few times doesn't mean you should give up. All the more reason for you to start over and attempt something else.'

Initially, the Dog and Dragon picked up custom very quickly, but it soon dived in popularity: first, the money the owners had spent on refurbishing the pub, and the salary they were paying Graham, meant that the prices of their dishes were distinctly higher than most people were prepared to pay, which didn't help the footfall; second, other gastropubs opened soon after we did, but they did it more cheaply; and finally, Graham was offered a job elsewhere in the capital at a restaurant aiming for Michelin status. The writing had been on the wall anyway for Graham, as his temper had started to spill out of the kitchen into the dining area, and on several occasions a customer had been on the end of his wrath; not a great thing if you want them to come back again. Or pay.

Andy broke the news to me at the end of an unusually quiet Saturday night that I was being 'let go next week'. He looked sad.

'I don't believe it,' I said. 'I love working here. Are you sure you can't keep me on?'

'I'm sorry, Vik,' Andy said remorsefully, 'I like you, I think you've got potential, but we're going to have to cut back on our expenses until we can sort out the financial mess we're in.'

For the first few days after I was let go, I sat in Ajay's lounge feeling numb and uninspired. I even phoned Andy to tell him I would work for less, but he told me he would never do that to any chef. 'You'll find something else soon, Vik,' he encouraged me. Yvonne also told me to 'get off your arse' and go and find another job.

I finally forced myself out of the flat and began to walk from restaurant to restaurant, from Shepherd's Bush to Bayswater, looking for work. But no one wanted me. My lack of experience was a hindrance, but it was made clear by some chefs that my skin colour was the underlying reason, although they never said it outright. It was my first introduction to the harshness and dogmatic attitudes of the catering sector. If I wanted to be a chef, then I was going to have to knock down some walls.

Unlike mine, Yvonne's first job, working behind the bar in a trendy Fulham pub, lasted less than two weeks. She was sacked when she threw a pint of lager over a customer who was drunk and tried to grope her. Which she followed by smashing a glass on the table in front of him and snarling that if he ever came near her again, then she would 'slice you open as quickly as a fisherman guts his catch – but without killin' yer first.' She was given her marching orders within the hour.

She then had a series of jobs, none of which she kept for more than a month and one or two which lasted a single day. She held down one job in an office for a whole week, as a receptionist for a large PR firm: this was an era when many men in an office assumed that the receptionists were fair game for tactile invitations even at their desk. The third time that happened to Yvonne, the executive's suit needed to be dry-cleaned to remove the coffee she had thrown at him.

It was three months before she got the only job which she stuck at before she met the band. We were in Soho for an evening, looking for a particular pub we had been recommended. Because it was pissing down, we ended up sheltering under a tattered tarpaulin on Denmark Street which was masking a stairway into a basement club. The bouncer who stood at the top of the stairs gave us the hard stare but as soon as we heard his Scottish accent, Yvonne went into full charm mode, and they were soon chatting away like old friends. We were just about to leave when we heard the guitars kick-in downstairs, and Yvonne persuaded the bouncer to let us in for free. Which is how we found The Ninth String.

Downstairs was the hottest, smokiest and loudest bar we had come across yet in London, but the band were good and the drinks, if not cheap, then almost reasonably priced for the centre of town. And best of all for Yvonne, when a fight broke out much later in the club, and the bar staff intervened, they weren't seen as the wrongdoers by the management or police. By the end of the evening, Yvonne had persuaded the manager to give her a try-out behind the bar the following night.

She started working at The Ninth String doing ad-hoc shifts when the club was short-staffed or a bigger band playing there called for more servers, and then moved on to more steady sessions once she had proven herself in her first bar brawl; ironically, not by fighting herself but by screaming so loud at the skinheads who were causing the melee that they fled of their own accord, without the need for anyone to physically throw them out. She got a round of applause from her colleagues for that trick.

July 1991

I was determined to find another permanent cooking job, but it quickly became clear that I wasn't going to immediately walk into another role. So although I continued to scan the local newspapers, and approach cafés and restaurants for work, I also signed-up with a catering agency. They found me ad-hoc jobs as a replacement kitchen assistant for the day, or washing-up at summer events in London's parks. It was boring work, long hours and crap pay, but at least I was earning a few quid. But it wasn't lost on me that on some days I had earned a better hourly wage in the Kirkstall Road chippie in Leeds.

Yvonne rarely talked to me about her life before Leeds. I knew she had grown up in Inverness and that her parents still lived there, but that was about it. It was as if she had split her life history the day she moved to Yorkshire. I didn't push her for details, and I was grateful that she didn't want to talk about ex-boyfriends. So, finding out about Dougie was quite a revelation.

I had been working at an outdoor event in Hyde Park all day, and I got back to Ajay's around eight o'clock, exhausted and ready to drop. I could hear voices coming from the lounge as soon as I walked in: Ajay's soft but a little tense, a loud male Scottish accent I didn't recognise and Yvonne, her accent also sounding distinctly more Scottish than usual.

I pushed the lounge door open and saw my brother and Yvonne sitting on the sofa opposite a man mountain: long straggly hair, a sea captain's beard and wearing a T-shirt two sizes too small for him. His biceps alone looked as broad as my thighs. He noticed me the moment I walked in, as if he'd been expecting me.

'Hey, there's the Rebrov I've been hearing so much aboot.'

He pushed himself out of the armchair he had been squashed into, and I swear I heard it sigh with relief.

'It's great to finally meet you, big man. I'm Dougie.' He held out his giant paw.

'Hi,' I said cautiously. I didn't fancy my fingers being crushed by his hand so I left it hanging. 'Sorry, a bit sweaty, just got off a shift. You know...'

'Oh, aye.' Dougie nodded knowingly and instead smoothed his hair back out of his eyes. I glanced at Yvonne. Her eyes were darting between us, and her knee was bouncing up and down like she had a nervous tic. She licked her lips.

'Vik, this is Dougie. He's er, he's...'

'Ah now, Von, don't be shy now. Ye must have told Vik about us, no?' Dougie turned towards Yvonne, but she looked away. The Scotsman smiled. 'Oh, I guess not. See, Von and me go back a wee while to when we were sweethearts back home in the Highlands. Aye, that's what, a few years ago now, eh, Von.'

Yvonne nodded but still didn't look at him. 'It is, Dougie. But –'

'Ah, dinnae worry,' Dougie snorted and waved his hand dismissively, 'I'm no going to embarrass you in front of your new friends. I can see that Vik's a wee bit surprised at my being here.' He grinned directly at me and sat down again heavily in his armchair. Both the chair and Ajay winced.

I had always assumed that Yvonne (Von?) would have had any number of boyfriends before I met her, but that wasn't the same as finally meeting one. I tried to look unconcerned. 'So, Dougie, what are you doing in London? Are you living here now?'

Dougie tapped his yellow stained fingers on the arm of his chair.

'Oh, I'm just passing through. At the moment.' He focused on Yvonne again. 'So tell me, Von, are ye still doing our Away Days?' Yvonne raised her head slightly as Dougie continued. 'Aye, they were great times, weren't they. Remember that time when we got into that castle? Eh man, we only just got out of there alive, didn't we! And when we kicked down the roses in the garden of that posh school. Jeez, I thought I was going to die laughing as the Dean or whoever he was came around the corner.'

I glanced at Yvonne, and for a moment I thought I saw her mouth twitch into a smile. But then she remembered she was angry with Dougie and the pout returned. To hear I wasn't the first man who had gone on Away Days with Yvonne was something of a surprise, although I don't know why I should have thought I was. But it hadn't occurred to me that she had enjoyed something so frighteningly intimate with someone else.

Dougie coughed. 'Your ma and da send their love, by the way. When did ye last talk to them? They said it's been years…'

'Dougie –' Yvonne started.

'I was only sayin' Von. Only because I just happened to be passing by their house recently and so I popped in for a wee cuppie, and they gave me the lowdown on where you were living now. Aye, it was great to see them again. We even looked at some old photos of you an' Kirstine, and –'

'That's enough, Dougie.' Yvonne stood up, and this time there was clear anger in her voice. 'Do not bring Kirstine into this. You hear me? No more.'

Now it was Dougie's turn to look down, and when he did speak a few moments later, he sounded genuinely abashed. 'Aye, sorry, Von. I hear you. That was wrong o' me.'

Ajay and I exchanged a bemused look. I had in the space of thirty seconds learned more about Yvonne's past than in the entire sixteen months I had known her.

Yvonne turned to face my brother. 'Ajay, despite the fact that Dougie is being a bit of a div, I canna just kick him oot. Not at this time of the evening. So look, if you let him crash here tonight, on the sofa, then I promise – promise – that he will be gone in the morning. Is that OK? Please?'

Ajay nodded. 'I'm not sure what I'm going to tell Riti when she gets back, but I'll think of something.'

'Thank you.' Yvonne sighed heavily. 'I think I can make that a bit easier. Dougie, get your coat and let's go to the pub. Just the two of us,' she added and looked at me. 'I think that's best, Vik, OK?'

'OK,' I said tentatively.

Yvonne picked up her fleece. 'You ready, Dougie?'

'Aye, magic,' Yvonne's ex-boyfriend said about going to the pub with my girlfriend.

Yvonne shook her head, but I could see a tiny smile on her lips, and I was worried again.

Dougie lifted himself from the chair and picked up a jacket which was dumped over a sports bag. He swung it around his shoulders. 'Don't wait up, big man.' He winked at me as they left the flat.

Ajay and I watched them go, heard the front door slam. I sank down on the sofa beside my brother. 'What the fuck just happened?' I asked him.

Ajay filled me in on what I had missed. He had got home at about six o'clock to find a huge man sitting on the doorstep outside with a sports bag, his breath stinking of beer. He had introduced himself as a friend of 'Von Anderson' and asked if he could wait for her inside.

'You should have seen the look on Yvonne's face when she walked in, bruv,' Ajay said to me.

'What was it?'

Ajay grinned. 'Don't look so worried, Vik, it certainly wasn't a look of delight. More as though she had just seen someone rise from the dead! He tried to give Yvonne a large bear-hug, but your woman pushed him away.'

That was some relief to me. I went to bed soon after Ajay's reassurances and tried reading *American Psycho* by Bret Easton Ellis, a new novel Yvonne had picked up. Yvonne had said it was compelling, but I found it disturbing. I turned out the light, and shortly after, I heard Ritika coming in. There followed a hum of words between Ajay and his girlfriend and then a loud thump on a wall where I guessed Ritika had thrown something at my brother and I trusted that he had managed to duck. It wasn't the first time. I'd seen a whole new side to Ritika since we'd moved in. We really needed to move out.

I lay in the dark and tried not to think about Yvonne and Dougie in the pub together. With alcohol. Despite Ajay's account of how she had reacted when her ex had turned up, I was still jealous. I reflected on all I had heard Dougie say about Yvonne's parents, which wasn't a lot, but even just those few words had been filled with substance and had left me with more questions than answers.

When I heard the front door of the flat open again, I pulled my alarm clock towards me; half past one in the morning. Jeez, where had they managed to find a pub that was still open until this hour? My whole body tensed as I heard them move into the lounge, someone putting the kettle on, teaspoons clanking in mugs. A few minutes later, our bedroom door opened with a gentle click and I saw Yvonne's silhouette as she crept in. She slipped off her jeans and wriggled out of her bra, and eased herself into bed beside me. Her hand brushed my shoulder.

'Vik? Are you awake?' She whispered the words as if she was hoping I might not be.

'Yes,' I whispered back. 'Are you OK?'

'Yes.'

'Good.'

A moment's silence.

'How's Ajay?' Yvonne whispered again.

'Fine. I think. I don't think Ritika's killed him yet.'

Yvonne muffled her laughter in the duvet.

We lapsed back into silence.

'Yvonne, I have to ask –'

'I know,' Yvonne interrupted me. 'And you've every right to. You want to know why I don't talk about my parents, right? I'm sorry, I just… I didn't think you'd be interested.'

'That's not what's bothering me,' I started.

'Oh, you mean Dougie,' Yvonne said quickly.

'Yvonne –'

'He's such a numpty. Crashing in like that and just expecting he could stay with me – us. Really, what a twat. And no, before you ask, I had no idea that he was coming. If I had, then don't you think I would have warned you?'

I thought about that. 'I guess so. Although now I've met him, I could also understand why you might not have wanted to tell me even if you had known he was in town.'

Yvonne jabbed me in the ribs and curled a leg across one of mine.

'Who's Kirstine?' I asked it quickly, before Yvonne could change the subject. I turned my head towards her and studied what I could see of her face in the dark. 'Yvonne?'

Yvonne stared balefully back at me, and then her eyes started to water and she tucked her face in my neck, and the next moment my throat was damp. It took her a few minutes before she stopped crying and then she spoke again in such a sad voice.

'Vik, please don't ask me about her.'

'Why not? Who is she?'

'She…she's someone who I was very close to when I was younger, that's all. Someone very, very special. But…but now I don't talk about her any more.' Yvonne rolled herself across my chest, propped herself up and looked down at me. 'Please don't ask me about her again, all right? I just can't do it. Is that OK?'

I gave the slightest of nods. 'OK…'

Yvonne pushed her body tight into me and I wrapped my arms around her. And we said no more.

What else could I say? Should I have insisted on talking about Kirstine? Would it have made any difference to anything that happened later? Maybe. I suppose it might have helped me understand.

Our time in Shepherd's Bush came to an end soon after Dougie's visit. Not only had Yvonne's ex turning up understandably pushed Ritika beyond her limit, we had also had enough of listening to our landlords' rows. We agreed one evening that enough was enough and it was time for us to move out.

We told Ajay and Ritika the next day, and they did nothing to conceal their joy. To be fair to them, they didn't whoop out loud, but they certainly didn't try to dissuade us.

'When?' Ritika asked eagerly.

'Can we help you find somewhere?' Ajay added.

I was a little peeved they were quite so happy, so I told them we would be fine finding somewhere ourselves, thank you very much. In the end, it took us two weeks to find a new place because, as I had predicted, the cost of renting anything within a reasonable distance of central London was way beyond our budget. We scoured the *Evening Standard* for cheap options, checked cards in newsagents' windows and I even visited one or two letting agencies - they all but laughed in my face when I told them our budget. In the end, we found something through a small ad in *Loot* magazine. We couldn't quite believe that the asking price was so low, but we confirmed it when we spoke to the landlord on the phone and went to visit it. Which is when we found out why it was so affordable.

The flat was halfway up a tower block on the seedier outskirts of Holloway in North London. The lifts had *Out of Order* signs peeling off the walls, indicating they hadn't been working for years, and the stairways smelt of piss and weed. However, the flat itself wasn't too bad, relatively speaking: one bedroom, a small bathroom and a combined lounge and kitchen. Well, an old fridge and a cooker in the corner of the room with an eyeline grill and an oven which occasionally worked. The bed was OK, although the sofa sagged in several places and the shower should have been called a dripper. But never has it been truer to say that beggars cannot be choosers and we ended up begging the landlord to give it to us. We used our meagre savings to pay the deposit.

Basically, the whole block was well on the way to becoming a condemned building, but the landlord was somehow keeping it propped up and renting out the flats where he could, at rock bottom prices. We stayed there for the rest of our time in London because even when the council did finally catch up with the landlord, the red tape required to get a tower block formally condemned and to evict all the tenants took for ever. Fortunately for us.

Four

August 1991

My time at the Dog and Dragon had made a big impression on me and strengthened my desire to work more in kitchens, and I knew by now that a career in food was what I wanted. As disappointed as I was to be let go by Andy, I was determined to get a permanent job cooking somewhere else. Although I continued to work for the catering agency, the crap jobs they found for me made me even more determined to search harder for a cheffing role. I finally managed to get invited to two interviews at new gastropubs, but they either deemed me not good enough, or my face didn't fit, even for the back of house, so I also began looking at jobs in more traditional restaurants. To my astonishment, it was at one of those establishments – Restaurant Le Jardin – where I finally found an opening.

Restaurant Le Jardin was on the edge of Hampstead, and although it wasn't far from our flat as the crow flies, it was tricky to get there by bus. I was almost late for my try-out, and when they asked me to make a bouillon, I was so flustered that all I could come up with was a basic pea and mint concoction. Not exactly haute cuisine. But ironically it was the simplicity which abetted me.

Chef Michel, the middle-aged, French owner, although you could barely discern any accent in his voice as he had lived in England so long, told me that he was getting fed up with 'would-be Escoffiers trying to impress me with more ingredients than you would find in an entire supermarket'. Consequently, my pared-back bowl of soup had apparently shown him I had the 'potential for greatness'. I assured him that was exactly what I had intended. 'Don't fucking push it,' he replied and promptly gave me a job as entremetier – entrée preparer – the chef responsible for hot appetisers, soups, vegetables, pasta and egg dishes.

I loved working at Le Jardin. If the Dog and Dragon had given me the groundwork for preparing contemporary cuisine, then Chef Michel introduced me to the classics. On my station, I had to learn how to make Salmorejo (gazpacho's richer, deeper cousin), Barigoule of Spring Vegetables, Quiche Lorraine and Piperade. And although it wasn't my responsibility, I was allowed to observe and assist with dishes such as cassoulet, coq au vin, apple tart, lemon mousse, moules marinière, veal, sole and much more. I'd eaten some of these dishes before, but at Le Jardin I discovered taste combinations that I never even knew existed.

Chef Michel was well-liked by his staff and customers. He was enthusiastic, usually calm, always remembered names and never seemed too busy to listen to a question or comment. He and the Sous Chef were mostly patient with me, although that didn't stop them from shouting and swearing in my direction if I was late delivering a plate or if I under-seasoned a dish. I learned quickly that the environment of the professional kitchen was no place to work for a sensitive soul. I once shared with Yvonne some of the newer, more colourful phrases I had learned, after she had told me that there was nothing in the English language that could shock her any more; some of the chefs' choicest expletives even caught in her throat.

Ironically, having hardly ever eaten puddings at home while I was growing up, other than Indian desserts on special occasions, I discovered that I had quite a sweet tooth. And although I still concentrated on my savoury food, I learned how to make chocolate fondant, profiteroles, and even how to spin sugar (not very well).

We all worked hard at Le Jardin, and there was pride in the food we presented to diners. London was undergoing something of a food revolution in the early 1990s, and every week, someone in the kitchen would hear of an astounding new restaurant opening or a radical young chef causing a stir. Names such as Antony Worrall Thompson, Marco Pierre White, Pierre Koffmann, Raymond Blanc, Rick Stein all became eponymous with the London eating scene, and we wanted Le Jardin on that map as well.

Once I had found my feet in Le Jardin's kitchen, I recalled Graham's encouragement at the Dog and Dragon, and I made time to experiment with dishes that drew on my heritage. Early on in my apprenticeship at Le Jardin, I told Chef Michel about my love for Indian-Jewish cuisine, but instead of laughing, Chef put down the notebook he had been scribbling in and asked me to show him my gefilte fish curry. With a feeling of impending embarrassment, I started to gather the ingredients at my station and compile the dish, but as I did so, I found I was sub-consciously altering what I had done previously at the Dog and Dragon, and I produced a less spicy and more delicate version of the curry. Chef Michel still turned his nose up, but it wasn't quite the humiliation I had anticipated. Most importantly, I realised that the Indian spices which I loved so much could be incorporated without losing the complex but beautiful flavours of the dish.

Over the following weeks, I continued to make my gefilte fish curry until it evolved into what was more recognisable as a fish soup but with a lighter stock and still with the influence of

Jewish-inspired quenelled fish and my own garam masala. The other chefs tasted it with grudging approval on their faces. The lunchtime service when Chef Michel added it as a Special to the menu was the proudest moment of my cooking career to that point. Sadly, it didn't sell well, but I received good reports from customers who did order it.

I began to realise that my experimentation and new understanding of fusion food meant that occasionally I could make suggestions for enhancements even for the standard dishes at Le Jardin. It didn't mean they were necessarily accepted by Chef, in fact, they were very rarely incorporated into an existing recipe, but they weren't dismissed out of hand. That made me feel I was really part of a team, something my working life had seldom given me.

During my time at Le Jardin I acquired a set of chefs' knives which would remain in my possession for many years, even after I left Chef Michel's restaurant. At the Dog and Dragon, Andy had lent me some basic knives, and I used those without being aware of how much better a good knife is. All I knew with Graham was that if anyone even as much as breathed on one of his personal knives, then he would go into meltdown and threaten them with the ten plagues of Egypt. It's a common attitude among chefs: whether you are a Head Chef or a Chef de Partie, your knives are your livelihood, and you don't borrow another chef's knife unless you ask; and even then, you probably need a written permission slip. In blood.

I had only written to my parents once since we had moved to our new place, but I had mentioned in that letter that I had just got my new job at Le Jardin. So, when a parcel arrived at our Holloway flat with a Yorkshire postmark, I was astonished to find inside three beautiful Sabatier knives wrapped up in a black canvas knife bag: a classic, eight-inch chef's knife, a paring knife and a boning knife. It came with a note: 'For our son, the chef. With love from your proud parents.' It shocked and delighted me. Although my parents had never discouraged me from my desire to work in kitchens, they hadn't positively supported me. I don't know how they knew what knives to buy or how they had even heard of Sabatier, but they made me so happy.

I immediately had them sharpened and the first time I used my new knives at Le Jardin, I instantly felt as if I could cook better. Good knives have that sort of impact. I treasured them from that day onwards.

While I was spending long nights in the kitchen, Yvonne was often happy to work extra hours at The Ninth String. Some of the bands who played at The Ninth String drew a politically overt left-wing crowd. Alcohol, music and politics, with a little weed thrown in, was Yvonne's idea of heaven. She often came back after such gigs happily riled up from an argument or buzzing from a long political debate.

'I thought you were supposed to be working behind the bar,' I asked her one night when she came home especially garrulous about the people she had met that evening.

'Aye, I do – I was,' Yvonne said quickly. 'But you get gassing to some of the customers, you know, between the sets – at the end when there's fewer punters around. That's when you meet the real interesting folk.'

One evening in August, not long after a MORI poll had declared the Conservative government's popularity was increasing again ('not as far as I'm concerned,' Yvonne muttered), Yvonne came back from a stint at the club on even more of a high than usual.

'You'll never guess who I met at the club.'

'OK.' I put on my best interested face. 'What happened? Who'd you meet?'

Yvonne thrust towards me a piece of paper she was holding. 'Look at this. Look.'

'What is it?' I took the paper from her. It was a pamphlet which looked like it had been designed on an old manual typewriter.

'It's a new socialist movement. It's so exciting.'

'OK.'

'Seriously, Vik, you've got to read their manifesto.' Yvonne jabbed her finger at the flyer. 'It tells you exactly what they're going to do to bring down the government.'

'Ah, the principles and policies of the Anglo-Italian Socialist Alliance.' I looked up at Yvonne. 'The Anglo-Italian…'

'Socialist Alliance! Exactly. It's a new international co-operation of socialist groups. We're no longer simply looking insularly and inwardly at just our own country and only our issues, but getting involved on a wider basis. We'll be so much stronger together. It's incredible isn't it.' Yvonne was almost out of breath as she reeled off her evidence. 'And look: there's a joint anti-fascist march here in London next month. We've got to go, Vik. Show our support.'

'But why are the Italians getting involved?'

'Vik! Don't you remember? Last month in Genoa?'

'Um…'

'Oh, ferchristsakes Vik, sometimes you are so scatter-brained. Remember, at the G8 meeting there were demonstrations in Genoa and the media accused the protesters of causing the violence. Gianluca says that's bollocks of course.'

'Hang on. Who's Gianluca?'

'He's the coordinator of the alliance here in London, didn't I say?' Yvonne swatted away an imaginary fly. 'No matter. You'll meet him when we go on the march.'

'When we go?'

'Come on, Vik. We have to be there. Gianluca says the BNP might arrange their own rally, so it's imperative we stand up to them.'

It seemed like my decision had been made for me.

The Anglo-Italian Socialist Alliance – AISA – *protesta anti-fascista* was held on the first Saturday in September and was planned to be a 'three-pronged' walk where the protesters would start in either Regent's Park, Holland Park or Battersea Park and all merge for a rally at Hyde Park Corner to hear a number of speakers. The walks wouldn't take much more than ninety minutes, but they would pass along some popular streets and there would be plenty of space for gathering in the park. There was also talk of various bands playing impromptu sessions en route.

The AISA were planning the march from Regent's Park, starting near the York Bridge and then winding through Marylebone to Marble Arch and down the eastern edge of Hyde Park to the finishing point. It should have been easy. Unfortunately, as Gianluca – a suave, confident, good-looking thirty-something Italian – had predicted, the BNP had decided to organise their own march from Oswald Mosley's birthplace in Mayfair to Hyde Park Corner. The police should have dispersed them as soon as they got together in Mayfair, but they didn't, choosing instead to let them walk along Grosvenor Square towards Hyde Park.

It was a warm, September day and the AISA marchers were in high spirits. As well as banners and placards and the inevitable megaphone, there were people with whistles and tom-tom drums and even a trumpet or two. It was noisy but friendly, and the police who accompanied the march kept their distance.

Rumours about the BNP march began to permeate through our ranks as we walked around Portman Square. I don't know how someone found out but it soon filtered throughout the protesters and although the whistles still whistled and the megaphone still urged the crowd to echo the calls of anti-fascism, there was a noticeable change in the atmosphere.

And then everything kicked off, ironically at the Joy of Life Fountain on the border of Hyde Park. A band was playing as we approached it, with a noisy but happy crowd dancing in front of them. More people were gathering from the marches which had taken the other routes. Gianluca, who was leading the AISA march, indicated we should pause and most of us wandered towards the music.

It was then that we heard the chants and noise of the BNP rally. At first, it was just that, shouts and deep-pitched howls accompanying the cries, but as the chanting got louder, so we turned to see what was happening. There can't have been more than twenty, twenty-five skinheads in their pack, but they were all running, charging down the path of the park towards where we had congregated around the stage. They were dressed in the far-right style: dark T-shirts with braces or bomber jackets, blue jeans tucked into high-laced bovver boots. As they got closer, I could see NF and crusader tattoos on the arms and chests of the men who were currently ripping off their T-shirts as they charged towards us. A few of the AISA men on the edge of the crowd turned to face them and held up their hands to ask them to stop. It didn't work, and they were simply punched in the face and knocked to the ground.

I looked around for Yvonne, but she was no longer standing beside me.

I started to run towards the Alliance leader, but at that moment, Gianluca called out orders in Italian and at least half the men in our group started charging towards the BNP. All of them looked angry, but I noticed that one or two were reaching into their pockets and pulling out what looked like knuckledusters. The shouts of the BNP were now being matched by those from the AISA, in English and Italian. The band tried to play on, but when I looked towards the stage, they were clearly struggling to decide if they should continue or not. The decision was taken by the young bass player, who tore off her guitar and jumped off the stage to run towards a woman who was being beaten by a BNP skinhead. I watched as she and two AISA members punched and kicked the BNP man until he ran off.

My eyes were drawn back to the fountain: people were fighting in the water. I saw Yvonne was at the edge of the fountain as two men approached her with raised fists.

'Yvonne!' I shouted, waving. 'Get over here!'

She didn't seem to hear me. I hesitated – I knew my skin would make me a prime target – but I couldn't just stand by either.

'Yvonne!' I tried again. 'Yvonne!'

She looked up and saw me. 'Vik!'

I was still fifty yards away. From the other side of the fountain, three or four AISA men appeared and they tore towards the BNP men just as they reached her. As they came together and punches flew, Yvonne took a step back. It was that one, small step that meant the first BNP man missed her and instead he received a sharp blow to his neck from one of the AISA guys. A few seconds later I was by Yvonne's side.

'Yvonne! Come on, let them fight. Let's get out of the way!'

'Vik,' she gasped, 'we have to stay and help.'

'No we don't,' I panted, 'and first –'

Something hit the side of my head. I collapsed on one knee. It might have been that which saved me from any further punishment because as I looked up and saw the BNP thug who had attacked me, Yvonne shoved him hard in the chest, and he fell backwards and tripped into the water.

Yvonne knelt down beside me. 'Vik, are you all right?'

I gingerly lifted my hand to my head. My fingers felt sticky, and as I lowered my arm, I saw my palm was covered in blood. My BNP attacker was sitting in the fountain holding his head. 'Jesus, we've got to get out of here now, come on.'

'But Vik, what about the others... I mean... Gianluca...'

I watched the fighting that was going on all around us. The AISA guys now outnumbered the opposition three to one, and a couple of BNP skinheads were lying on the ground receiving punishing kicks. I saw Gianluca jump up on to the roof of a car and swing his arm back with a burning bottle in it. Another member of the AISA ran towards the police holding some sort of metal bar. It was like something out of a film.

'Gianluca's a big man who can look after himself, Yvonne. Now come on.'

I staggered in a half-run away from the fountain, further into the park, and sank to the grass, staring up at the sun. We could still hear shouts and calls, but now I could also hear the wail of police sirens. I don't know how long I lay there; it felt like ages, but it can't have been more than a few minutes before Yvonne was back at my side dabbing at my head with a piece of cloth that she must have wet from the fountain. I winced as she dabbed at my cut.

'I'm sorry, Vik, I'm not trying to hurt you, but – hang on – I have to get the grit out of your wound. Now just bite your lip.'

Yvonne carried on wiping my wound quite roughly until I couldn't bear it any longer and I swatted her away.

'Enough, Yvonne, really. Enough.' Yvonne sat back on her haunches. She wouldn't look at me. I patted my head again; blood didn't seem to be seeping out any more.

'You took your time,' she said in a quiet voice. 'Joining in, I mean. Gianluca and his crew were already there. We shouldn't have deserted them.'

'You think I should have got involved?'

'You promised me once that you would protect me. Do you think you did?'

I was shocked. How had Yvonne suddenly remembered our conversation from that night in Wesson?

'What was I supposed to do? Someone clouted me over the head with a brick.' I waved at the cloth Yvonne was still holding. 'What is that anyway?'

Yvonne looked down at what she was gripping. It was balled up in her hand. 'I don't know. It was just lying on the ground.' She started to unfold the cloth. 'Well would you look at that!'

It was a grey T-shirt with a red flag of St George in the middle and a crude swastika inked on by hand.

Yvonne smiled for a moment. 'I think that's poetic justice, don't you? A BNP T-shirt helping a Jewish Indian,'

'I'm not sure. I hope I don't get septicaemia from it. Or rabies or something.'

Yvonne threw the T-shirt at me. As much as I was repelled by what it stood for, I needed it to soothe my aching head. I held it back over my wound. Yvonne glanced over her shoulder. 'Vik, how are you feeling? Do you think you're strong enough to walk now?'

I nodded and then winced again. 'I think so –'

'Good. Because I can see a lot of policemen now and they are soon going to start rounding people up and asking questions, and I don't need to tell you that they are going to take one look at your skin and think you are one of the agitators, not just a victim. So I think we should get out of here while we can. I'll find a payphone and call Gianluca later to explain why we've gone. I'm sure he'll understand.'

We got up and shuffled away slowly, so as not to bring any attention to ourselves. One hundred and eighty degrees in the opposite direction of where herds of police were now rounding up the AISA and the BNP, waving truncheons and pushing them into two separate groups who continued to gesticulate at each other. Yvonne propped me up, and we made it to Knightsbridge tube station, and into an underground train without dripping too much blood on the floor. We tried to look inconspicuous; fortunately this was the London underground, and people would rather look anywhere than at two bloodied demonstrators. We finally made it to the A&E at UCH, and after only a three-hour wait, the medics patched me up and gave me six stitches. Yvonne told them I had gone over the handlebars of my bicycle; I don't think they believed her.

Yvonne stopped going to the AISA meetings after the *protesta anti-fascista*, and returned to The Night String. 'The BNP are a bunch of thugs,' she told me, 'but that doesn't justify AISA's premeditated attacks, and Gianluca and his mates going in with knuckledusters and Molotov cocktails. It's not the way I believe in protesting. If that's how Gianluca thinks he should act then it won't be with me in future.'

I didn't let my wound stop me cooking and carried on working hard at Le Jardin all winter. I was determined to show Chef Michel how good I could be.

Five

Following the success of my gefilte fish curry, Chef Michel allowed me to continue to experiment with my fusion of Jewish and Indian food. I tried using Indian dishes as the base and then adding Jewish influences, but they never seemed to work.

So instead I started with Jewish dishes, devising ways to add an Indian twist to them. It was trial and error. This resulted in some foul concoctions: Lamb Kishke, based on the traditional Jewish beef intestines, stuffed with a mixture of matzah meal, spices and schmaltz, but Indianed-up by adjusting the seasonings, but which I quickly confined it to the fusion bin; an acceptable but uninspiring variant on pierogi (dumplings of eastern European origin); and even an attempt to use chopped liver, chrain and pickled herring in a thali. I did have some success with savoury profiteroles, which Chef half-praised but still dismissed as sub-standard, and I never felt they really represented what I was trying to achieve, a contemporary fusion of two different traditions.

One day, Chef Michel approached me while I was working on another, ultimately semi-disastrous attempt at mixing pickled herring and spices, and gingerly picked up the herring, gently squeezing it. He sniffed. 'Maybe you are going about this the wrong way, Vik,' he ventured.

Chef dropped the herring on my chopping board and wiped his hands. 'Perhaps you are looking at the Indian aspect in a… too classic way.'

'Classic?'

'Yes, you are I think drawing on your knowledge of Indian food from the sub-continent. But there is more to Indian cuisine. You also have Indian cooking in South-East Asia – Malaysia, Singapore, Indonesia, you know. They have variants on classic Indian dishes, but they also have their own fusion recipes. For example, Nyonya cuisine.'

'How do you know about that?' I asked, somewhat incredulous at Chef's knowledge.

Chef Michel shrugged. 'Oh, I worked in a Malaysian restaurant for a while when I was younger. I picked up a few things here and there. And I read books about cooking all the time. Don't you like cookbooks?'

I felt embarrassed. 'I didn't even know there were Malaysian restaurants in London.'

He smiled. 'Time to do some research. This city is a huge melting pot of different cultures.'

The following morning before work, I went through *Yellow Pages* looking for bookshops that might be able to help me. I soon found Books for Cooks in Notting Hill and visited the following day. I bought several recipe books for South-East Asian food, hoping to find inspiration. I was surprised by how much of it I recognised, although it was presented in unfamiliar ways. I collected lots of ideas. For example, the approach to cooking fish and Singaporean crabs Malaysian-style opened up new avenues for me for Jewish adaptations, and the Nyonya use of sambal instantly got my fusion juices flowing.

In the end, my dish which did make it to the menu of Le Jardin for 'special occasions' was my version of Kneidlach, a Jewish dumpling made of matzah meal, eggs and, traditionally, schmaltz, generally boiled and served in a chicken soup stock. I left the matzah balls almost as they were, with a tweak here or there, but I spiced up the stock. I wasn't sure that the Kneidlach could take the spices, but they gave it a pleasant piquant. Chef Michel insisted on a few modifications as the dish progressed, which elevated it to the standards expected in Le Jardin.

I found that I was learning how to balance flavours better, and the more I learned, so I found I was creating dishes in the kitchen that I would never have dreamed of back in Harrogate.

I was clearing down after service at Le Jardin one lunchtime in March when Pete, one of the junior chefs, told me that Chef Michel was lunching with a big name in the restaurant world.

'Better make sure you don't serve him any of your freaky fusion dishes,' he said with a wink.

I peeked into the dining room, at the corner table, where a tall, smartly dressed man sat by himself, toying with an espresso cup as if swirling around any remaining coffee. He had a full head of wild, white hair but his face was very lined, and his eyes looked tired. He looked familiar, as if I had seen his photograph in a magazine.

'Roger Raybourne,' Pete said, nodding at the diner. 'Him and Chef go way back. Recognise him now?'

'Of The Three Rs?'

The junior chef grinned at my awe and returned to his station.

I continued to hover at the entrance wondering if I could wangle myself an introduction. So Chef Michel was friendly with the owner and Executive Chef of one of London's most exclusive restaurants, Restaurant Roger Raybourne. Or The Three Rs as it was often referred to by the media. This was the big league, the world I wanted to move into. How could I make this happen without looking ungrateful, or worse, a fool?

I could hear Chef Michel's voice ringing through the kitchen. Risking another glance into the restaurant, I realised that Raybourne was still alone. Quickly, I approached his table, brushing down my whites. He looked up.

'Mr Raybourne? I'm Vik – Vikram Cohen,' I said in a rush. 'I specialise in Jewish-Indian fusion dishes and I'd love you to try one for lunch.'

Raybourne pushed back his chair to straighten his back and regarded me with hard eyes; he must have been at least six feet four.

'Jewish-Indian?'

'They're based on my heritage.'

'How fascinating.'

'Sorry to keep you, Roger,' said Chef Michel, stepping out of the kitchen. 'I see you've met our latest chef, Vikram Cohen.'

'Mr Cohen, a pleasure.'

Roger Raybourne held out his hand and smiled broadly, revealing the teeth of an ex-boxer: two gaps and a single gold tooth.

'Mr Rayb – Chef Raybourne, good to meet you too.' I shook his hand and immediately regretted it as I realised how sweaty my palm was.

Impressively, the famous chef did not wipe his hand on his trousers and simply pursed his lips into a half smile. 'Chef is fine, Mr Cohen. Or can I call you Vik?'

'Of course, Chef.'

'Good. Join us.'

It wasn't a question.

Chef Michel pulled up an extra chair for me with an intrigued glance at his friend. I sat, hunched over, hardly able to look such a great restaurateur in the eye. Chef Michel sat back lazily in his chair.

'Roger and I go back a long way, Vik. Did you know that?' I shook my head. 'Indeed. We trained together in Paris, and then we worked together briefly in New York. They were fun times, eh, Roger?'

'They were tough times. André had us working all hours in that goddamn furnace.'

'You loved it! You're always telling me so.'

'Ah, you know. It made me the man I am today and all that.' Chef Raybourne swept his hand through his hair. 'Enough history. Vik tells me that he specialises in Jewish-Indian dishes. I'd like to try one. What do you recommend?'

'You see, Vik?' Chef Michel boomed, making me jump. 'You put the time in for many years to become a great chef, and you never know where it may lead. This boy could be really good,' he said, slapping me on the shoulder. 'But,' he added, holding up a finger, 'he is still learning of course.'

'I can recommend the Kneidlach, Chef,' I said quickly. 'Let me prepare that for you now.'

Roger Raybourne nodded and waved me away. 'Go. Show me what you can do.'

I returned quickly to my station. Ignoring the rest of the staff, I chopped, seasoned and sautéed, eager to cook Roger Raybourne the best food I could; but conscious that I had overstepped protocol, worrying how Chef Michel would react later.

I nervously sent my dish out.

After Raybourne had finished my Kneidlach, he sent for me. As I approached his table, I noticed that thankfully his plate was empty. He indicated I should sit down. While Chef Michel finished eating, Raybourne spoke to me as if we were the only two people in the restaurant.

'I am impressed,' he declared. 'I have not tasted anything like that before. That is something you should be very proud of.'

I rubbed my hands on my whites. I was conscious they were stained with spices and splashes from the stock. Some chefs prided themselves on keeping their whites clean; I hoped Roger Raybourne wasn't one of those.

'Thank you, Chef.'

Raybourne lent back and tapped his fingertips together. 'Of course, it could certainly be improved, but it was exciting. Quite visionary even.'

I could feel Chef Michel's eyes burning a hole in the back of my head but I kept myself focused on his guest, although I wasn't sure how to respond to his praise. My mind started to drift, and I wondered if I should mention my gefilte fish curry or my other amalgamations I had been considering. Maybe I should ask him how he would suggest I develop it, would that be too impertinent to request of such a great chef?

'Vik? Are you listening?' Raybourne's voice was curt.

I was suddenly aware that the two chefs were both scrutinising me.

Chef Michel shook his head. 'Vik, did you hear what he said? Roger is offering you a job.'

'I – what?'

Fortunately, Chef Raybourne seemed to find my agitation amusing.

'I was saying, Mr Cohen, that although I think you still have a lot to learn, you have great potential and I love having chefs in my kitchen with new ideas. Not to mention a good palate and someone who can place their own mark on their food. And I like a man who seizes an opportunity. Not many junior chefs would introduce themselves like you did. So what do you say? Would you like to come and work for me as my Poissonnier?'

Would I like to work for Chef Roger Raybourne as his fish chef? At The Three Rs? I dared not look over at Chef Michel, and concentrated on my feet. I had only been at Le Jardin for seven months. In that time, Chef Michel had taught me so much and given me a chance, and the other chefs were easy enough to work with. Should I really turn my back on all that for a highly pressurised and unpredictable new workplace? Or was this too good an opportunity to decline, one which would enable me to step up to the next level of fine dining? I turned to my current employer.

'Chef Michel, I'm not sure if –'

The Executive Chef held his hand up. 'Vik. Listen. Here at Le Jardin you have limited openings. Roger can give you opportunities and teach you even more than I can. And he can pay you more too! If you want to be a great chef, you should take Roger's offer and run with it. Run like hell. Just remember that with more responsibility and a higher salary comes greater pressure. Much greater pressure.'

Chef Michel stopped and sat back in his chair, looking weary, as if he had said these words many times before.

Two weeks later, I said my goodbyes to Chef Michel and the staff at Restaurant Le Jardin in Hampstead and went to work for Chef Roger Raybourne at Restaurant Roger Raybourne in the heart of Mayfair.

April 1992

There is a Jewish joke that one of my uncles taught me: a man dies and goes to Gehenna (in the Hebrew Bible, a destination for the wicked). There he is told he will spend one day in Heaven and one in Hell and then he can decide where to spend the rest of eternity. His first day is in Hell, and while he is there, he has a wild time, partying, drinking, enjoying whatever pleasures he chooses. The following day he goes to Heaven, where it is serene and pious, and people pass him in the street and smile benevolently at him, but it is otherwise dull. Consequently, he chooses Hell, but when the Gates of Hades are opened to greet him the next day, he is immediately yanked in by his collar, chained to a burning scaffold and Beelzebub approaches him with a cat o' nine tails. 'Wait!' the man says, 'I don't understand. When I came here before, it was all fun and parties. What is happening now?' 'Ah well,' says the demon, 'yesterday you were a potential employee. Now you actually work here.'

I recalled this allegory on my first day at The Three Rs. Roger Raybourne's restaurant was very different from my previous experience. The kitchen was larger than any other I had been in: there were more stations, more worktops, more pans and plates, more Chefs de Partie; the walk-in fridges were huge, the vegetables piled high, and the stacks of raw meat made it seem more like an abattoir; and there were much bigger charbroilers, food mixers and meat grinders.

My inaugural shift started innocently enough: Chef Roger greeted me and introduced me to the Sous Chef and the other Chefs de Partie. I registered immediately that I was the only non-white person in the kitchen, other than a couple of plongeurs. It didn't bother me, but for a moment I did wonder why, in a large, internationally renowned kitchen, this was still the case. I was to find out by the end of my first day.

For the first hour, while Chef Roger was in the kitchen and the mise en place was underway, the atmosphere was loud but unaggressive. That changed the moment Chef Roger left the restaurant.

Although the noise level didn't increase dramatically, there were more threatening tones, the language deteriorated, and the commis chefs and the apprentis bowed their heads and took without question whatever orders were barked at them. I saw one young apprentis get a slap from the Sous Chef, but the boy just winced and resumed his work. The only men – and they were all men at The Three Rs – who didn't seem concerned were the other Chefs de Partie. Thirty minutes after Chef Roger had left for the morning, I received my baptism to The Three Rs' in-house style.

I was coming to the end of preparing the fish for the lunchtime serving when I met the Chef de Cuisine, Chef Kevin Tyndall. After collecting my final ingredients, I saw a large man standing at my station, tossing my morning's work from one side to the other. I had already been warned by Jake, the rôtisseur, to watch out for Chef Kevin, and his subsequent description of the Head Chef had not been wrong. He was indeed a burly man, with a thick neck, impressive biceps and hair shaven to a number one, making the tattoos on his scalp clearly visible. Another tattoo of a snake started on his neck and disappeared inside his chef's whites to reappear on his left bicep. On his right arm was a St George flag, and his hands had knife scars crisscrossing the fingers. My new boss was engrossed in examining my work, so I stood behind him. He reeked of tobacco, the Gauloises he smoked during his breaks, I discovered later. I introduced myself.

'Hello, Chef, I'm Vik Cohen. Is there anything I can help you with?'

I might as well have been invisible. Chef Kevin didn't acknowledge I had even spoken, let alone that I was standing beside him, and instead he continued to sort through the fish I had been preparing, throwing some to one side and giving other pieces a cursory glance before slapping them down on the worktop. I realised all the staff within a few feet of my station had gone completely quiet. The junior staff continued to work, but the other Chefs de Partie crossed their arms and watched their boss as if it was some form of entertainment.

Kevin left it another sixty seconds before he spoke. 'This is shit,' he said very quietly. 'Your work is all fucking shit.' He finally looked me in the face, and although he was no taller than me, I felt like the proverbial mouse standing in front of the lion.

'I'm sorry, Chef,' I started. 'If you can show me what's wrong then I –'

'What's wrong,' Kevin interrupted, still quietly, 'is that I have been given a fucking Paki as my new Poissonnier, who doesn't know a fish's arse from its head. That is what's wrong.'

He thrust his face in front of mine. I tried not to flinch, but I took a step back, I couldn't help it. And then he did shout.

'Or am I wrong? Are you, in fact, a fucking yid? Because I can't tell. All I know is that all this,' he planted his left hand on the stack of fish in front of him, 'needs to be done again.' And he swept his hand off the counter, scattering most of my prepared fish on to the floor.

I looked down at the now inedible bass and turbot which lay at my feet. 'But I –'

I didn't get any further. Chef Kevin reached out and with one enormous hand grabbed me by my collar. Instinctively, I tried to pull his hand away but he just tightened his grip.

'Maybe I didn't make myself clear,' he said slowly. 'If I say that this all needs redoing then this all needs redoing. Comprende, Paki Vik?'

I nodded, and after glaring into my eyes for several seconds, Chef Kevin released me. I staggered backwards and lent against the counter. When I looked up he had gone. The kitchen hubbub returned, and with a sympathetic look, one of the plongeurs helped me clear up the fish from the floor, and I started the long job of preparing a new batch for lunch.

I was still reflecting on what had happened and what I was going to do about it when Jake, the rôtisseur, sidled up to me. 'I warned you,' he said, half smiling. 'No one wants to get on the wrong side of Chef. You should watch your step.'

Everyone else acted like nothing out of the ordinary had happened.

I worked hard for the rest of my shift, going over my fish preparation in my mind, wondering if Chef Kevin had been justified to dress me down or whether he was, as Yvonne would say, 'a racist prick'. Finally I decided that it was more important for me to prove myself to the team rather than whinge or worry any more about it.

When I got home late that evening, Yvonne was still out working at The Ninth String. I lay in bed and made a decision. I wouldn't tell Yvonne what had happened. She would no doubt fly off the handle, tell me I had to stand up to Chef Kevin's racism. She wouldn't understand my approach. This was something I had to manage on my own.

Six

Even though Yvonne enjoyed watching the bands which performed at The Ninth String, I could tell that she missed the energy and excitement of playing in a group herself. So when Yvonne met The Libertine Dolls, her life, and therefore mine took a whole new direction.

It was a Saturday night and Fergus, a friend of my brother, was having a birthday bash in a pub in Archway, and Yvonne and I tagged along. It was one of those big pubs where the main room has high ceilings and a stage for a band. Yvonne was looking stunning in a checked shirt with the top two buttons open, worn over a tight-fitting tank top, black jeans, and sporting deep, crimson lipstick.

Fergus and Yvonne immediately hit it off, while I chatted to a couple of Fergus' mates and vaguely watched the band preparing on stage. Fergus eventually got pulled away by other friends and I got Yvonne back, just as the band launched into their first number, and our attention was drawn towards the stage.

The band were made up of three female guitarists, one of whom played bass, and a male drummer. Two of the women wore tank tops, short leather skirts and knee-high boots. The third, the lead singer, wore a denim shirt and jeans. They were loud, not particularly refined, but the music had fire and edge.

They finished their first song, a cover of a Roxette track, and launched straight into their second, just about recognisable as a rough and ready version of Divinyls' 'I Touch Myself'. What it lacked in musical ability, it made up for in noise and shrieking guitars, along with some less than subtle touching of themselves by the guitarists. I noticed Yvonne was watching them intently, nodding her head to the music. Unfortunately for the band, she was in the minority; most people in the pub were still talking and barely paying any attention. No one clapped when the song finished.

The lead singer pulled the microphone closer to her. 'Well, gee, thank you, Archway,' and shook her head. 'So, we are going to play a few more songs for your entertainment, oh, and by the way, we're called The Libertine Dolls.' She adjusted her tuning keys.

'Do you like them?' Fergus had rejoined us.

Yvonne half-nodded. 'They've got attitude. I like that. But they need something more.'

'I know Jane, the lead singer,' Fergus said. 'We spent one year at art college together.'

'She's good. Got a decent voice. Just needs to sing songs more appropriate for it.'

'She's a feisty one, that's for sure.' He raised his voice as the band kicked-in to another song. 'Do you want me to introduce you?'

After playing Status Quo's 'Down Down' (which included two girls in the band incorporating hand and mouth actions which made Yvonne roll her eyes), Jane announced they were taking a short break and sat down on the edge of the stage, ignoring two lads who tried to talk to her. Fergus led Yvonne towards the guitarist and introduced them. I watched as they shook hands. They couldn't have known it of course, but it was a key moment in both their lives. Yvonne appeared to ask a few questions, and both girls laughed. Fergus left them, and I saw that Jane began to listen more keenly as Yvonne spoke to her. Then they shook hands again, and Yvonne walked back to where I was standing.

'What were you talking about?' I asked.

Yvonne shrugged. 'You know, this and that. I gave her a few suggestions. We'll see if she takes them up.'

'Suggestions?'

'Yes, ideas. Don't look so worried, Vik, we were just having a chat.'

'I'm not worried, I'm just surprised.'

'Hey. I've been in bands myself, you know. I do know something about singing.'

'Well, yes, but –'

'Vik. Just shut yer geggie.'

I shut it. The Libertine Dolls started to play again, a tune I didn't know, and after a couple of songs which no one in the pub acknowledged, Jane stepped up to the microphone. 'Thank you *so* much. Now we would like to invite a special guest to join us.'

Yvonne winked at me. 'Seems she liked my idea.' She handed me her drink.

'A Scottish siren. Please welcome Yvonne Anderson.'

After all the time I had been with Yvonne, I shouldn't have been surprised. When I asked her later how she had persuaded Jane to let her sing, Yvonne looked a bit coy and said, 'Oh, you know, I told her I played a bit. And I…might have kind of insinuated that I once played with Joan Jett.'

'You didn't. Did you?'

Yvonne gave me one of her speculative looks. 'Might have done,' she said. 'Chatted to her once after a gig. I asked her if she was looking for a backing singer.'

'Really?'

Yvonne flashed me a knowing smile.

Ignoring the odd cat whistle, the 'Scottish Siren' walked towards the stage and stepped up. Slinging a wireless guitar around her neck, she accepted a similar microphone from the drummer, which she clipped to her shirt. But rather than immediately start playing, Yvonne instead jumped off the stage, walked to the side of the room and dragged a small bar table into the middle of the floor, ten feet or so from the stage. With a few punters now watching her curiously, The Libertine Dolls' temporary band member climbed on to the table and faced the band.

'You ready, Jane?' she said loudly into the mic. The feedback made me wince, but it also ensured a lot of people looked towards her elevated position. Yvonne grinned. 'Well, let's hit it.'

So saying, the three guitarists struck up the first chords to Joan Jett's 'I Love Rock n Roll'. It was a good choice. People standing closer to the band began to nod their head, and as Yvonne started to sing, she also began to stamp her foot up and down on the table. I half expected the old furniture to collapse under Yvonne's dancing. As The Libertine Dolls hit the first chorus, more people gathered in a circle around Yvonne, looking up at her, swaying, a few even dancing. Yvonne and Jane continued to exchange power chords and by the time the song came to an end, it seemed that close to half the drinkers in the pub's main room were watching now. A round of applause rang out, the first of the evening.

'Well, hello, Archway,' Yvonne said into her mic, and wiped her forearm across her forehead. 'Man, is it me or is it hot in here? I think I need to cool down.' With a wink towards the rest of the band, she untucked her shirt and flapped the front of it up and down. That earned her a few more whistles and shouts. She looked down at the people standing around her.

'You know what fellas, what say we cool down some more.'

And with a quick shimmy of her guitar strap, Yvonne unbuttoned the rest of her shirt and without pausing, pulled it off over her head, revealing just her tank top beneath.

That got the whole pub's attention, men and women. And to accompanying whoops and calls, Yvonne shouted into her mic, 'Jane, give me some guitar!' and the band kicked straight into Wild Cherry's hit song, 'Play That Funky Music', a sure-fire favourite for pub bands. Bellows of delight went up all round the room, and as the band played and Yvonne danced on the table, swinging her shirt around her head, her skin glistening with sweat under the pub lights, I realised that now most of the tavern was watching, dancing, singing or waving their arms in the air.

I stood at the back of the room wondering what the hell Yvonne was doing, unable to join in with the cheering, watching my girlfriend jump up and down on the bar table, the focus of so many eyes. Someone knocked the glass I was holding, but I ignored them. I was uncomfortable with what I was seeing, but at the same time, there she was, converting a previously apathetic room of average pub-goers into an animated arena of dancers and fans. Yes, the rest of the band was playing with her, but she had been the driving force and that did give me a sense of pride. I couldn't help it. She might be half naked, but she was still the one who was controlling the situation.

Halfway through the song, Yvonne jumped off the table, ran towards the stage and bounded up on to it. Automatically, people followed her and within seconds, there was a throng of people dancing in front of the musicians. Yvonne grinned and tied her shirt to the end of her guitar neck, smoothed her hair back and wiped away the sweat. Now standing in front of a fixed microphone, Yvonne gave a signal to the band, and as the chorus culminated, Jane and Yvonne stopped playing, and only the drummer and bass player carried on the beat. Yvonne grabbed her mic in one hand and looked out from the stage. The lack of guitar, now seemed to make the crowd even more attentive.

'OK, men of Archway,' she said calmly into the mic, 'I've shown you how to do it. Now it's your turn. Are you ready? On the count of three, I want to see your shirts off and swinging around *your* heads. OK.' She licked her lips. 'Ready? One… two…three!'

The drummer stopped. For a moment, there was silence. No one moved. No one took off their shirt, and everyone just stared at the band. Yvonne turned to the drummer and signalled him to start again. Then she readdressed the audience.

'Well, that was absolutely fucking pathetic. What the fuck are ye all doing? Look at me! Come on, fuckin' well get involved. This is 1992, fer Chrissakes. All right? All right…'Yvonne looked at Jane. 'Jane, you and me this time, we'll count them in together. And you lot,' she swung her arm in an arc towards the audience, 'this time, I want to see your tops off and some serious jumping up and down and waving your shirts around your heads. OK? OK… Now. One, two…three!'

As Yvonne and Jane yelled out three, they both started running up and down the stage, shouting and signalling to the men to get their shirts off. Gradually, it started to happen. The other guitarist struck up again, and the first few men in the crowd removed their shirts. Then more shouts and then more men ripped off their tops and started swinging them around their heads, and then even more. By the time the whole band had launched back into the Wild Cherry cover, guitars turned up to max, Yvonne and Jane screaming out the final words, the pub was going wild. The last chords of the track were powered out, and everyone started cheering and hooting. Yvonne grinned at Jane; the Libertine Dolls' lead guitarist gave her the thumbs-up.

They played two more songs together: Guns 'n Roses 'Sweet Child O' Mine', followed by just the first verse and multiple choruses of Free's 'All Right Now', and as The Libertine Dolls moved on to the opening lines of Frankie Goes to Hollywood's 'Relax', Yvonne nodded to Jane, put down her guitar, grabbed her shirt and eased herself off the stage. She had to push through the crowd to get back to the bar, but amidst lots of back-slapping, cheers and whistles, she headed straight back towards me, buttoning up her shirt as she walked. When she reached me, she stopped, cracked a broad smile, wrapped her arms around me and gave me a long kiss. Around me, there was an even louder cheer. Any doubts and uncertainties I had from earlier disappeared, and I kissed her back. As I watched her smile and shake hands with people who came up to congratulate her, still with her arm draped around my neck, I was reminded again that if I wanted to be with Yvonne, then this was how it was going to be. Yvonne Anderson had announced herself to London and London wanted to see more.

Yvonne and the band swapped phone numbers at the end of the night, and a few days later they all went out for a drink and discussed Yvonne joining the group on a permanent basis.

Yvonne said yes, of course. But she wanted them all to rehearse more. They had to be tighter, more focused, and although she had no problem with the sexual innuendo, she felt it could be done more professionally. 'It's not about giving the microphone a blow job,' is how she explained it to me, 'it's the music and the power of the lyrics which is going to really make the crowd watch and want to come back for more.'

She found a back room of a Camden pub, and they started rehearsing there over the following weeks. Jane welcomed the energy which Yvonne brought and loved the suggestions that their new member gave to the group. Yvonne was so keen for the band to improve and 'really reach their potential', that she insisted they keep on rehearsing even after hours of practice. This wasn't welcomed by all the band, and it was only a matter of days before one of the guitarists quit and the drummer failed to show up.

There had also been some initial tension when the bass player, Steph, had got very drunk one evening when the band and their other halves were drinking together and admitted to Jane that she quite fancied Yvonne. Unfortunately, H, Steph's girlfriend, overheard and there followed ten minutes of accusations as Yvonne, Steph and H circled each other. It finally ended in hugs once Yvonne had shouted at H, 'Look, you know I like Steph, but there is more chance of me jumping into bed with Norma fucking Major than your girlfriend.' It turned out that was precisely the right thing to say.

The departure of the other band members left Jane, Yvonne and Steph on their own, but they decided that they didn't need another guitarist and set about simply auditioning for a new female drummer. They eventually found Keisha, a black woman living in South London, whose stories of her rebellious teenage years made even Yvonne do a double-take. 'That's our USP,' Yvonne emphasised, 'four feminists with attitude in a sexually charged rock band. Just like Kathleen Hanna and Bikini Kill. That is what we are going to be, but on this side of the Atlantic.'

The new line-up of The Libertine Dolls played their first gig a week later. Yvonne knew that The Ninth String had nights when there were no acts booked to play at the venue, and she persuaded the management to give them a try. They hastily printed up some flyers, stuck a few small ads in the local free magazines and on May 15, as John Smith announced his intention to stand for the Labour leadership, The Libertine Dolls proclaimed their intention to take over London's music scene.

It was a raw gig, and despite their rehearsals, they were not yet a tight unit. There can't have been more than fifty punters downstairs watching the band that evening, but Yvonne and Jane did manage to cajole some of them into dancing, and there were a few sweaty bodies in the bar before the end of the night.

Despite the small audience, Yvonne loved every minute, and when we went home that evening, she was bouncing off the ceiling with leftover adrenalin. We didn't get much sleep. Two days later, she asked for fewer shifts at The Ninth String so that she could dedicate more time to the band. Then she told me what she had done.

'I know the band are going to be a success, and your income from The Three Rs should be enough for both of us, right?'

I hoped she was right, about my job and the band.

My life at The Three Rs continued to be difficult. Chef Kevin maintained his antagonism and aggression towards me, and I was subjected to periodic racism, both blatant and underhand. I think the only reason he didn't sack me was because I produced a good standard of food.

'Is he like this with everyone?' I asked Jake one morning.

He shrugged. 'Everyone goes through it. You've got to be able to take a joke in this game.'

'Has anyone ever said anything?'

'About Chef? Are you mad? You want to keep your job?'

'But there are other restaurants.'

Jake put down his knife. 'The Three Rs is one of the most prestigious places in London. You work here, you can go anywhere next. And Chef is a brilliant cook. You want to learn, you accept his way of working. Even Chef Raybourne gives him some slack.'

Jake's words resonated. I didn't think any more about walking out because I had no intention of appearing weak. Chef Michel had warned me about the pressure, and there was plenty of that. Chef Raybourne was rarely in the kitchen and Chef Kevin ruled. I had only been there two weeks when he gave me a verbal warning for slightly overcooking some mackerel.

'What do you think this is, catering college? We sack people for less than that.'

He threw it in the bin. The kitchen was silent except for the tap running.

'I'm sorry Chef, it won't happen again,' I said, and waited for his anger to blow over.

'No. It fucking won't.'

With that, Kevin marched off to see Roger Raybourne. All the kitchen staff could hear them arguing in his office, the words 'not good enough' and 'want him out' clearly audible. I put my head down and continued to fillet my fish.

'You know that Chef Raybourne never consulted Kevin about your appointment,' Jake told me while we worked. 'That really wound him up. You didn't even have an interview like the rest of us. So you were a double whammy.'

Now the chilly atmosphere in the kitchen made more sense. So far my work had been checked and double-checked by Chef Kevin and I was forced to remake anything he claimed was even remotely sub-standard. I was shouted at, screamed at, and verbally abused every few days in my first month at the restaurant. I was given the worst shifts and I often worked until quite literally my fingers bled. I knew that Chef Kevin would have loved to sack me, so I worked harder than I had ever done in my life. I was convinced I could win him over once he saw past the colour of my skin. Chef still had to run his kitchen and he needed a Poissonnier, so he had to put up with me.

At the end of the month, I gained a tiny bit of recognition from the Sous Chef, who finally admitted I had done a good job. That almost made the previous four weeks worthwhile.

Yvonne noticed the difference in me. I came home either so exhausted I could barely talk, so indignant about a specific piece of abuse I had received or so elated that someone had actually said thank you to me during service, that it was hard for her to know how to approach me after each shift. She told me I was being exploited (I knew that), putting myself at risk (I doubted that – this was a professional kitchen) and stupid to stay there as I was clearly good enough to cook somewhere else where they did appreciate me.

'I'm worried about you, Vik,' she confided in me after one shift where Kevin had thrown a cookbook at me, narrowly missing my head. 'I know it's important to stand your ground to racist bullies like your Chef, but there comes a time when you have to ask how best to do it, when you can't do it on your own.'

I had never heard Yvonne talk like this before. She even suggested that I should talk to Roger Raybourne about it, but I wasn't going to do that.

'There's no way in hell that Chef Raybourne is going to sack his Head Chef,' I reminded her. 'He might give him a slap on the wrist, but that would be it. And you can imagine how Kevin would react with me if he found out I was telling on him. That really could get dangerous.'

Late May 1992

The week before The Libertine Dolls' next gig, Yvonne invited the other three members of the band for dinner at our flat. After eating, Yvonne picked up her heavy old ghetto blaster and positioned it in the middle of our kitchen table. She slipped a cassette into the tape deck and pressed play. Punk music blared out.

'Girls, listen. Have you heard of this band?'

The other women shook their heads.

'Who is it?' Steph asked.

'An American band from Washington state called Bikini Kill. They're part of the riot grrrl scene in the US. Groups like them, Bratmobile, Heavens to Betsy, they're all saying what I think we want to say: songs about sexuality, female empowerment, racism. But, of course, we're doing it in our own way.' She let the music play for a few bars. 'They also publish a zine called *Girl Power*. Girl Power. There – that is our style.'

Jane nodded. 'Girl Power. I like it.'

'Me too,' added Steph. 'You're right, it's concise and packs a punch.'

'Exactly.' Yvonne was excited. 'We should be the leaders in the UK with this, yes?'

'Which means what?' Keisha asked.

Yvonne opened her arms. 'When we play, we're not just Jane and Steph, Yvonne, and Keisha. We should allow ourselves to adopt on-stage personas. Let yourself go! That's what we're about. That's Girl Power.'

The four women raised their glasses to the music.

The Dolls introduced their new style a week later, at a pub in Finsbury Park. It was their best performance I had seen.

After the gig, I was sitting with the band at the bar when a portly man with a Bobby Charlton comb-over joined us. He was wearing an old, baggy grey-checked suit, his tie hanging halfway down his neck.

'I didn't know we were trying to attract fifty-somethings to our gigs,' Jane murmured.

The man stood in front of us. 'Good gig, that,' he said. 'Vibrant.'

'Glad you enjoyed it,' Yvonne said obliquely.

'Terry Duke,' he continued. 'Artist management.' The other girls glanced at each other as Jane grudgingly shook hands with Terry. 'Listen, you've got promise. Got any more gigs lined up?'

Yvonne shifted in her chair. 'Maybe.'

'Cool. So where is it? Another pub like this? Somewhere else where you need to drag the punters in?'

Yvonne glared. 'The Fox and Hounds in King's Cross.'

'I know it. An average sort of place.'

'Yeah? Well, wait till we play there.'

Terry smiled. 'Believe it or not, I know how difficult it is for a band like you, just starting off, wanting to play your music and change the world, to do all the boring things like book gigs and sort out payments. That's best handled by someone else. Someone who knows the scene and knows who to approach.'

Yvonne crossed her arms. 'Are you saying you want to be our *manager*?'

Terry held Yvonne's gaze. 'What if I told you I know Vince Power.'

Jane gasped. 'Who runs the Mean Fiddler?'

'That's the one.'

'Could you get us a gig there?'

'Not immediately, maybe. I think you need to work on a few things before Vince would give you a slot. But sure, in time.'

'Cool,' said Keisha. All of us were sitting up now.

I could tell Yvonne was still not convinced. 'Knowing someone isn't everything. Who else have you managed?'

Terry ticked off on his fingers half a dozen names of artists which even I had heard of, as well as several I didn't know but which seemed to impress Yvonne and the others even more. 'And before all that, I was even involved in the classical music scene, and let me tell you, that's a tough nut to crack for artists. I thought I knew my classics, but there are a lot more talented violinists and flautists than there are drummers in rock bands. No offence, Keisha,' he added quickly.

'None taken,' the drummer said sullenly. 'Is it true what they say about Kazuko?'

Terry grinned. 'I couldn't tell you that now, could I. Let's just say that there's no smoke without fire.'

Keisha threw back her head and laughed. 'I like this man,' she declared. 'I say we give you a chance.'

Jane and Steph nodded. Yvonne bit her lip. 'I don't know…'

'Look,' Terry lowered his voice, forcing the women to listen more carefully. 'I really like you girls, I think you've got something. The guy who runs this place said you were good, that's why I dropped by. And having seen you, I agree. I think you can go places and you can be big. But you need someone to help you.'

Then Terry played his trump card. 'Yvonne, I know Derek who runs the Fox and Hounds. We go back years. Shall I tell you what he normally pays his bands?'

Yvonne nodded. Terry said a figure.

'How much?' Yvonne clenched her fists. 'The little gobshite. He's not even paying us half that.'

'Like I say,' Terry said calmly, 'you need someone with a bit of inside knowledge to make sure you're getting the best deal.'

Yvonne pursed her lips. 'So how would it work then? You become our manager? You organise the gigs?'

'Me and my wife, Terry and June Artists Management Limited.'

Now it was my turn to be shocked. 'Terry… and June?! As in the seventies sitcom?'

'Well yes but not exactly. We're not those actors.'

'You don't think that's a bit lame?' I continued.

'You'd think so, wouldn't you? Actually, it gives us something of an edge. If you go in somewhere with a name like Terry and June, then half the time the guy you're dealing with doesn't think you're anything serious. So we offer him a contract, give him a deal, and you know what – he barely looks at it. Thinks he's taking us for a ride.' He grinned. 'Too late he discovers that we're the ones who have got him over a barrel. Let me tell you, June has the talons of a panther.'

He proceeded to tell us the story of how he manipulated the BBC so that one band he managed were booked on *Top of The Pops* without their single even being in the top fifty, with a rider that included champagne and cream cakes. By the end, all the band were laughing, Yvonne included.

'Of course, Auntie B was always a bit wary of June and me after that, but they still dealt with us. They just read the minutiae of the contracts a bit more carefully.'

They shook hands on a deal that evening and formalised it contractually later that week.

Seven

June 1992

As one of the more exclusive restaurants in London, it was comparatively common to get celebrities at The Three Rs. Regulars included several Hollywood actors, a fair few pop stars, and numerous footballers with their wives and girlfriends. We often received special requests from such parties, usually a supposed food intolerance or a demand to leave out some ingredient or other. Most of the time it used to piss off the whole kitchen, and I know that on several occasions when the request wasn't something which would harm a customer if we left it in, the ingredient was still included. I don't think a customer ever complained.

There were also the A-list celebs who asked for a dish which wasn't even on the menu. Depending on who it was, Chef Kevin was either delighted or enraged about such wishes. If he liked the person, then he would pull out all the stops and make the dish himself, even delivering it to their table if he could get away with it. If he disapproved of the requestor, then he would delegate the fare to one of his staff to create, but woe betide them if news got back to him that the customer had not enjoyed it.

It was early summer when a somewhat nonplussed Maître d' stalked into the kitchen to talk to Chef about a new cover.

Apparently, Lisa Constance, an emerging British movie starlet, had walked in without a reservation with three fellow actresses, and was demanding to speak to the Head Chef himself to discuss her meal choice. Kevin was thrilled to hear that such an entourage were dining at his restaurant, and ignoring his Maître d's indignance, he positively scampered out to meet them. When he returned ten minutes later, his mood had darkened, and he barked out orders to the Sous Chef and several Chefs de Partie. Then he approached my station.

'Come here, Cohen.'

I wiped my hands and joined him. Chef Kevin glowered at me. 'Lisa Constance has asked for a particular dish and I damn well hope you know how to make it.'

Clearly Chef didn't know the recipe, and it was so specialised that he couldn't make it up.

Chef stared me down. 'Do you know how to make Ikan Bakar?'

I don't know what Chef Kevin would have done if I had not known the dish. Would he have returned to the famous actress and told her he couldn't make it? Or would he have tried to cook it himself? And would he have punched me on the nose first?

Fortunately, I did know the fundamentals of Ikan Bakar – Malay burnt fish – certainly enough to make the sambal which is the key to the dish. It's basically grilled fish served in banana leaves in the authentic South-East Asian version. But if you get the balance wrong, then it will either be tasteless or blow your head off and kill any flavour in the fish. And, of course, the fish needs to be grilled to perfection.

I nodded at Chef Kevin. 'I do, Chef. I know how to make that.' Just for a moment, I thought I saw Kevin's cheek muscles flinch as if he was relieved.

'Fucking good thing,' he sneered and clicked his fingers at two other chefs. 'Andrew, Mac, help Vik here make the Ikan Bakar. And if he needs something doing, then do it. OK?'

The other two chefs nodded, as surprised as me at his command.

I cleared my throat. 'Chef, one more thing. Do you know why she is asking for this?'

'Why?'

'Yes, I mean, why Ikan Bakar?'

'Because she fucking wants it. Why the fuck does that matter?'

'Yes, I – I realise that. But, I don't suppose she explained why she wanted this specific dish, did she? Because,' I added quickly as Chef prepared to swear at me again, 'it would help me spice it correctly if I knew what version she liked.'

'What version?'

'Yes. You see, there is a classic Borneo recipe and a slightly different Singaporean variety –'

'She mentioned she had once had it in Malaysia, but she had never found anywhere in England that could replicate it to the exact taste.' Chef Kevin sniffed. 'So you're just going to have to get it right, aren't you? Does that help?'

'Yes, Chef.' I turned to the two chefs assigned to me. 'I need the following ingredients.' I started reeling off the core ingredients for the fish sambal: red chillies, shrimp (to make the belacan – shrimp paste), shallots, lime. 'And I really hope we have lemongrass. Do you know if we have any fish sauce?' I asked.

Mac nodded. 'I think so. We serve the occasional Thai dish.'

'Be careful with it. Don't drop the bottle because it stinks to high heaven.' Mac started to run to the shelves. 'And look for some turmeric powder too,' I called after him. I turned to

Andrew. 'Bring me a pestle and mortar, please. We could use a food processor, but we can control the sambal better in a mortar.'

Ikan Bakar is often served using stingray wings, but I knew we didn't have any such fish in our kitchen, so I substituted it with fresh sole. It would have to do. The harder part was knowing how to present the fish as we certainly did not stock banana leaves. I discussed the issue with Mac.

'I guess there aren't any Indian supermarkets in Mayfair, are there?'

'None near here. What else can we use?'

I thought for a moment. 'Have we got any fresh corn on the cob? With their husks still on?'

'I think so.'

'Then let's give this a go. We can try to use the husks in place of the banana leaves, but they need to be dried. Try stripping a few off and put them in the oven between two baking trays. We'll see how close we can get to making them semi-authentic.'

Thirty-five minutes later, Chef Kevin was calling out for the main courses. 'Two minutes to the pass, yes, Cohen?'

'Yes, Chef!'

'Two minutes?'

'Yes, Chef.'

Kevin grunted without meeting my eye. I couldn't tell if he was pleased I was on-time or furious that I seemed to be pulling it off – maybe both. Two minutes later, I presented the fish to the Head Chef. The corn husks were not perfect, but Mac had done a decent job getting them as usable as possible. The sole was cooked well, and I just hoped that the sambal was not too spicy for the actress.

Kevin took my serving without a word, and nodding to the Maître d', he indicated it was ready along with the other meals for the same table. Chef then turned his back on me without a further glance. I returned to my station and crossed my fingers.

Fifteen minutes later, the Maître d' returned and whispered to Chef Kevin. The Head Chef's face went from his default grimace to a look of thunder in five seconds. I watched as he glowered in my direction and beckoned me over with a single, crooked finger.

'Customer wants to see us,' he said. 'Follow me.'

My heart sank. She was clearly a high-maintenance diner. What hadn't been to her liking? The leaves, the sole? I was pretty sure that the sambal had worked. I did as I was told, and followed the Chef de Cuisine into the restaurant, behind the Maître d'. He led us to a table of four women, all beautifully groomed in dazzling dresses, dripping jewellery, laughing at a joke. When we reached the table, I glanced at their plates, and noted they were all more-or-less empty. I let out an inaudible breath. The Maître d' coughed politely. One of the women looked up; she had Jennifer Aniston hair and a Julia Roberts smile. I had seen her face on film posters, but she was even more beautiful in the flesh.

'Miss Constance,' Chef Kevin started, 'you wanted to see us.'

Lisa Constance put down her champagne glass and gave him her hundred-watt smile. 'I did, yes. Are you the chef who made me the Ikan Bakar?'

Kevin paused. I could tell he so wanted to claim ownership of my dish, but knew that he couldn't pull it off. If I hadn't known better, I would have thought that he might burst into tears. Chef cocked his neck muscles.

'No, I'm the Head Chef, Miss Constance. The chef who made your Ikan Bakar would be my Poissonnier.' Slowly, he nodded at me.

'Well,' said the actress. 'Then let me say this, Mr Poissonnier. That was without a doubt…the best Asian fish dish I have ever eaten outside of Malaysia. It was absolutely divine. Where did you learn how to cook like that?'

Lisa Constance sat forwards in her chair, propping her chin on her hands, as if I was the most fascinating person on the planet. Behind me, the Maître d' gave me the tiniest of nudges in the back.

'I just love cooking fish,' I said quickly. 'I'm so glad you enjoyed it. Thank you.'

'No, it is I who should be thanking you,' Lisa Constance replied smoothly. 'I have requested this dish at many good restaurants in London since I had it in Kota Kinabalu and none of them has come close to what I ate in KK. But you have cracked it. You must be a special chef in great demand – do you do private catering? I would love to use you one day. And I'm sure,' she added waving in Kevin's direction, 'that your Head Chef must be thrilled to have you on his staff. He might even have to watch his back if you're producing dishes that good!' Her fellow actresses laughed with her.

I risked a glance at Kevin. It was like watching a slow-motion action replay of a car crash as ever so slowly, Chef forced a smile and nodded at the customer.

'Thank you, Miss Constance,' I said again. 'Ladies, have a lovely evening.'

'You too,' they chorused, all eyes still on me.

As soon as we walked back through the kitchen doors, Chef Kevin ripped off his apron, flung it to the floor and stormed off towards the fridges without a glance at me. I took a deep breath and walked back to my station. Although Mac and Andrew were kind enough to say well done under their breath, the rest of the staff looked away. I knew why: in the Chef de Cuisine's eyes, he had been shown up. Not merely by one of his Chef de Parties, but by a 'Paki'. He probably couldn't imagine anything more intolerable. It was ironic: in what should have been my proudest moment in The Three Rs, I was thanking my stars that there was nothing that could make it any worse.

I was wrong.

We barely saw the Head Chef for the rest of that service, and when I arrived at the restaurant the next day, he point blank ignored me. That didn't surprise or worry me, and I got on with my mise en place.

Then Roger Raybourne arrived. I didn't see him enter the kitchen, but one of the apprentis nudged me and flicked his head towards the pass. The restaurant owner was standing there in his business suit instead of his whites, talking to Chef Kevin. I didn't think it was possible for Kevin to look any angrier than I had seen him in the past twenty-four hours, but I was wrong. I couldn't hear what they were saying, but I saw the Head Chef gesticulating wildly, while Roger Raybourne stood there motionless, hands in his pockets, talking down to Chef with his distinct height advantage and occasionally shaking his head.

After a few minutes, the Executive Chef spun on his heels and headed towards me. Chef Kevin slouched behind him. The usual hubbub of the kitchen dulled to the occasional whisper.

'Hello, Vik.'

'Chef Raybourne.' I wiped my hands on a cloth.

'No need to stop what you're doing, chef. I thought you might like to know that Lisa Constance rang me today as she wanted to tell me personally how gorgeous, her words not mine, your food was last night. She thinks we should promote you right away. Well done, Vik, good work; if you carry on excelling like this, the sky's the limit.' Chef Raybourne placed his hand on my arm. Then, nodding to Kevin, they left the kitchen together.

I should have felt on top of the world, ecstatic that the owner of The Three Rs should deliver such a compliment in person (and despite my misgivings, a tiny part of me was elated), but it didn't take Jake the rôtisseur's shake of the head in my direction for me to know that I was in trouble. If Kevin had been seething the night before, then today he would be breathing fire.

After Lisa Constance's visit, I had to walk a fine line with Chef Kevin. I didn't want to abdicate my responsibilities, but I didn't want to give him an excuse to push me around. But inevitably we had to work closely together during some shifts.

Soon after the success of my Ikan Bakar, another celebrity asked for an adapted fish dish, which Chef told me to make. It was a Saturday night, always our busiest. I think Chef Kevin might have refused the request if it hadn't come from one of his favourite footballers. But it meant that Chef began working right beside me, ostensibly because he was making another dish for the table which had to go out simultaneously; I was sure it was because Kevin relished the opportunity to pounce on any mistake I made.

It began well enough; we were both chopping and dicing ingredients, watching each other's moves, and at one point, Chef even grunted satisfaction while observing my knife skills. I wondered if this might even be a turning point in our relationship. Unfortunately, as I was finishing my prep, Kevin leaned across me to reach for a herb, and as he did so, his elbow swept across my station, scattering leftover vegetables. I think it was an accident but as he pulled his arm back, he knocked my fish and it slipped on to the floor.

'What the fuck, Cohen?' Chef slammed his knife on to the countertop.

'Sorry, Chef, but you–'

'I don't fucking care, Cohen. We've got five minutes to get this out. Throw that shit away and get another bass prepped now.'

He turned away to deal with another chef's question. I looked at my station – it was a mess. I couldn't tell what was edible and what couldn't be used. I pushed it all to one side, thinking I would clear it later, grabbed a knife and prepared a new dish faster than I had ever done before. Two minutes later, Chef was back at my side, breathing down my neck.

'Come on, Cohen, come on. Faster. I want that fish on the pass in three minutes.'

'Yes, Chef, but I–'

'Now, Cohen, now.'

And with a furious gesture, Chef Kevin waved his arm at the front of the kitchen. In doing so, he hit my elbow. That wouldn't have mattered normally, but I was panicking, and my knife handle was slippery from the fish, and as he knocked me, the knife slipped out of my clutches and clattered on to the floor at our feet, point first. Around us, voices lowered. If there is one thing which any chef hates, it is knives being dropped on the floor. Not only is it dangerous, but it's your livelihood. It should never happen. At least the knife had missed our feet.

It seemed that everyone but me knew what would happen next.

Chef Kevin faced me, looking angrier than I had ever seen him. 'Cohen, pick that up now,' he said quietly. His softer voice was more terrifying than if he had shouted at me.

I bent down, half expecting to get a knee in the ribs while I did so, reached for the knife and placed it on the counter in front of me. We both looked at it. The point of the knife had chipped off. It was ruined. I cursed myself. My parents had only just given me my own set of knives and already I had broken one. What a fool.

Chef Kevin was still staring at the broken knife. His face was turning even redder than before and a muscle in his cheek twitched. He looked, if it was possible, angrier than I had ever seen him before. Slowly, he moved his hand to the knife's handle, his fingers hovering over it. I frowned, surprised at his concern for my equipment, and looked again at the knife – and my heart dropped. I'm surprised it didn't stop beating.

It wasn't my knife.

It was Chef Kevin's.

My mind raced. How could this have happened? After Chef had knocked the food on my station, in my rush to get the dish prepared, I must have picked up his knife by mistake. Christ, yes. That was it. My Sabatier knife lay to one side, untouched.

I heard a whisper at my elbow and I realised that everyone around me knew what had happened. Within seconds, the kitchen was silent. The other chefs seemed to have backed away from us. It was just Chef Kevin and me standing at my station: me, terrified and not knowing what to say or do; the Head Chef now trembling as he lifted his knife from the counter to examine it. For a few seconds he turned it round, caressing it with his fingers as if it was as precious as a new born puppy.

'You better get that dish out in thirty seconds, Cohen's Chef said quietly.

And then, without even looking at me, he walked very slowly across the floor towards his office.

The noise levels gradually returned, the plongeurs helping me tidy my station. But the other Chefs de Partie didn't talk to me, no one came near me except when they had to ask for an order, and I spent the rest of the shift expecting to receive any manner of verbal or physical retribution at any moment. It never happened.

I went home that night knowing I had dodged a bullet, but not sure how.

Early July 1992

During the first weeks after he was appointed as manager of the band, Terry kept his word and started to book The Libertine Dolls into a series of pubs and clubs across London. The first few gigs were still in venues where the band had to compete with the beer, loud conversation and the fact that most of the punters hadn't come to see The Libertine Dolls play. It forced the band to hone their set, adding and removing songs as they discovered which were more popular. Yvonne and Jane had started writing their own songs and they incorporated a few into their performances. Yvonne introduced a concept on some nights of theming a song around whatever was in the news at that time. The stand-out example was when ex-prime minister, Margaret Thatcher, became a Baroness in the House of Lords and The Libertine Dolls dedicated a one-night-only cover of Raven's 'Blind Leading the Blind' – that was greeted with such approval when they finished that they had to stop playing for a minute or so to let the cheering die down.

The more they played, so they began to increasingly acquire a reputation as a band that would guarantee a good evening. There was no one else on the scene like The Libertine Dolls. Gradually, other gig offers came in, supporting small acts who already had a following and playing in dedicated music venues rather than pubs. They concentrated more on the music and less on the sexual theatrics, although they maintained their on-stage personas and played the songs which had created all the attention. They began to be recognised for their music as well as their 'stage show'.

The Libertine Dolls had concentrated on gigging exclusively in London for the first couple of months since Yvonne had joined. This was partly because the opportunities were far greater in London pubs and clubs, but it was also pragmatic because that's where all the women had their day jobs. But come July, Terry mooted the idea of the band playing at festivals outside the capital.

'So where are you going to get us a gig,' Jane asked. 'Glastonbury?'

'You're too good for Michael Eavis,' Terry said deadpan and then smiled. 'Maybe not quite yet. Have you heard of SaxFest?'

'Is that a jazz festival?' Steph asked.

It wasn't. It turned out that SaxFest was a rock festival which attracted up to two thousand people to a site just outside Saxmundham in Suffolk, in the expansive grounds of a large, private manor house where the owners needed the money to be able to afford the upkeep of the building. (Not that they lived there when the event was happening.) The event flyers advertised it as a Hunting Lodge, and Terry told us that the main house was full of old coursing and shooting equipment, portraits and memorabilia from the 1920s. The stage set-up was modern, though, with an excellent sound system.

I watched from the side of the stage and crossed my fingers. Being a small, unsigned band, The Libertine Dolls had been given an early afternoon timeslot, when the venue was still not full. The Libertine Dolls came on, played a few songs and got a decent reception. Yvonne and Jane wanted to do something to make the audience remember them, so Yvonne had come up with one of her one-time-only songs and introduced it from the front of the stage.

'I'm guessing you guys have heard of Hank Stone, yes, the so-called porn king of America. He produces films and magazines for the adult industry and earns millions. Well, let me tell you, what he actually does is exploit women. His pornography kingdom is a pile of shit.' And she spat on the stage. Some people in the front cheered. Yvonne continued: 'Earlier this month, another magazine in the States published a photo of Mr Stone on the front cover with a gunsight superimposed over his face.' The crowd cheered a bit louder. 'And that gave me an idea. So let me tell you what I want to do to him.'

And with a signal to the rest of the band, they struck up AC/DC's 'Shoot to Thrill'. It encouraged more of the crowd who had been lounging in the field to come closer to the stage. After singing a couple of choruses, Yvonne nodded at Steph and Jane, and they carried on with the regular beat of the song while Yvonne unstrapped her guitar. She went behind the drum-kit where Keisha was sitting and returned a moment later, holding up some copies of *New Scarlet*, Hank Stone's own porn magazine. There were a few derisory catcalls from the front of the audience.

Yvonne put her finger to her lips. And as the band continued to bang out the song, she started to rip up the magazine and hurl its pages into the audience. Then she turned around and wiped a few pages up and down her bottom before throwing them on the floor and jumping up and down on them. With a final swipe of her arm, she went back to her mic, and the band finished the song with a concluding chorus.

They hit the last chords and among the cheers, launched straight into two final numbers. They left the stage to whistles and applause.

That should have been that for The Libertine Dolls at SaxFest, but it wasn't. Two hours later, the band and I were sitting in the sun enjoying our beers when Terry walked up.

'I have news', he said. 'Tonight, as you may know, The Charlie Bridge Band were supposed to be the penultimate act, but unfortunately, Charlie has fallen sick. Appendicitis or something. But he won't be playing, that's for sure. So...' the band's manager looked serious and then broke into a smile. 'The organisers have asked if you will do an extra set instead of them.' He held his arms out. 'What do you say? Fancy another bash?'

For a moment, the girls looked at each other and then Jane let out a whoop, and they all started hugging each other and then jumped on their manager as well.

'Terry, you are a fucking genius!' Jane laughed. 'How the hell did you pull that one off?'

Terry smiled. 'I know someone who owes me a favour. And they heard how well you went down in your early set – the field has been buzzing about your stunt with *New Scarlet* magazine, Yvonne – and they think you can step up.' Yvonne laughed. 'It's your chance to really make an impression. Don't blow it.'

I looked at Jane, Keisha and Steph and they were all grinning like Cheshire Cats. Then I looked at Yvonne; she was frowning.

'Yvonne, you OK?'

Yvonne nodded. 'Mm? Yes, I'm fine. Actually, I've got an idea.' She turned to her manager. 'Terry, can you get me into the Hunting Lodge? I'd like to have a bit of a look around.'

We didn't see Yvonne again until thirty minutes before the band were due on stage. She was carrying an old hessian messenger bag.

'Jeez, Yvonne,' Jane snapped. 'Where the fuck have you been? We were starting to think you'd had an accident or something.'

Yvonne ignored Jane's remark, dropped the bag at her feet and slung an arm around my neck.

'Guys, listen. I've come up with a slight adjustment to the Hank Stone song. I can't tell you about it all now so you'll have to trust me, OK? But I promise you – we will make an impact.'

Steph sighed heavily. 'Why do I think this is more than a slight adjustment?' Yvonne winked at her. 'Oh, good God. Yes, OK. What do you want us to do?'

Yvonne smiled broadly. 'It's very simple. During the song, when I ask you to stop playing, you stop. OK?'

'For how long?' Jane asked. 'How will we know when to start again?'

'You'll know,' Yvonne said flatly and gave Terry a wink. Then she ran her fingernails down the nape of my neck. 'Oh, and Vik? I need you to do something too.'

Half an hour later I stood at the side of the stage and watched the four women walk on, Yvonne dropping her bag behind Keisha's drum-kit. They plugged in their guitars, Keisha clicked her drumsticks above her head, her bangles glinting under the stage lights, and the band launched into their opening Divinyls cover, followed by a Status Quo number. By the end of their second song, the crowd were already cheering, and when they played two heavied-up Abba covers, it was clear that a rock festival audience had never seen anything like it. I swear half of them were laughing. Although most of them seemed to know the words to 'Gimme! Gimme! Gimme!'.

After another few songs, I saw Yvonne beckon Steph and Jane towards her, where she said a few words and then she nodded to Keisha who held up her drumsticks in acknowledgement. Then Yvonne faced the audience. Where there had been five hundred or so people earlier in the day, now the field was full to capacity, and the sun had just dipped over the horizon. The lights on stage were shining brightly, and the spotlight focused on the lead singer.

Yvonne pulled the mic towards her with both hands. 'I'm guessing all of you guys have heard of Hank Stone, yes?' she said calmly and repeated her soliloquy of earlier, disparaging him for his exploitation of women. The crowd booed and cheered with Yvonne as if it was a pantomime. As before, with a signal to the rest of the band, The Libertine Dolls struck up AC/DC's 'Shoot to Thrill', and as before, it went down well.

After singing a couple of choruses, Yvonne nodded at Steph and Jane, unstrapped her guitar and slid behind Keisha's drumkit. The rest of the band carried on playing. When she returned to the front of the stage, she was carrying what looked like a hunting rifle. She hoisted it up with one arm and grabbed the mic with the other hand.

'Do you know what this is?' she asked. 'It's something to blow Hank fucking Stone's head off.' The audience cheered.

Then she signalled to Jane to ease back on her guitar, so all you could hear was Steph's bass and Keisha's drums stomping out the beat, with an occasional swipe at the strings from Jane, a few whoops from the crowd. Which made her next actions all the more audible.

'In case you hadn't noticed, we think that Girl Power is great. We think that empowering women to have sex when they want to is great. To show off their bodies when it is their choice, is something which all you women –' she swung her arm around in an arc in front of her, '– can do if you want to.' More cheers. 'But when a nasty old man is preying on young girls' vulnerability and making money solely for him and his cronies then we say that it's time to *stop*.'

Yvonne held up her hand, and the band ceased playing in an instant. She brought her hand down and they started again. Yvonne smiled and looked down at the gun she was holding. 'I thought you might like to know that I just found this in that big house back there. Do you think it works? Should we find out?'

The crowd cheered. Yvonne looked to her right and caught my eye. I shook my head. Yvonne had said she wanted me to come on stage, but she hadn't mentioned that there was to be some theatrics with a gun. She crooked her forefinger in a come-here motion, and I shuffled on to the stage. I got within a few feet of Yvonne and then she held up her hand. I stopped and stood stock still. Yvonne raised her palm in the air. I nodded and held up the copy of *New Scarlet* magazine high above my head.

'Girls,' Yvonne said into the mic, 'Stop your playing for a moment. Terry – give me some Rossini.'

The rest of the band stopped playing, and for a moment there was silence, even the crowd didn't hoot or call out – they were transfixed, and probably as confused as I was; this certainly wasn't turning out to be your average rock gig.

Then, out of the speakers, at full volume came the opening trumpet blast of the finale of the 'William Tell Overture', and as the music kicked in, so the entire crowd, or at least as far back as I could see through the sweat now running into my eyes, started pogoing to the music. It was more like a punk version of Last Night of the Proms. I glanced back at Yvonne, and the mad woman was now waving her rifle around her head as if she was conducting the audience. The rest of the band seemed as nonplussed as I was, and then Jane, followed by Steph, started clapping along and geeing up the crowd. It was as if we were back in the Archway pub on the night Yvonne had met them, but twenty times bigger.

Slowly at first and then faster and faster, the violins and brass picked up the pace, and as they did so, the crowd grew more frenzied and Yvonne's gun-waving more and more exaggerated, and as the orchestra built up to the crescendo with the last crash of the cymbals, so Yvonne turned to me, blew me a kiss, cocked her rifle and pointed it directly above my head. Then with an equally theatrical pull of the trigger and a recoil which would have done any ham actor justice, she fired the gun.

There was a sudden crack above my head, and the *New Scarlet* magazine I was holding burst into flames and a flash of white light shot upwards into the air. Somehow, I kept hold of the tattered shards of the magazine, before involuntarily dropping to my knees.

Out of the corner of my eye, I could see Yvonne, Jane and Steph standing at the front edge of the stage, holding hands and waving them above their heads at the crowd, Keisha joining them a few moments later. All I could hear was a non-stop cacophony of cheering and whooping and screaming from the crowd.

I discovered later that Yvonne had indeed found the gun in the Hunting Lodge and concocted the whole affair with Terry. The magazine I had been holding contained an envelope of sparklers, bangers and magnesium strips and was doused with lighter fluid. Terry had sneaked on to the stage as the overture came to an end, and as Yvonne 'fired' the gun, he had fired up the mini-Molotov Cocktail I was holding.

The band couldn't continue with their set after that. They tried to finish 'Shoot to Thrill', but Yvonne said that they could barely hear themselves sing, so they just thrashed out the final few chords and decided to call it a night. The audience, however, had different ideas and demanded two encores.

Late July 1992

For the two weeks following the incident where I broke Chef Kevin's knife, I found the atmosphere at The Three Rs to be quite surreal. I knew I was cooking good food, the other chefs were cordial with me, and I didn't get any abuse at all from Kevin. But I noticed that no one said a word to me that didn't have something to do with the dishes or the food preparation, and hardly any of the staff would look me in the eye if I attempted to engage them in everyday conversation. If I tried to join in with general staff banter about football or who they had shagged the night before, the chatter just shut down and people returned to their work.

My last shift for the week was the Friday evening, with Yvonne and I having managed to plan a rare weekend together when neither of us was working. It had been a busy serving, and I was still clearing down late after service had finished. The other staff began drifting out, one by one, on their way to parties or late-night drinking sessions. Just as I thought that I was on top of my work, Chef Kevin stalked towards my station.

'Cohen. Go and help Jake finish his meat preparation for tomorrow.'

I was surprised. 'Can someone else help Jake? I've got to check my fish, Chef.'

'Everyone else has left. Just do as I fucking say – chef,' Kevin snarled.

I nodded glumly. Jake told me to start mincing steak with the large, electric meat grinder as he didn't have time to do that, and promptly disappeared. Fifteen minutes later, with the meat grinder winding down, Kevin was back with another demand.

'The ice crates containing tomorrow's fish have toppled over in one of the walk-in fridges, Cohen. Go and sort it out.'

'How did that happen?'

'Do I look as if I fucking care? Just fix it.'

None of the apprentis was around – it seemed everyone else had left now – so I went to check. He was right. Someone, I never found out who, had knocked over the fish crates and there were fish and ice all over the floor. It took me over half an hour to sort out all the mess. When I finally stepped out of the fridge, I realised that the kitchen was a lot darker than usual. But as it was so late, I presumed that whoever was locking up was waiting for me.

I started to walk towards the exit, realising that not only was it dark but it was also abnormally quiet. I was aware of my own footsteps, and I had never heard any kitchen so noiseless. The only other sound was the hum of the fridges. I called out to make sure there was someone still in the kitchen, in case I had been locked in accidentally, but there was no response. Gingerly, I edged my way along the side of the vegetable racks, trying to work out where the remaining light was coming from. I had just walked around the last corner when I heard a cough. I started to turn around but then I heard footsteps behind me, and just as I was starting to wonder if someone was playing a practical joke, I felt someone grab my shoulder and kick me hard in the back of the knees, followed by a shove in the back. I fell forwards and desperately tried to break my fall, but I had been pushed hard and my wrist buckled. I yelped with the pain and rolled on to my side.

Somebody grasped my armpits and hauled me up, and as I struggled and tried to break free, I received another crack across my shoulder blades, and I toppled forwards again. A rough cloth was pulled over my head; I knew instantly what it was, I could smell the potatoes that had been in it. I reached up to pull it off but received a hard whack across my fingers from something like a pastry roller. I yelped and pulled my hands away. I shook my head violently from side to side, but there was no shaking it off. Someone pulled it further down over my neck. I stopped trying to shake it off and concentrated on just trying to breathe, not panic. Easier said than done.

The man holding me, I presumed it was a man, wrenched me forwards. Even under my sack hood, I could tell it became brighter over the next few seconds as the kitchen lights were turned back on. 'What's going on?' I called out, my voice muffled by the sack. 'What are you doing?'

For an answer, my assailant punched me in the stomach, which knocked all the wind out of me, and I fell forwards again on to my knees. I tried once more to rip off the sack but as I did so, it was again pulled back over my neck. And even though I couldn't see the fingers stretching the sack over me, I could smell them. They smelt of Gauloises – Chef Kevin's choice of tobacco.

My breathlessness increased. The man started to physically drag me along the floor by my forearms. Then he yanked me upwards and bent me over what I guessed was a kitchen counter, and before I could reach out to break my fall, my chin hit the worktop. I yelled out in pain. I slumped down on my knees, still winded, and scrabbled across the floor, trying to rip off my hood, which seemed to be fastened somehow. I bumped into another obstacle and stopped to catch my breath. It was ominously quiet.

It was at this point that I realised I was in deeply serious trouble. Assuming this was Kevin, it was clear that I was going to get beaten up badly. But surely it couldn't be anyone else but Chef Kevin: no one else could get in, the back door of the kitchen couldn't even be opened from outside, and anyway, I'd smelt the tobacco on my assailant's hands. Evidently, this was why Chef had let everyone else go already. I wondered if he was going to identify himself or tell me to 'quit the restaurant or else', and how long I could hold out before I acquiesced. I had made my point in terms of sticking it out at the restaurant for this long, perhaps it was now time to call it a day at The Three Rs.

I wish it had been that simple.

The silence was broken by the sound of one of the kitchen appliances starting up. Suddenly, I went from being scared to feeling truly petrified. I recognised the noise: I had been using the machine earlier that evening.

I started to crawl away again, any direction would do, but it was to no avail. Kevin grabbed me and hauled me up to my feet, forced my hands behind my back and tied them and pulled me forwards towards the metallic groan of the meat grinder. I began to scream for the first time, calling out for help and trying to fight back, and instantly a hand reached under my hood and my mouth was muffled with a cloth. Within seconds, I was thrown forwards on to the metal counter, and as I turned my head sideways, I smelt Kevin's sweat as his face came down to meet mine.

Still without saying a word, the chef untied my hands and yanked my right arm towards him, and pain tore through my shoulder as he leaned against me. I couldn't move.

I only remember some of what happened next. Kevin seized my right wrist, the volume of the meat grinder increasing as he dragged me towards it, closer and closer to the blades of the machine. My shoulder felt as if it was on fire, and I was pulling back so hard that I thought my tendons would snap. All my pleas and screams were muted by the cloth in my mouth. I do remember the initial pain as the blades met my first finger and I can still hear the sound of my bones as the grinder started to do its work... But that's it.

I must have passed out with the pain before the rest of my hand went in.

The next thing I remember was waking up in a bed which wasn't my own, lying on my back, not being able to recall where I was. I blinked; everything seemed overly bright, and I squeezed my eyes open and shut several times – which triggered pain to shoot across my forehead – before I could focus on where I was. I was in a hospital bed in a ward, wearing a full-length gown. A needle and syringe was attached to the back of my left hand, and my eyes followed it up to a drip bag which hung above my bed.

I turned my head to the right, and as I did, a wave of nausea rushed over me. I groaned. Then I heard 'Vik! You're awake!' Yvonne threw her arms around my neck. 'Vik! I was so worried! Vik, oh, Vik!' and then she buried her face into the side of my neck and sobbed. For ages.

I lay there in shock and, with my left arm still attached to the drip bag, I tried to return her hug with my other arm, but I could barely lift it. It felt as if there was a heavy weight attached to the end. I glanced down: it was wrapped tightly with bandages.

Sunlight was streaming through the window behind my bed. It was only when the pain of Yvonne's embrace became worse than the pain in my head that I tried to ease her off me. I couldn't of course, so instead, I croaked, 'Yvonne. Please…' and she lifted her head again. I could see the tears still streaming down her face, and I tried to smile, but instead, I felt tears come to my eyes too. We lay there for a few moments, our foreheads just touching, before Yvonne pushed herself up, dragged the back of her hand across her nose and sniffed loudly. Then she managed a smile and very gently stroked my cheek. I blinked back as I stopped crying.

'Miss Anderson, I think you need to sit back down now.' I craned my neck to see a doctor at the foot of my bed, holding a clipboard. She smiled gently. 'I'm sure that was welcome, but now he needs to rest again.'

She pulled some curtains along the railing above my bed. The doctor came round to the other side where my drip bag was and, I noticed, other equipment with lights and numbers emitting a low hum. She looked at the flashing digits and adjusted something on the wire which led to my drip bag.

'How *are* you feeling, Mr Cohen? I don't think you had a chance to answer Miss Anderson.'

'Confused,' I said. I thought for a moment. 'I hurt all over, my head, my shoulder, my arm.'

'Do you feel drowsy?'

'I do.'

'That'll be the morphine helping, nothing to worry about. Not after what you've been through.'

After what I... Wait, what was she saying? What had I been through? I felt so shattered.

'Where am I? What's happened to me?'

'Don't worry about that for now.' The doctor raised her eyes and looked at Yvonne. 'Two minutes, OK. Then you need to let him rest.'

I watched the doctor walk away, wondering if I should be asking more questions, before realising that Yvonne was talking to me again: '... thought you were going to die.' I looked back at her, wondering what she meant but suddenly I felt extremely sleepy.

'Yvonne, I...'

'Shhh,' Yvonne whispered and stroked my head again. 'You do need to rest. Don't worry, I'll be here when you wake up again.' And she bent over and kissed me on the lips.

As Morpheus worked his magic, I wondered what I was doing here in hospital.

When I awoke again, no one was standing by my bed, and the chair in which Yvonne had been sitting was empty. I lay still and looked back at the machine quietly buzzing above my head. There was something about that noise…

I felt more awake than I had previously, and I surveyed where I was. In hospital clearly, but with the curtains around my bed drawn back again, I could see I was in a small ward with three other beds, two of which contained sleeping patients. There was a large seascape hanging on the wall; it was terrible, with a harbour and a few boats supposedly bobbing on its waters but looking as if they were anchored fast, unlikely to bob even a few inches. It was a painting which I was to grow to dislike over the days to come.

I shifted my weight and grimaced as my right shoulder spasmed again. Then I examined my right arm. It lay alongside my torso more like a pipeline pinned to the sea floor than a living appendage. I peered at the bandage on the end of it. It was a large, well-wrapped dressing, covering my wrist and at least six inches of my arm and it puzzled me; what was it doing there?

Then I noticed the machine again, buzzing above my head. I looked at the bandage and raised my eyes to the machine. Then I studied the dressing again, focused on the buzzing and then I remembered: The Three Rs kitchen, Chef Kevin, the noise of the kitchen appliance, the meat grinder.

I screamed.

Within seconds, a nurse was by my bed, checking the machine, putting her hand on my chest, but I carried on screaming. I don't know for how long. More medical people came, and I thought

I also saw Yvonne at one point at the foot of my bed before I found my eyes closing again.

The next time I woke up, the room was darker. Dim light glowed softly in the ceiling. My left hand, with the drip in it, felt sore. Yvonne was back in her chair, her legs tucked up under her, reading. She didn't appear to have noticed that I was awake and so I didn't say anything. I watched her for a while, flicking through a magazine, biting her nails between flipping the pages. Yvonne rarely read magazines, and I wasn't convinced she was really reading this one. I still felt sleepy.

Then I looked at my right arm and remembered again why I was here. I opened my mouth wide, but this time I didn't scream out loud. I just closed my eyes and re-ran in my mind my final scene in The Three Rs kitchen with Chef Kevin: the walk-in fridge, the kitchen counter-tops, the vegetable racks, the meatgrinder. The meat grinder. Kevin had asked me to help Jake…

The morphine kicked in and I fell asleep again.

Yvonne told me later that I carried on waking and calling out and then falling asleep again for another thirty hours before I finally woke up and 'spoke normally' to her. She had been there the entire time, except when a nurse had forced her to go home for a few hours. But she returned while I was still sleeping and in her inimitable style managed to persuade the medical staff to let her stay by my bedside even when all the regulations said that she shouldn't. I think my doctor agreed that it would be better for me if someone I trusted were present when I came round again.

The morning I properly woke, Yvonne and my doctor – she introduced herself as Dr Washington - pulled my curtains around my bed and told me what had happened two days before.

Someone had seen a taxi dropping me off outside University College Hospital in Euston, where I was now, with my bleeding arm in a makeshift bandage, gaffer-taped to a champagne cooler half-full of ice. Apparently a man in bloodied, chef's whites had guided me into the hospital and made sure I was looked after. I must have looked quite a sight, staggering through the doors into A&E and collapsing on the floor, floating in and out of consciousness, wearing a badly applied tourniquet. The tourniquet and ice were the only reason I hadn't died from severe loss of blood, with the ice staunching the bleeding. Even so, it had apparently been touch-and-go for a while. The doctors rushed me into surgery and did what they could, but Kevin and the meat grinder had done their evil; my right arm now finished at my wrist. Or, technically speaking, where the radius and the ulna met in my forearm – I was to learn a lot about carpal anatomy over the following weeks.

The official cause of my injury was recorded as an accident. Of course, Yvonne, knowing what I had told her previously about Kevin Tyndall, didn't believe for a second that this was the case, but it was another two days before I could bring myself to tell her or the police what I recalled. The officers who visited me in hospital listened to my account of Chef Kevin's racism and what I remembered about the attack. They took notes and subsequently visited the kitchen where they interviewed the staff – none of whom purported that my working relationship with Chef Kevin had been anything other than genial – and checked the meat grinder for fingerprints, but reported back that they had only found mine. That's when I discovered that it was Kevin who had allegedly discovered me bleeding in the kitchen, applied a temporary tourniquet and called a cab to take me straight to A&E. It was beyond belief.

Predictably (but I loved her for it), after crying and gasping, Yvonne swore and stamped around the room, screaming of injustice. It was ironic that Yvonne's fury, rather than make me even angrier, somehow tampered down my rage. My life already felt as if it was slipping away from me. How would I cook now? Who would want me in their kitchen any more?

Thoughts of revenge surfaced and then floated away again. There was a part of me that was also frightened. If slicing off my hand was Chef Kevin's first action against me, what else would he be prepared to do?

Dr Washington was equally as horrified as Yvonne when she heard my account. She sat by my bed after the police had visited me. 'Just so you know, Vik, the police talked to me too.'

'Good,' Yvonne cut in. 'I hope you told them what a racist psychopath Kevin Tyndall is.'

'That's not my job, Yvonne. I gave them information on your condition, and they asked me for my opinion on how it could have been caused.'

'Well that's OK,' I said. 'You know how it was caused. My Head Chef rammed my hand into a meat grinder.'

'Yes, I know that's what you told me, Vik.'

'Wait.' I tried to push myself up on my bed. 'You sound as if you don't believe me.'

'I'm sure that you genuinely believe that's what happened, but...'

'But what?'

Dr Washington clutched her clipboard to her chest. 'One of the questions they asked me was whether, in my professional opinion, someone could have forced another person's hand into such an appliance –'

'And the answer's yes. Because he did it.'

'And if so,' the doctor continued, 'then what sort of damage it would have inflicted.'

I held up my right arm. 'You can see that. Everyone can see.'

'The problem, Vik, is that the injury you received infers something else.'

'What do you mean?' I said angrily. 'How can there be any doubt as to what happened?'

'I have to look at it from a medical point of view. And I studied the trauma to your metacarpals and trapezoid.'

'I don't understand.'

'Well, if you were assaulted, and your assailant had really wanted to cleave off your whole hand, then he probably would have used more force and you would have suffered even worse injuries towards your lunate, and beyond.' She pointed to my left hand, close to where it met my wrist. 'But most of your injury was not in that area. Yes, we had to remove the rest of your hand, right up to here,' she touched my wrist again, 'but it could have been worse.'

'Worse?' Yvonne interrupted here. 'How the fu–, how could it have been worse?'

Dr Washington shifted in her chair. 'I'm only telling you this because I want you to know the full situation. And because this is what I told the police.' I nodded sullenly.

'Think about it,' Dr Washington resumed. 'Would a man really risk a potential murder charge by trying to remove your whole hand? Because that's what might have happened if you had lost any more blood. If the tourniquet or ice hadn't helped. If you had arrived at A&E even a few minutes later.'

I shook my head. 'He cut off my hand and he obviously meant to do it. I don't know why you're trying to defend him.'

'I'm not. My job is to give you the facts. And as I said, to tell the police too. That's why I'm here. But equally the police need sufficient evidence to press charges. Bear in mind that the man you claim was your assailant was also the man who packed your arm in ice and got you to the hospital.' She stood up. 'I'm so sorry, Vik.'

Dr Washington left Yvonne and me alone. Unsurprisingly, Yvonne didn't accept a word of the doctor's theory. She was convinced that Kevin Tyndall was a 'racist shit' and he had meant to do everything he had achieved.

I sank back on my bed. How could Dr Washington believe that my injury was an accident? After all that I told her. Was the truth too hard for her to accept? Did she think I was making it all up in my mind?

I closed my eyes. I reached a conclusion very quickly: it didn't matter any more what she thought, or what happened to Kevin Tyndall. I had lost my hand, regardless. That was going to affect me for the rest of my life.

Yvonne had phoned Ajay as soon as she had found out what had happened. So my second visitors were my parents and my brother. I hadn't seen Mum and Dad since I had left Leeds. They had caught the train down to London the day after Ajay had called them, and at King's Cross station they met Yvonne for the first time, with Ajay doing the introductions. Ajay and Ritika gave them their spare room, and many months later Ajay told me that by the end of the following fortnight, Ritika would have gladly welcomed Yvonne and me back to her flat if it meant that her unofficial mother-in-law would move out. It wasn't an easy time for anyone, I guess. My father put on a brave face when they visited me, although I could tell he was hiding his anguish, whereas my mother cried constantly.

Ajay came to see me a lot, but Ritika only visited me once in hospital as she was so freaked out by my hand. I couldn't say I blamed her. Yvonne also brought Jane, Keisha and Steph. The shock on their faces when they saw me was enough to make me laugh for the first time since the attack, which was a bloody hard thing to do. They brought Terry and June with them once or twice, but Terry looked so grim, and June so horrified that I told Steph to let them know that they didn't have to come any more. Chef Michel came once, although he barely stayed more than half an hour. He looked miserable, and I knew he thought it was his fault because he had let me go to Roger Raybourne's restaurant. When he left, I made Yvonne go after him and tell him that I didn't blame him.

It was a whole week before Chef Raybourne came to visit me. He phoned the hospital first to request whether we could meet in private to discuss what had happened, and I subsequently asked if he could visit out of hours so that Yvonne wouldn't know. I didn't want her to go off like a steam train if the man she hated walked into my ward while she was there.

When he arrived with a bouquet I could tell he was trying not to stare at my bandage. He looked pale. He sat down and gingerly patted my arm.

'So how are you, Vik?'

'Well I've still got my left hand. That's one good thing.'

He nodded uncertainly. 'Tell me what happened.'

I described the events of the evening in the most matter-of-fact way I could, and by the time I came to the end, the chef's face was a mixture of disbelief, shock and a pasty greyness.

'The police have talked to all of my staff. You know, Vik, many chefs have tripped up before when using those machines. Lost their balance when pushing in the meat. You have to be so careful.'

I stared at him. 'It wasn't an accident, I already told you.'

'It must have been.'

'So why would I pretend otherwise?'

Chef Raybourne looked away. 'You had a traumatic incident, Vik. You lost a lot of blood. Your mind must have concocted another story to make it easier for you.'

I stared at him, incredulous.

'And Kevin got a taxi for you.' He sighed. 'I know Chef can be tough on the staff but he's not a psychopath.'

Roger Raybourne seemed to be studying the wall. 'Kevin says that you must have slipped on some minced meat which fell on the floor when you were operating the machine. It was the first time you had used it, yes? Well, he blames Jake for letting you operate it unattended. Kevin heard your scream, applied your tourniquet and phoned for a taxi. The man saved your life, Vik.'

I couldn't believe what I was hearing, but it seemed that was the story which Kevin – and Chef Raybourne – was sticking by. The Three Rs' owner said he had interviewed each of the other chefs de partie individually, but all of them said they had already left the restaurant that evening, and every one of them had told him that Kevin's reported bravery was exactly what they would have expected from him. When he stood up to leave, the Executive Chef still found it hard to look me in the eye. He asked me if there was anything he could do for me.

'Actually,' I said, 'I do have one question.' Roger Raybourne nodded. 'Is Chef Kevin still working for you?'

'Yes, of course he is. I can't just sack him with no evidence that he did anything other than help you. And I have the restaurant's reputation to consider.'

'You could,' I replied coldly.

Roger Raybourne looked out of the window. 'He's a fantastic chef, Vik. The restaurant needs him.' His voice started to break up as he finished his words and he cleared his throat before continuing. 'Anything else?'

He stared at me for a few seconds, but I refused to break eye contact. And before the owner of Restaurant Roger Raybourne did finally look away, I saw in his eyes such a hollow callousness that I knew I didn't want to ever see him again. Chef Raybourne would do anything to avoid a scandal in his flagship restaurant.

At the end of the week, when one of the policemen I had talked to returned, he reiterated that they had interviewed all the kitchen staff who had been working at The Three Rs that night and that they all confirmed Chef Kevin's rectitude. They had found nothing to indicate a struggle. None of the other chefs said anything incriminating against Chef, so it was just my word against his. There was nothing else they could do with insufficient evidence, so they weren't going to press charges or pursue the case.

Kevin Tyndall had got away with it.

When I told Yvonne, she declared the police were all a bunch of racist pricks and the entire force was a corrupt group of cowardly, white twats. I agreed but I now realised I couldn't expect anything else from them. They probably didn't care enough that a Jewish-Indian man had been assaulted in a workplace and had his hand chopped off in a violent and racially motivated attack, and both they and the perpetrator should have been held to account; but this was 1992, and it seemed to me that Kevin's account was so watertight, that even if I tried to make a complaint about the police, I wouldn't get anywhere. I was just a footnote on a report that would end up being filed in the wastepaper bin.

However, if the police weren't going to pursue the case, that left me with one thought-provoking option, or at least the threat of it. I phoned Roger Raybourne for one final discussion.

'Mr Raybourne, you have no doubt heard that the police have dismissed my incident as any sort of attack.'

'That's because it wasn't, Vik,' Raybourne replied calmly.

'That's because they don't care enough to investigate the word of a "Paki",' I answered sharply, 'not because they're right.'

'Strong words, Vik. Be careful what you say.'

'Oh I will, Mr Raybourne. In fact, that's why I'm phoning you.' I paused deliberately.

'Go on,' Raybourne said after a moment.

'So, if the police aren't going to charge anyone, then I have no choice other than to initiate a private prosecution against The Three Rs.'

'A private prosecution?'

'Exactly. It's the only way I might get justice.'

'You wouldn't have a chance,' Raybourne said slowly. 'You've no evidence that anyone attacked you, and the police haven't arrested anyone.'

'You might be right. But I have nothing to lose.' I let those words sink in before continuing. 'Even if I don't win the case, I would feel I had done the right thing.'

'Now listen, Vik–'

'Of course,' I said quickly, 'It would take a lot of time and it would be very public. And I don't really want to drag your name through the courts if I can help it. But as I said, I don't have any other option. Do I?'

Roger Raybourne wasn't stupid. Two minutes later, he had agreed to pay me a generous lump sum as a 'discretionary sickness payment' while I was off work – not that there was any question of me returning to cook for him – but only if I promised not to pursue the prosecution. This at least meant that if I couldn't get any employment for a few months, then Yvonne and I wouldn't starve.

It was three weeks before I had the bandage permanently removed from my right arm. Dr Washington had hoped it would be less, but the shock to my radius proved greater than expected, and the wound took longer to heal. The dressing was, of course, changed frequently, but each time the nurses replaced it I looked away; I wasn't ready yet to see whatever remained. Yvonne made herself look the first time she saw them changing the dressing, but when they had finished, tears were streaming down her cheeks. After that, she too avoided watching the nurses while they worked on my wound.

But there was no getting away from it once Dr Washington had declared that the bandage was ready to come off permanently. Yvonne sat in the chair beside me and held my left hand tight as the nurse removed the dressing, and when she had finished, we both stared at what was left. Where my right hand had been, now my arm ended at my wrist and, well, that was it. No hand. Just an ugly stump with a skin graft. I waved it around a bit like a light-sabre and touched it gingerly with my left fingers. It didn't hurt so much now. I held it out towards Yvonne, and she put her hands around it, smiled and then brought the stump up to her lips. One of us cried again, I don't remember who – there were a lot of tears during that time.

'There is one thing I don't understand,' I said later as I unsuccessfully tried to hold a book with my arm.

Yvonne glanced up from her magazine. 'Just one?'

'Well, one specific thing. Why would Kevin mangle my right arm when I'm left-handed? Surely if he had wanted to truly hurt me, then he would have attacked my left hand.'

'There's an easy answer to that,' Yvonne snarled. 'Because he's completely fucking stupid and he paid so little attention to you while you were cooking for him that he never even saw what hand you work with. Seriously. It just shows what a moron he is.'

I considered that.

'But thank God he is a moron,' she continued, 'because you can still use your left hand, can't you?'

'Of course.'

'And that's the most important thing for you as a chef, yes?'

I didn't answer her. At that moment, I wasn't sure that I ever wanted to cook again.

Following my discharge from UCH, I spent weeks in and out of a rehab centre. It wasn't until September before I was fully signed-off, and by that time my emotions were completely fucked. I went from anguished crying and resigned acceptance, to fits of rage and screaming, swearing I would get even with the bastards. Sometimes quite literally inside one minute. But more and more I stayed quiet, feeling depressed and wondering what on earth I would do next; and could I cope with whatever that was. Dr Washington prescribed me antidepressants, painkillers and sleeping pills that she swore would knock-out an elephant. I asked her if they would knock-out a psychopathic, racist chef who continued to run a top London restaurant, and she smiled at me uncertainly and changed the subject.

The hospital did discuss with me as to whether I would like a prosthetic hand. I hadn't thought about that as a possibility as I had assumed that replacement limbs were little more than ornaments, and I couldn't see the point of a plastic appendage; how would a fake hand help me work in a kitchen, even if I wanted to? Dr Washington confirmed that most prosthetics were still simple devices, although she told me that there were far more advanced, myoelectric prostheses being developed in North America, where you could control an artificial limb with the electrical signals generated naturally by your own muscles. It was exciting but the cost was clearly prohibitive for the NHS. I told her that I didn't want any plastic prosthetic attachments just yet, it was too early, but I would let her know if I had a change of heart.

I did go through a phase of planning in my mind all sorts of retribution on Chef Kevin. I didn't discuss this with Yvonne because she would quite likely have started to make tangible plans and found dodgy pubs in the East End where she could buy from disreputable blaggards all the equipment I dreamed about using. In my heart, I knew that I wouldn't go through with any of my plans, but there were occasions when I would lay awake at night – or even just lie on our sofa for hours during the day – and seriously contemplate it.

I didn't know how best to dress for months. To start with, I would wear gloves on both arms when I went out, but the glove on my right arm would often slip off. I tried taping it on, but that was just bloody stupid because it was a right faff getting it off. I almost always wore long-sleeve shirts and pullovers, and when I was out in public, I would usually have my right hand thrust deep in my pocket. One time in the check-out queue at Sainsbury's a small girl saw the end of my arm and started to scream and point, and nothing her mother could do would calm her down. Everyone else began to stare at me, and in the end, I dumped my shopping basket on the floor and half-ran out of the supermarket. On another occasion, I was in a pub with Yvonne and two guys started laughing at me. Yvonne told them to shut their traps and threatened to make them 'wear their beers', but they didn't stop mocking me behind their pints. I wasn't ready yet for such shows of fear and antagonism, and I put away my short-sleeved polo shirts for the time being.

I started to count the practical problems of living with one hand. All the things you do every day which you take for granted, you suddenly find you can't, like tie your shoelaces (I bought ankle-high slip-ons and wriggled my way into laced shoes which I didn't untie), open a can of soup, squeeze toothpaste without making an unholy mess, even putting on a pair of socks: these were all new arts I had to learn with one hand.

The one thing I could still do was cook in my own kitchen. But I didn't. Not because I wasn't able to – I could use a frying pan with one hand, and I could, just about, chop some soft vegetables – but because I didn't want to. I had no desire to cook again. Ever. It seemed uninteresting and, at times, even repulsive. When she noticed I wasn't cooking, Yvonne initially encouraged me to do so, but I just told her I wasn't feeling well or I couldn't do it, or I just plain sulked. Which meant I stuck to bacon and eggs, and baked beans on toast. When Yvonne tried to push the subject one day, I actually yelled at her, and for the only time in our relationship we had a blazing stand-up row. I had never shouted at her so vehemently before (even our arguments in Wesson never reached this level of intensity), and we were both so shocked, that moments after one of us finally stopped screaming, because whoever it was couldn't think of another original or nasty insult quickly enough, we were hugging and apologising and saying we didn't mean it. And five minutes later we were in bed.

Sex was one of the few things which ultimately didn't suffer, although it took us a while to not feel awkward. In the end we just drank a bottle of wine and let our alcohol-induced hormones do the rest. In fact, now that I wasn't working or cooking, when Yvonne wasn't out with the band, sex was something that we had more time for than ever. One day, Yvonne came back with a sly smile and pulled out of her bag a book which she tossed towards me. I caught it one-handed (I was getting quite good at that) and held it up.

'*The Kama Sutra.*'

'Well,' Yvonne said quietly, 'I thought we could try to replicate a few positions in a three-handed kind of way. How does that sound?'

I threw the book back at her, but I was laughing. It sounded great.

Eight

October 1992

Terry began to get The Libertine Dolls more paid time on stage. But now he wasn't looking for small pubs, now he wanted to move them up a rung on the ladder, and he started to get them gigs as support acts with much bigger bands with larger audiences and well-established fans. Groups like Stradlin, Persistence of Time, the up-and-coming Suede, an Ocean Colour Scene gig just before their tour with Paul Weller. They started headlining their own shows at Dingwalls and The Marquee; and Terry finally picked up the phone and called Vince Power. When I started to attend their gigs again, I could see just how tight the band had become. I think at that time it was one of the few things that did make me feel alive.

Yvonne and Jane continued to write their own songs. They were a combination of politically motivated songs and those with more blatant sexual connotations. One of the songs Yvonne wrote on her own was simply called 'K'. It was a song about a girl called K who grows up being stigmatised and abused because of a tough family background, and ends up taking her own life. In the lyrics, Yvonne blames different parts of society for K's circumstances. Yvonne claimed it was a song about a random girl, hence the use of the initial, but it was clear to me it was more than that because I saw her crying on several occasions when she sang it on stage. Despite my questions, she wouldn't tell me any more about what had inspired her to write it.

The band's big break came at the end of the month when Terry negotiated a support slot at the Town and Country club in Kentish Town, opening for Tabitha's Secret. After the gig, the band spent some time out front on The Libertine Dolls' merch stall which June had put together for the show. I was standing nearby, chatting with Terry, my stump concealed by my shirt sleeve, watching the band sign T-shirts and flirt with some of the punters, and as ever, glancing across at whoever Yvonne was talking to. Which was why I noticed that she was paying close attention to one particular man who had approached the stall. He was tall, dressed entirely in black and wore Police shades, even indoors. As he spoke to her, he swept back his long hair and Yvonne giggled slightly. They only talked for a couple of minutes, and then the man wandered away, but after he left, Yvonne remained standing where she was, biting her lip and staring into the distance. It wasn't how she usually reacted to men who tried to engage her. I walked across anxiously.

'Vik, guess who I was just talking to.'

'I have no idea,' I replied as casually as I could. 'Who was he?'

'An American agent, called Wilton Pine or something. He promotes bands in New York and on the East Coast. He said he would be interested in working with us if we ever came to the US. Isn't that amazing!'

'Incredible,' I agreed flatly.

'I've always had a thing for the States. All my favourite films were set there: *Paris Texas*, *Mississippi Burning*, *Cool Hand Luke* – God, Paul Newman was gorgeous in that - and *Breakfast at*

Tiffany's of course. Oh, and that new film, *Thelma and Louise*, that was incredible.'

I mentioned *Terminator*, and Yvonne laughed.

'Yes, that too.' Despite my attempts to look calm, she must have realised I was concerned because she clasped her hands around my neck. 'Hey, don't worry. I'm not about to up sticks and leave just because one man has told me he knows a few people across the Atlantic. We've got too much going on here.'

I smiled and said that I knew that and I wasn't worried. I was of course. But I wasn't going to admit it. How would I cope if Yvonne did go? I could barely drum up enough enthusiasm to look for work now, let alone consider how I was going to support myself after Raybourne's 'sickness pay' ran out.

Winter 1992/93

Over Christmas and New Year, Yvonne and I spent some time together in London, and then I visited my parents in Yorkshire. Yvonne had intended to fly up to Scotland to see her family, but after a tense, difficult phone call with them, she decided not to go. Jane then joined us both for a short break in February, in Dublin to celebrate my twenty-third birthday.

When we all returned to London, Terry gathered the band at his house to give them the news that he had organised a nationwide tour. All their hard gigging in London had paid off, and they would hit the road in spring. Uncontrollable screams of delight greeted his announcement.

The Libertine Dolls' manager then announced that Channel 4 had been in touch, and had invited them to appear on *The Night Train*, their live, contemporary music programme for unsigned acts, which was hosted by Radio 1 DJ, Kel Davis. The band screamed again.

The following week, we all went to the TV studio, a large warehouse in Docklands. To keep the momentum of the show, Channel 4 erected several stages, which meant they could cut dynamically from one band to the next.

The Libertine Dolls were asked to open the show, and their song received a good reception from the audience in the studio. Following two more bands and a section of VT, the programme then returned live to the warehouse, and Kel Davis introduced The Libertine Dolls again, this time standing on stage with his arm draped around Yvonne's shoulders. I could see the tension in her body; she was just itching to shrug him off. Davis stepped down, letting the back of his hand trail down Yvonne's arm as the band struck up the first chords of 'I Love Rock 'n' Roll'. They launched into the song with Yvonne still grimacing at him.

After the first chorus, the band slowed the rhythm down mid-song, and Jane and Keisha got the audience to clap along. At this moment, the camera panned in for a close-up of the lead singer. Yvonne, clasping her mic, licked her lips, winked, and instead of singing the chorus as usual, mimed the words 'I love cock and ball' straight into the camera. And then she slid her fingers from her mouth slowly down the length of the microphone. The director must not have believed she really did it, or otherwise he would surely have cut to another shot, but he didn't. So Yvonne repeated it.

Just as The Libertine Dolls were winding up, I saw the floor manager desperately grab Kel Davis, and when the DJ jumped back on stage after the song finished, you could see that he looked somewhat rattled. Stupidly, he put his arm around Yvonne's neck, and as he began talking to the camera, she turned and whispered in his ear. For a moment, Davis looked shaken, before recovering his poise and quickly removing his arm. Yvonne smiled angelically into the camera and accepted the second round of applause.

I asked her later what she whispered. 'Oh,' she said lightly, 'I told him that if he didn't take his hands off me in three seconds, then I would rip off his balls live on TV and shove my guitar up his arse.'

In April, when the band set off on their tour, I had had every intention of staying in Holloway while they cavorted around England; even though I was no longer moping around the flat, I was still in no mood to show myself off in front of hundreds or thousands of people in remote English towns. But Yvonne wasn't having that, and I was formally drafted as assistant sound engineer to the band.

A nationwide tour sounds grand – it was anything but. It was a hard slog of driving around the country, squashed into a minibus, and many hours of cooped-up boredom. And in the evenings, having to put all your energy into the gig no matter how knackered or pissed off you are. Although my engineer duties took up my evenings, I had little to do in the daytime other than wait around for Yvonne and run errands for her, and there were days when I felt little more than a groupie. But it meant that I didn't have to think about my life or my future – what possible job I could do with one hand. We stayed at crappy motels and ate at cafés and motorway service stations with the occasional pizza delivery or 'luxury alternative' at an Indian restaurant. In eight weeks, we travelled over 1 400 miles to twenty-five different towns. We saw Colchester, Norwich, Peterborough, Leicester, Nottingham, Hull, various other northern towns I can't remember, then more of the Midlands followed by Bristol, Exeter and back along the south coast up to the capital again.

The nights that were shit were hard to take but the gigs where the audience got into it, where the band were up for it and where it all just took off made all the travelling worthwhile. The university towns were probably the best, where the crowd raved, and all four women let their hair down and tore it up.

After the gig in Bristol, I suggested we detour to Weston-Super-Mare to see our old mates, Gary and Miles.

Yvonne gave me a suspicious look.

'Really?' she said. 'And why would we want to do that?'

'I loved it there before we had to leave,' I said. I looked at my left arm. 'Happier times before I started trying to make a name for myself in the restaurant world. Maybe I should have just stayed in hotel portering.'

Yvonne hugged me. 'I'm sorry I can't go with you,' is all she said.

Part of me was scared that I might be identified as the person who bottled the old man in the bus stop, so I didn't arrive until after dark, and I met Gary in an obscure pub on the edge of the town. He said the hotel business was challenging and a number of the temporary staff had been let go the year before. Miles was still busking but supplementing that meagre income with the occasional paid gig in Bristol, and he claimed he was writing a book. I told Gary about Kevin's attack on me and updated him on what Yvonne and I were doing now; Gary was so shocked, he barely said a word. I could see tears in the corner of his eyes. He, in turn, updated me on James Peters, the man Yvonne had hit with her bottle. It turned out, thankfully, that the local papers had exaggerated his injuries, and he had made a full recovery.

I wanted to visit Wesson pier for old times' sake, so the two of us walked down Beach Road and then ran down the wooden boards of the pier, pausing only at the end of the jetty to get our breath back while we stared at the waves crashing over the groynes.

'Yvonne and I spent many evenings sitting down here, getting drunk,' I said.

'Do you miss it?' Gary asked.

'I don't miss the cold, and I don't have any desire to sit in freezing bus stops. But I still loved just being with Yvonne. Things were simpler then.'

Gary nodded. 'I preferred getting drunk in Miles' flat.'

'Yeah,' I said. 'They were good times.'

'But what about you now?' Gary nodded at my left arm. 'Don't let a little thing like that hold you back. Yvonne doesn't let anything get in her way. I'm sure you could still become a great chef if you wanted. You just need to find your way. I'm sure Yvonne's said all this already.'

I turned Gary's words over in my mind on the train journey back to Bristol. It occurred to me that Yvonne hadn't mentioned my career for a while. She hadn't urged me to get another job as I was still paying half of the rent and bills. She never talked about my future, or whether I could still cut it in a professional kitchen.

June 1993

With fame, comes new opportunities, and Yvonne's prominent position in the band often propelled her into the spotlight. This became clear when Yvonne was offered a photo-shoot by

Boudicca, a new glossy magazine aimed at the young professional woman.

Yvonne asked how the rest of the band would be included, and that was when the editor said that they wouldn't be, it was solely Yvonne they were interested in. To give her some credit, Yvonne wasn't comfortable with this and thought about the offer for the next twenty-four hours, but her ego overruled her heart and the next day she phoned the magazine back and told them she would do it. She knew that Jane, in particular, would be annoyed, and so she didn't tell her or Terry until she had finished the photo-shoot the following week.

'Here,' she said, tossing some prints on the table after the band's rehearsal. 'They wanted to do a portrait of just one of us, but I mentioned all your names and banged on about The Dolls endlessly. All good publicity.'

Jane sifted through the black and white prints. 'Maybe for you. I can't believe you would do this without telling us first. The band not good enough for you any more, is that it?'

Terry looked disappointed and said, 'Oh, Yvonne', but Jane continued arguing and made several snide remarks about how obviously Yvonne wanted to go off and do her own thing.

Yvonne had expected Jane to react in this way and she had told me the evening before that she intended to placate her, rather than argue. That plan lasted all of two minutes before she lost it.

'You know what?' she snapped. 'The fact is the magazine didn't want to interview you or the other two. I actually tried to persuade them to do a group photo-shoot but they didn't want to, because I'm the public face of the band. Just enjoy it – and think of it this way, you won't be the one with the stalkers when we're playing Wembley Stadium.'

Jane stood up suddenly as if she'd been slapped, and left the room. She made sure we all heard the door slam.

Jane's bluster didn't last long, and by the following week, they were once again standing on stage side by side, grinning inanely at one another as a bunch of fans in the audience tore their shirts off and tried to jump up on stage. At least at that point, the two of them were still in synch.

Yvonne was increasingly being accosted by fans and flunkies after gigs, and journalists would come to her for quotes before the other band members. She was fine with this, of course, and most of the time the rest of the band (except Jane) were too. And most of the time I was still flattered and still surprised that she still chose to come home with me each night. But my insecurity about my position and my future was resurrected after a gig at the Marquee.

Yvonne was sitting on the edge of the stage after the gig, sipping from a water bottle. I noticed that she was talking to a familiar character, dressed entirely in black with a pair of Police sunglasses tucked in his pocket. As he spoke to her, he frequently swept back his long hair, as Yvonne fiddled with her earring and swung her legs to and fro.

It took me a moment before I recognised him as the man who had approached Yvonne after The Libertine Dolls supported Tabitha's Secret at the Town and Country club – now The Forum – the previous year. I watched them from the other side of the bar. At the end of their conversation, he handed Yvonne his business card and gave her a kiss on each cheek. That surprised me, partly because of the gall of the man, but also because Yvonne would rarely let anyone kiss her after knowing them for just a few minutes. She stared thoughtfully at the card and twiddled it around in her fingers, then looked up and saw me, and waved. I walked over and handed her a bottle of Amstel.

'Who was that?'

'Oh, Vik, that was Wilton Stratford Pine.'

'Oh yes. Didn't he come to one of your other gigs in London last year, at the Town and Country?'

Yvonne looked up at the ceiling. 'Oh, yes. You're right, I'd forgotten that.'

'What did he want?'

'What makes you think he wanted anything? He's a US promoter. He was just telling me about his business.'

'Handsome bugger though, wasn't he?' Keisha had been standing behind Yvonne, earwigging.

'Was he?' Yvonne replied. 'I hadn't noticed.'

Keisha snorted. 'I'd watch out for him, Vik, if he's giving your woman his business card.'

I waited until Keisha had stepped down off the stage and gone to find a drink herself before I continued.

'And what did he really want?'

Yvonne looked around furtively and lowered her voice. 'He made me an offer, Vik…he thinks I could go solo!'

'Solo? Really?'

'Yes. He manages several acts already, and he said I have all the qualities necessary to become a huge star. Quote unquote. And get this: he said that if I were interested, then he would invite me to New York and get me a job singing there. Imagine that!'

I tried not to. If Yvonne went to the States, what would I do? There was no way I could afford to go with her. I would be left on my own. The potential of that reality bit in.

'But…I mean…why? Why would you want to do that? Don't you want to sing with The Dolls?'

'Of course I do, Vik. And that's what I told him.' Yvonne shifted her gaze back towards the door. 'I'm not going anywhere.'

Yet, I just stopped myself from spitting out. I looked around just in time to see Wilton Stratford Pine stooping to kiss goodbye to another woman before turning back to catch Yvonne's eye a final time. He gave her a charming smile and made a 'call me' sign with his thumb and little finger. Then he disappeared out of the door – but not out of our lives.

Nine

People always say that they remember exactly where they were when they heard that Elvis had died or when the news reported the fall of the Berlin Wall. For me, I will always remember the day when June phoned to tell us that Terry had had a heart attack. Yvonne and I rushed out of our flat in less than thirty seconds, hailed a black cab and told the driver to get us to Charing Cross Hospital as quickly as he bloody well could. We burst in through the main entrance and found June on the fifth floor in a tiny lobby, sitting on a cracked plastic chair, staring at the wall as if she were hypnotised. Then Steph and H appeared, having already been at the hospital, trying to get an update on Terry, and we all embraced.

June updated us on what had happened: they had been at home, fortunately, and Terry had started to complain about a pain in his chest. Within minutes he was clasping his ribs and June said he sank to the floor on to his knees, before rolling over and gaping at her like a freshly caught fish. The ambulance she called arrived in minutes, and it might only have been the vicinity of the hospital to their home which saved Terry.

The next few hours were torture before we were learned that Terry was through the worst of it. The next few days weren't much better, but at least we felt that Terry would live.

Five days after Terry's cardiac, Jane phoned us to say she wanted to call a meeting with the band and they all came round to our flat in Holloway. We sat in a slightly awkward circle around the kitchen table, toying with cups of coffee.

Jane leaned forwards. 'Girls, listen. We have some decisions to make.'

'About Terry?' Keisha asked after no one else spoke.

'About Terry.'

All the women sat, staring at the floor or at their mugs, avoiding each other's eyes.

'Go on, Jane,' Yvonne said after a moment's silence.

Jane looked up. 'We all love Terry, I know we do. But we have to ask ourselves whether he can still be the man he was.'

'That seems a bit premature,' Keisha broke in. 'Plenty of people have heart attacks and then go back to doing whatever they were doing before perfectly well.'

'That's true. But I'm not sure if Terry will be able to keep up the pace he set before. Or at the rate that we need him to if we are going to keep building on our success. Hell, in the last three days alone, June has passed on five messages to me from promoters and magazines.'

'Really?' Yvonne sat up now. 'I didn't know about that. Why didn't you tell us?'

Jane flung out her arms. 'Hello! Because our manager has just had a heart attack, yes? It hardly seemed important that we should worry about a radio interview or a magazine article. Although I know they are crucial to *you*.'

Yvonne crossed her arms. 'And what is that supposed to mean?'

'You know very well what I am talking about.'

'Well tell me anyway.'

'OK –'

'Girls, stop this.' Steph held up her hands. 'Have a bit of respect here. Our manager has just had a heart attack, and you two are squabbling like a pair of teenagers. Come on.'

Jane and Yvonne glared at each other for a moment longer and then looked away.

Steph sighed. 'But sadly, I also think we have to talk about whether Terry can still manage us.'

Jane nodded.

'So, what are our options?' Keisha asked. 'Can June manage us on her own?'

Jane and Yvonne shook their heads in unison.

'I doubt it,' Yvonne said, 'not only will she have to look after Terry, but she was never the driving force that Terry was, and I can't see how she could take over his role. Jane?'

Jane puffed out her cheeks. 'Agreed.'

Keisha held out her palms. 'OK, so as I was saying, what are our options?'

Jane coughed. 'I do have one thing to, er, bring to the table.' The other women looked at her. 'One of those messages I mentioned from June, I did call back.'

'You've got a nerve,' Yvonne spat instantly. 'Telling me not to think about talking to journalists and then you go and talk to one anyway. Cheeky cow.' She sat back in her chair, rocking its back legs.

Jane held up a hand. 'Wait a second, Yvonne, let me explain.'

'I'm waiting.'

Jane ignored her. 'It wasn't a journalist I was talking to, it was…the owner of another artists' management company.'

'A what!' Yvonne crashed forwards on her chair.

'Let me explain!' Jane repeated, raising her voice this time. 'This wasn't completely out of the blue.'

'Oh, this just gets better and better.'

'Yvonne, do you want to hear what I have to say or not?'

I reached over and touched Yvonne's arm. She pulled away from me and gave Jane the most fleeting of nods.

Jane took a deep breath. 'Two weeks ago – before Terry's heart attack – I met this guy after the gig at The Astoria. Fellow called Louis Vance. Any of you heard of him?' The others shook their heads. 'I recognised him from a photo in the *NME*, which is why I approached him. I knew he already manages a number of acts, mostly pop but a few alternative rock bands too. We got talking and he said he wanted to discuss an idea he had. I told him that we already had a manager but I gave him my phone number just to shut him up.'

'To keep your options open you mean.'

'To keep our options open, Yvonne. Anyway, he called me again three days ago. He hadn't heard about Terry's heart attack; by the way, I mean, we haven't publicised it have we, so he wasn't just being a nasty opportunist. And actually, once I told him what had happened, he said he would call back another time. But I told him to carry on, and he asked if he could meet me. So I did.'

Yvonne shook her head again and blew out a long breath of air. Steph and Keisha ignored her. I could see that although Yvonne felt hurt, the other two were interested in what Jane was saying.

'What did he want?' Steph asked.

Jane continued. 'He told me that he was putting a new girl band together, based around the whole Girl Power thing – I mean, it's not just us that's been exploiting that is it – and he loved our individuality as well as our music. He's keen to emphasise the idea of stage personas as part of his act, and he's got serious money behind him. He wanted to know if we would like to be in his group.'

'But we've got a group. We are a group.'

'Yes, we are. Well, we have been. But Terry, he is as much a member of this band as us. In fact, in some ways, he is more important. I mean, can you really see us carrying on without him?'

'We might have to get another manager,' Steph said.

'Maybe. But I don't know if they would ever get us like Terry does,' Jane said solemnly. 'There is something about him and us. He's our fifth Beatle if you like.'

No one spoke until Keisha finally asked, 'What do you think, Yvonne?'

Yvonne grimaced. 'I think it's a bit bloody cheeky of him, that's what I think. This Louis Vance bloke, it seems to me he's just ripping us off. Did he say why he wanted us in particular?'

'He likes us,' Jane answered. 'He said he had come to two of our gigs and he was impressed by our stage presence, our attitude, the fact we can sing and that we play our own instruments.'

'Well at least he's right about that,' Yvonne said. Then she frowned. 'Hang on a second, how come he only talked to you? Why didn't he want to talk to me?'

Jane looked embarrassed. 'Well, what he said was that although he loves you as a performer, he thinks you are clearly volatile, those were the words he used, and he thought I would be a better person to make a business proposition to. Sorry.'

Yvonne nodded slowly. I could see that although she wanted to disagree, part of her couldn't.

'Listen, Yvonne.' Jane pushed her chair back and squatted in front of her key collaborator. 'I have loved, absolutely loved the last year since we met you. You have helped us go from being a decent pub band to a bloody good stage act. More than good. With so much potential in front of us. And I couldn't see any reason why Terry wouldn't be taking us forwards. Until this. Until I saw Terry's fragility, and until I talked to Louis and he explained what he could do for us and how we could do it. And now,' Jane stood up again, and suddenly she had tears in her eyes. 'Now, I think this is the right thing to do. And I…I want to do it. With you. Or…or without you.'

No one said anything for a long time. Then Yvonne spoke again, her Scottish accent emphasising her anger. 'Youse are quite something, Jane, aren't you. Quite something. Not only are ye burying Terry even before he's had a chance to say anything for himself, but you are now making a decision for all the rest of us without any of us saying what we think. And that's nae right, Jane. In fact, it's downright focking wrong.'

'Jesus Christ, Yvonne!' Jane exploded, getting to her feet. 'You fucking hypocrite. Who suddenly made you the sole leader of the band? It was our band first, remember, before we let you join us. Who suddenly changed the rules so that you can tell me what I can and can't do? If I want to go and play in Louis' band, then I fucking well will, OK. And don't you start being so high and mighty about who is speaking for who. What about your exclusive exposé in *Boudicca*? You're perfectly happy for it to be all about you when you want it to be.'

Yvonne stood up too, facing Jane, her chest heaving. 'You're out of order, Jane. You are so fucking selfish.'

'Me? How the fuck can you say that? What about that American that Keisha saw you talking to at the Marquee? Don't tell me that wasn't some self-centred, underhand business offer which you were cooking up with him. Because I bet it was, wasn't it? Wasn't it!'

And then all hell broke loose. Yvonne and Jane started to scream at each other, Steph tried to act as peacemaker but got shoved by Yvonne, and so she got aggressive herself. Keisha watched for several minutes with her head in her hands before also trying to say something, but then Jane told her to fuck off because she didn't have the right to any say, and then Keisha let loose a stream of swear words.

As for me, I stood to one side and decided that I would only get involved if anyone actually hit anyone else. That would be my time for intervention. But if they just screamed and raged and swore at each other, then I wouldn't do anything. It was their call, their decision to make.

It took ten more minutes before it was silent again in our flat. Then two more minutes of ice-cold discussion before a plan was agreed. Just like that. Jane and Steph both said that they wanted to negotiate with Louis. Keisha said that she didn't want to be in a commercial girl band and that she would go and find some other lunatics to play proper rock music with. And Yvonne said she was quitting.

And that was the end of The Libertine Dolls.

Two weeks later, Yvonne rang up Wilton Stratford Pine and accepted his offer to sing in New York as long as he agreed that I could come too, and he bought us both tickets. He said he would organise everything and agreed on the spot.

So we all went our separate ways.

The other women went to spice up their lives in England, and Yvonne and I gave up the flat in Holloway, ordered tourist visas and headed to America, both of us yearning to breathe free.

Part 3

New York

Ten

August 1993

My first impression of New York was of a giant film set. The skyscrapers, the yellow taxis, the steam vented into the streets, the brownstone buildings of Greenwich Village and their metal fire escapes, the rattling of the subway, Times Square; I'd seen it all in a hundred movies, in dozens of sitcoms, in too many police dramas. The first time I saw an NYPD cop in his full regalia go into Dunkin' Donuts, I looked around to make sure I hadn't accidentally walked on to a film set. It's a city to get lost in and to never get lost in. As for the weather, it can be extreme, from blizzards in winter to blazing hot summers.

When Yvonne and I arrived, it wasn't unusually hot by New York standards, but with ninety per cent plus humidity, Yvonne (pale, blonde, used-to-the-cold Scottish girl) found it tough going for the first few weeks. When you buy an ice cream and it starts melting before you've finished your second lick, then you need to find some shade quick.

It wasn't just the daylight you had to watch. Manhattan in the early 1990s was a place where you had to know the streets that you could and couldn't visit after dark. Wilton Stratford Pine gave us some initial pointers, and after dire warnings from other locals, we clicked pretty quick where the no-go areas were.

We were even advised by several folk not to stand on a street corner with a map in your hand looking like a goddamn tourist, not unless you wanted a switchblade to slice the map in two.

When Yvonne had phoned Pine after the final Libertine Dolls summit, she had explained that as much as we wanted to come to New York, we could never afford to rent anywhere, so did he have any suggestions...? Without hesitation, Wilton provided us with an apartment rent-free. Our accommodation was in the Lower East Side, which Yvonne told me had been one of the most vibrant parts of New York in the early twentieth century: where the Marx Brothers, Al Jolson and Irving Berlin had grown up, not to mention the Beat poets ('Who are they?' I asked her innocently and received a verbal clip across the ear). It turned into a rougher place in the sixties, but by the 1990s, the district was home to students, artists and immigrants from all over, including Bangladesh, China, India, Japan. It wasn't exactly Holloway, but once again we had stepped into another multi-cultural world. Sadly, plenty of white Americans resented the influx into their neighbourhood, and the racism was evident.

Pine had assured us we would be fine there. He had personally bought several apartments in the Lower East Side which he was already renting out: 'I tell you, this place is going to become a hot place to live in the years to come, and when it does, pow, my investments are going to go through the roof, baby.' Even Wilton Stratford Pine's lexicon was a Hollywood caricature to us.

Our apartment was on the fourth floor of a well-looked-after block and contained a bedroom, shower, a small space which only an estate agent could have called a lounge, and a tiny kitchen which quite literally only one person could stand in. When you opened a cupboard door above you, you had to bend backwards like a limbo dancer and at the same time stretch forwards like

American icon, Stretch Armstrong, to pull out a can of soup. Pine also provided us with a phone line in the apartment, so he could call Yvonne whenever he wanted her.

Despite the minute apartment, the somewhat dicey neighbourhood and the initial temperatures, we loved New York. I had never dreamed I would live anywhere outside Britain, let alone in one of the greatest cities on Earth. Yvonne took it in her stride, but it didn't stop her from gazing in awe at the Manhattan skyline when we walked through Central Park, laughing as the ketchup and mustard dripped on our fingers as we ate our first hot dogs from a street vendor, or staring like a star-struck teenager the first time we saw an entourage of blacked-out limousines driving slowly down Broadway; the woman behind us swore that it was the President's own cars – or maybe Tom Cruise as 'he definitely has whips like that'.

After we had been in Manhattan for a couple of days, Wilton Stratford Pine invited us out for dinner. He took us to a trendy restaurant in the Village: loud, expensive (we were glad we weren't paying), rather average Asian fusion food, where it seemed that most of the customers were more concerned about checking each other out, rather than the gastronomy. Pine immediately began to tell Yvonne of his plans to 'introduce you' to New York. He had friends who were looking for new acts to play at their clubs, agencies who needed new models and he knew several bands who would give their left arms for a vocalist like Yvonne.

'Oh, sorry, Vik,' he added quickly. 'I, ah…'

'S'OK,' I said, 'it's my right arm which I lost.'

'Ha…' Wilton Pine's laugh trailed off, apparently unsure if I was joking or offended. I didn't add anything to help him out. I had forgotten how good looking he was and how charming he

161

could be, and now here he was chatting up my girlfriend and filling her head with dreams of stardom.

'Actually,' Pine continued, focusing again on Yvonne, 'I've got a couple of auditions lined up for you already which I wanted to discuss with you.'

'Really?' Yvonne was genuinely taken with the man.

'Really.' Wilton Stratford Pine gave her a broad, perfect smile.

Yvonne nudged me excitedly. 'D'you hear that, Vik? Wilton's getting me in front of the right people already!'

I nodded unenthusiastically and crammed a monstrous but drab shrimp in my mouth.

Pine began to scan the room and continued without looking at Yvonne. 'And if you need some immediate money then I can set you up with a couple of modelling contracts no problem.'

'Modelling?' Yvonne glanced at her reflection in the mirrored wall. 'I've never done any modelling. Don't you need any experience?'

'Hmm?'

'You know. Surely I would need to know how to walk and show off the clothes if I was asked to model.'

'What?' Pine turned his attention back to Yvonne. 'Clothes? Baby, you won't need to worry about that for these modelling contracts.' He winked. 'I know you don't have any of those British hang-ups.'

Now it was Yvonne's turn to sit back in her chair, crossing her arms tightly across her chest. Pine raised his eyebrows.

'Wilton, I am no doing any of that sort of modelling, and I am not going to take ma clothes off for anyone – apart from Vik. Do ye understand?'

Wilton Stratford Pine looked genuinely surprised. 'Sure, ba– Yvonne,' he said. 'So no lingerie photo shoots?' Yvonne shook her head vehemently. Pine nodded, unruffled. 'No problemo. There are other gigs in town too, which you might prefer. If you don't mind singing in sessions or doing backing vocals for the odd MTV video, then I can find you those opportunities instead.'

Yvonne glanced at me and back at Wilton Stratford Pine, and a smile broke across her face. 'That would be fine. Thank you!'

Pine picked up his wine glass and tilted it towards hers. Yvonne returned the gesture, and they clinked glasses.

'What about a working visa?' I said hurriedly. I thought I had better say something to make sure Yvonne remembered I was there. 'You said on the phone that you would help Yvonne get a visa which would let her work here.'

'I did. And you are right – Vik. I will obtain a temporary Visa for Artists and Entertainers for you, Yvonne. Don't worry about that, just leave it with me.'

Leaving Yvonne with Wilton Stratford Pine was not something I wanted to do, but I had little choice over the coming days.

I, of course, had no legal right to work in the US and if I wanted to earn any money, then I had to accept that I was going to get some piss-poor employment from someone unscrupulous enough to hire somebody without a visa and on any terms my prospective employer wanted to give me. I briefly considered if I should look for work in the catering industry but I guessed that if a one-handed, Jewish-Indian, illegal immigrant walked into most restaurants looking for a job (even if he had his own set of Sabatier knives) then most likely he wouldn't get past the front door, let alone be offered an interview. Not unless he wanted to be a dishwasher.

So I was lucky when I did find a job with Vid-u-Missed. Vid-u-Missed was one of those businesses which worked for a few years but was never going to make the owner a million dollars, no matter how much he told you it would.

The idea was simple enough: if Joe Public living anywhere in the New York area went to work and then realised s/he had forgotten to set their video recorder to tape their favourite show, then s/he could phone Vid-u-Missed, and they would tape it for them in their offices and send the tape to the client.

There were three categories of membership: bronze, where we put the video in the mail; silver, where we would deliver it personally and post it in your mail-box; and gold membership, where the suckers who did sign up for this actually gave us a key to their house or apartment, and we would let ourselves in and leave the video on their TV stand, ready for them to watch as soon as they got home that evening. Although many new punters signed-up for the gold service, it didn't take them long to work out they were being royally ripped off.

My job was to take the orders and enter them into the company's ageing and deathly slow Commodore Amiga A3000 personal computer. Jeff, the owner of Vid-u-Missed, was incredibly proud of his Amiga, and I suppose that when it was first introduced, it would have been state of the art. By the time I was using it, it was forever crashing, and it would take five minutes to boot-up. I couldn't believe that Jeff employed me, a one-handed operator to enter the orders on to the computer, but I guess I was cheap (he certainly paid me a pittance) and eager, and he said that my British accent swung it for him as he thought that I would sound sophisticated when I answered the phone. I didn't personally trust Jeff's judgement too much, but I wasn't going to argue with his assessment.

Apart from me, Jeff employed Paolo to deliver the gold members' videos, as Paolo had his own bashed-up motorcycle which he was incredibly proud of. The best part of my job was when we got a gold member request which had to be delivered asap in Manhattan, and if Paolo was already out on another call, Jeff would ask me to do the drop-off. My birthday present to Yvonne that year was to persuade Paolo to cry off sick on the day of her birthday, when I knew that one of our top customers who had recently moved to a penthouse on Fifth Avenue would be out of town. Yvonne came with me and we spent three hours there. There is something special about having sex (several times) in a spacious, open plan, luxury apartment on the top floor of a New York skyscraper, looking down over the city through tall, glass windows, while hundreds of feet below you, people walk past like ants, oblivious to what is going on above them.

While I was educating myself on how to use the Amiga PC at Vid-u-Missed and learning Manhattan's grid system to deliver videos, Wilton Stratford Pine began to introduce Yvonne to New York's alternative music scene. 1933 in America was mostly about Prince, Guns 'n Roses, Garth Brooks but there was a thriving alternative rock scene which, although it primarily heralded from LA, saw bands like BLind MeLoN and fIREHOSE come to the East Coast. New York had its own local alt-rock scene with groups such as Rain on the Matador, Paramnesia Abstraction and Claviger. Hip-hop was also migrating from the West Coast with artists like Black Moon heading east. Pine introduced Yvonne to a young black man from Brooklyn called Christopher George Latore Wallace who Pine said was just about to break through with his alias, The Notorious B.I.G.

It was far removed from Finsbury Park and Terry and June (and a million light years from Inverness), and despite Yvonne's intentions and desire to keep her feet on the ground, she couldn't help but get swept up in the scene. During the first month or so, I would often go with her and Pine to see bands and hang out in clubs where the bar tab was taken care of, and although we both smoked weed, neither of us wanted anything harder. But it became difficult not to. Pills and powder were passed around more than bottles of Budweiser at some venues. I never succumbed, and Yvonne told me that she didn't; but there were nights when I was working, and she went out networking with Pine and when she came home in the early morning she was so wired that I found it hard to believe that she hadn't sniffed a line of coke or been dabbing speed.

But I never suspected her of infidelity. I trusted her.

Wilton Stratford Pine was a smart man. He had seen in London how Yvonne could turn heads and how she could own a stage. Combine that with her Scottish accent (which could get dramatically more brazen when required), and he claimed that she was made for New York.

Rather than frustrate Pine, I think he found Yvonne a challenge. Not simply to break her into the big time but to break her for himself too.

So Yvonne accepted the gigs as a temporary backing singer, willingly auditioned for bit-part singing roles in bizarre TV commercials (although she never got offered any), appeared on a few second-rate MTV videos for mediocre bands, and even sang in a few studio sessions for the kind of music that you might end up hearing in hotel lifts and shopping malls.

Some days, after such a session, she would come back to the apartment so disillusioned that she wouldn't want to speak to me or go out or do anything except watch some bland TV and neck JD straight from the bottle. I would try to comfort her, reassure her that she was bound to get her big break soon. But I am sure that there were times when she wished that she was back with Jane in a London club causing havoc with The Libertine Dolls. Then the following day she would get an invite to a new bar that was opening in the village, and it made the flight across the Atlantic worthwhile again.

It was on those nights, when Yvonne was out with Wilton Stratford Pine, that I started to wonder what it would mean for me if she did get her big break. Would I still figure in her plans?

Despite the auditions and the bit-parts in average MTV videos, Yvonne was increasingly frustrated that she wasn't able to sing and perform as she had been doing in the UK with The Libertine Dolls. We had been in New York for six or seven weeks and although she knew that recognition in America wasn't going to happen overnight, I think the promises from Wilton Stratford Pine had made her believe that she would be gigging regularly by now, either as a solo act or with some funky east coast outfit. Singing muzak tracks was not what she had come to the US to do.

Yvonne finally got her break in a show Pine had invested in, an off-Broadway show called *Boon!* – a dystopian rock musical about a businessman who becomes the President of the United States and then starts World War Three with the flick of a switch. But although the plot was poor, the sets worse and the costumes a poor man's rip-off of *Terminator* meets *Rocky Horror*, the score was great. There was a live band in the theatre, and the acoustics were astounding.

She managed to land the lead female part. It helped that Pine, as a lead financier, could put some of his acts in front of the casting director, but the rest of the selection process was down to

Yvonne: her voice, her charisma and unabashed stage presence, which the director loved.

As the weeks went by, she began to have a lot of fun rehearsing with the cast, and she threw herself wholeheartedly into the madness and energy of the production. The show was deliberately edgy, with more fake blood than an Alice Cooper concert, lyrics intended to make the theatre district feel uncomfortable, and even the audience was encouraged to dress up and interact with the cast on stage.

One evening, Yvonne came home after rehearsals and told me there had been an almighty bust-up at the theatre that afternoon. She stood in the middle of our lounge area and lit a cigarette and it all tumbled out of her.

'Honestly, Vik, I thought at one point there was going to be a mass brawl.'

'What happened?'

Yvonne examined her fingernails. 'It was all because of Wilton, well him and Brad. Well, mostly Brad really.'

Brad was Yvonne's leading man in *Boon!*, a charming African American whom I had met once when Yvonne had started rehearsals. I had found him a lively and entertaining guy.

'Go on.'

'It was so stupid, really. It started when Brad and Wilton were discussing one of the scenes. It isn't up to Wilton or Brad, of course, to direct the cast, but because Brad had a suggestion which would mean we would need to spend more money on the scenery, Wilton got involved. In no time, the discussion became an argument. You know how men are.'

I let that go. 'It doesn't sound so bad, just handbags at three feet. Not exactly a mass brawl.'

'Hmm, yes, well the brawl nearly broke out because of what happened next. Wilton took a full swing at Brad. But Brad is pretty nimble on his feet, he was a mean basketball player at high school, and he just swayed to one side, and Wilton fell arse over tit in front of half the crew. Then, unfortunately, someone laughed, and Wilton started swearing and shouting…'

Yvonne paused and bit her lip. I held out my arms to encourage her. Yvonne took a deep breath.

'And then…and then, Wilton called Brad a stupid cotton picker. *That's* when there was the threat of a mass brawl.'

I shook my head; what an idiot Wilton Stratford Pine was.

'At least a fight didn't break out in the end,' Yvonne continued, 'but at one stage, half the cast were threatening to quit unless Wilton apologised. Some of them even wanted him to be kicked out of the show altogether. Which would be difficult, seeing as he is the lead investor. Anyhow, I took Wilton outside and asked him what he was playing at. Finally, after half an hour, I got him to see sense, and he calmed down and went back inside, and stood in front of the entire cast and all the crew and said what a dick he had been, and how sorry he was and how he felt so embarrassed. He laid it on pretty thick. But he meant it, you could tell.

'In the end, Brad told him to shut the fuck up and gave him a hug.' Yvonne inhaled deeply on her cigarette. 'Man, it was touch and go for a while. There was genuinely a point where I thought that might be curtains for the show.'

'But now it's OK?'

'Yes, now it's OK, I think.'

I blew my cheeks out. 'And all because Wilton was being a dickhead. A racist dickhead.'

'Yes…' Yvonne paused. 'Yes, he was. But, you know, Brad was riling him, really winding him up. So although Wilton shouldn't have said what he said, I don't entirely blame him for saying it.'

I stared at Yvonne. I couldn't believe it. Had she just said that? Had she just defended Wilton Stratford Pine's racist attack on *Boon!*'s lead actor? It was inconceivable. I took a step towards her. She was still standing in the middle of our lounge, watching the ash at the end of her cigarette build up.

'But, Yvonne…'

She looked up at me. 'Actually, Vik, can we not talk about this any more. The whole episode has exhausted me, and I just need a drink. Is that OK?'

'Well, yes, but –'

'Good. That's that then.'

And that was that. Yvonne cut me off, didn't want to talk about it any further, refused to answer why she was defending a racist shit like Wilton Stratford Pine. Yes we were staying in his apartment for free, which may have been connected, but the Yvonne I knew wouldn't have sacrificed her principles for that. At least, not in the past. It made me feel simultaneously insecure, curious and angry. And I didn't like it.

Eleven

My job at Vid-u-Missed only lasted a few weeks, before the company went bankrupt. I spent several days looking for an alternative job, but as I had found when we arrived in New York, it was a significant challenge for a one-handed man with no working visa. I realised that with Chef Raybourne's pay-off fast running out, I needed money quickly. I could only think of one thing: my Uncle Neel.

Uncle Neel, was my mother's only brother, very much the black sheep of the family. When my mother and her family had left Kenya for Leicester, Neel initially went with them, but within a year he had left England and emigrated to California, where he was offered a job in what was to become Silicon Valley. Some years later I learned that this happened because he had met an American woman in the Midlands, they had fallen instantly in love, and moved to the States together. When my brother and I asked our parents why we hadn't been told this before, what was so bad about marrying an American, they clammed up. It seemed so hypocritical to me, as it was very nearly a replica of my parents' own story. It was Ajay who eventually cajoled our Aunt Prisha into explaining why Uncle Neel was never talked about: his bride was white and she was rich. Uncle Neel had been accused of selling out his family and heritage, marrying for money and forgetting his roots. She said he had boasted about the great life he was going to have, and badmouthed the shitty little life he was leaving behind.

My parents had always encouraged Ajay and me to accept people for who they were, regardless of colour or creed, and the whole anecdote didn't sit right for either of us, but we didn't have any evidence to refute such a story. Neither Ajay or I had ever met him or his wife, and the few photographs which we saw of Neel while we were growing up only showed him as a teenager. The last thing Aunt Prisha had heard, Neel and his wife were living on the East Coast, somewhere near New York.

I hoped that Aunt Prisha was right and that my uncle was living nearby. If so, maybe he could help me find work, or even lend me some cash. I phoned Ajay and asked him if he could contact our aunt to see if she could give me any further clues as to our estranged uncle's whereabouts; maybe I could then hunt him down in a phonebook.

Two days later, Ajay called me back. 'You're not going to believe this, bro, but Aunt Prisha has had Uncle Neel's phone number all along. She says he is living in Long Island.'

'You're kidding. I thought no one knew where he was.'

'That's what I thought too. You'd better ask him for the full story if you get to meet him.'

I phoned my uncle's number the same evening. A man answered.

'Neel Jayashankar?' I asked.

'Yes?'

'This is Vikram Cohen, your nephew.'

There was a long pause.

'Vikram? Really?'

'Yes, Uncle. I am calling you from Manhattan.'

Another pause.

'Oh my God! Vikram. I can't believe it. What are you… why…I mean, my God. Is it really you? It's so good to hear from you.'

'You too, Uncle.'

'Wait, did you just say you are in Manhattan?'

'Yes.'

'But I am in Long Island. That's practically next door!'

I couldn't help but laugh. 'Yes, uncle, I know. That's why I'm calling. I, er, I hoped we might be able to meet up.'

'Yes, we must! As soon as possible.'

'That would be great.'

Uncle Neel told me that his wife, Elizabeth, and he were going to be in Manhattan that weekend, meeting friends at the Waldorf Astoria, and he would love to meet Yvonne and me at the same time.

Then we talked a little more, Neel reeling off a series of stories about my mother and two of her sisters which only their brother could have known. I had to ask him to stop or he might have continued for hours.

I had never told Yvonne about Uncle Neel before, I had never needed to, and, rather than tell her I was going to ask him for help, I said that my aunt had given Ajay our uncle's details out of the blue when he mentioned I was in New York. Yvonne listened engrossed that evening as I recounted the phone call to her and revealed all I knew about his history. I had thought that Yvonne would be adamant that I should snub him because of his wealth, but much to my surprise, she was supportive of me meeting him and, she said, to give him the benefit of the doubt until I heard his side of the story. Thankfully, she agreed that it might be better if she didn't come with me, so that Neel and I could get to know each other without being worried about looking after her too.

Knowing that the Waldorf was one of New York's most high-class and iconic hotels, I bought a tie before I met my uncle that Friday evening; a new experience for me. When I arrived at the hotel I was directed to Sir Harry's Bar, the sign at its entrance indicating that it was hosting a private function for a charitable foundation. I had my name checked against a long list, walked into a high ceilinged, art deco-styled room past a long, twenty-foot ebony bar into a throng of people and was instantly offered a choice of cocktail. I liked it so far.

I had wondered how Uncle Neel and I would recognise each other, but I needn't have worried; I was the only guest under thirty who wasn't white and there was only one Indian man who could have been my mother's brother: a slight man, dressed immaculately, looking a good few years younger than a man I knew to be in his mid-fifties, he was nevertheless a male version of my mother. Uncle Neel rushed over and his genuine smile of delight relaxed me more than any words. He held out his hand and then looked shocked as I offered him my right arm.

'It's a long story,' I said, shaking my shirt sleeve down so that it was covered again.

Uncle Neel took my left hand in both of his. 'We have all the time in the world,' he said.

He guided me towards a table in the corner of the room. After a few minutes of pleasantries where we agreed how hot New York was and how amazing the Astoria was, Uncle Neel sat back in his chair and gazed at me intently.

'You know, Vik, I wasn't sure that this day would ever come.'

'Oh. Why not, Uncle?'

'Oh, you know. Because as far as your mother is concerned, I barely exist any more, do I? I mean, does she talk about me much?'

'No...'

'Exactly. So why would I have expected that we would ever meet?'

'I don't know.' I shook my head. 'Uncle Neel, can I ask you a question about that?'

'Of course. You can ask as many questions as you want. And I want to ask many things about you too. We have so many years to catch up on.'

'How come Aunt Prisha knew where you lived?'

Neel beamed. 'I will tell you, Vik, but I don't know if you should pass this on to your mother. We may have to find a different story for her. The truth is that your Aunt Prisha and I still write to each other. I don't think your mother knows that.'

'Wow. OK, but hang on, I thought it was Aunt Prisha who told Ajay all about how you married a rich white woman and then spurned the rest of the family.'

Uncle Neel looked downcast, and he swirled his ice around in his glass. 'The only truth in that is that I did indeed marry Elizabeth, and yes, she comes from a very wealthy family. However, it was her family who was more upset, as you might imagine if you think about it for a minute. Their only daughter marrying out of her class, and not only that but to a bloody Indian to boot!' Neel smiled sadly. 'When Elizabeth and I got married, her father cut off all communication with her and froze all her bank accounts, and we spent five years living hand to mouth in California.'

'With income from your tech job?' I asked.

This made Neel laugh. 'My tech job? Is that what you were told?' I nodded. 'Well, yes, I did work for IBM but my job for the first two years was a cleaner while I did a night course in IT and robotics! Elizabeth worked in a café, waitressing. We didn't have much money, but we were in love, and we had a lot of fun.' Neel chuckled. 'God, listen to me, I sound like some stereotypical hippy.'

'I think it sounds cool,' I said.

'It gave us an income!' Neel said. 'But then Elizabeth's father had a heart attack. Elizabeth heard about this from her cousin, and she flew back to the East Coast. Her father recovered, thank goodness, and while he was recuperating, Elizabeth spent a lot of time with him. He started to understand how happy she was with me and, of course, how much he had missed her, until finally, he announced one day that he had accepted our marriage and formally welcomed me into the family.'

'So it wasn't the easy option for you to move to the States,' I said thoughtfully. 'I don't understand why Mum hasn't stayed in touch with you.'

Neel shook his head. 'It's because I didn't marry the woman our parents wanted me to. Our parents had their hearts set on her, but I felt we had nothing in common.'

'I didn't know you were expected to have an arranged marriage,' I said, truthfully.

He nodded, looking melancholy.

We carried on talking while the waiters circulated with cocktails. Neel told me how sad he had felt when my mother and her sisters had assumed he was marrying for money, and how it was, of course, doubly awkward because he was moving away with a white woman; and how, after several fruitless and angry arguments, he had decided that it was simply easier to let sleeping dogs lie. ('I never dreamed that I would be estranged from my family for the next two decades, or I would have tried harder to have made them understand how much I loved Elizabeth.') Except for Aunt Prisha, nobody wrote to him.

'We have kept in touch for twenty years and I have every letter,' Neel said proudly. 'Think of the family history chronicled in those dispatches.'

'But why didn't you ever fly back to see us?' I said. 'They would have listened to you.'

'Sadly, I don't think they would have. Your grandparents have long memories and blood runs deep. No one would have wanted to see me.' He paused. 'I always hoped that you or Ajay, or one of your cousins, might contact me one day. And now you have done that. I'm so happy!'

He tapped my glass with his, and I had to fight back my own tears.

I told Uncle Neel about growing up in mainly white Harrogate, how Yvonne and I met, my growing desire to become a chef and then I told him about what Chef Kevin did to me. Neel listened without once interrupting, and when I had finished, I could see his eyes were damp.

'I'm proud of you,' he said, 'and so glad that we have finally met. And you've never wanted a prosthetic hand?'

I shook my head. 'I can't do much with a fake hand, it wouldn't feel like part of me.'

Neel nodded. I took a sip from my drink and decided that now was the time to ask for his help.

'The thing is, Uncle Neel–'

Before I could continue, an elegant woman with her blonde hair piled high on her head, wearing a long red dress and a glittering necklace, glided over to us. Neel stood up as she arrived at our table, and I followed suit. Uncle Neel introduced her as his wife.

'I am so pleased to meet you, Vik,' Elizabeth said in a broad New York accent. Compared to her appearance, her voice was so incongruous.

'Thank you for inviting me, Auntie,' I replied.

Neel's wife laughed and shook her head. 'Just call me Elizabeth, please. Auntie makes me feel far too old. Are you enjoying living in New York?'

'I am.'

'I'm so glad. Neel, can I borrow you for a moment? There are a few donors I'd like you to meet.'

Uncle Neel turned to me.

'Can we continue this conversation another time, Vik?'

'Well, I was hoping to ask–'

'Maybe next week?' he said, handing me a business card. 'Elizabeth and I are having a party at our place in Long Island. Please come. And bring your girlfriend.'

I thanked him and said we would love to come.

I had to persuade Yvonne to go to Neel and Elizabeth's party. She was well aware that it would be full of 'high society eejits' as she referred to them, far removed from anyone she normally mixed with. I agreed but reminded her that this was my long lost family and an important occasion for me. She reluctantly agreed.

I kissed her. 'Thank you, Yvonne, this means a lot to me.'

'I know,' she said, stroking my cheek, 'and I promise I will be on my best behaviour. If anyone does say something stupid about the homeless or gun control or anything, then I swear I will bite my lip.'

I said that she could bite mine if that would help her. She said she would like to practice on me, and it wasn't long before we ended up in bed.

Neel and Elizabeth lived on Sunset Drive, Sayville on Long Island, although my uncle had also told me that they had a pied-à-terre just east of Greenwich Village. If you look at a map of New York, then Long Island seems like it's next door to Manhattan, but if you have to take public transport and walk, it isn't so straightforward. By the time Yvonne and I had changed buses, got off at the wrong bus stop, and found our way to their house, it took us over two and a half hours. We were not only exhausted, but with the temperature still in the high-eighties we smelt like we had walked all the way. I was wearing a heavy, long-sleeved shirt, and the sweat was running down my back. Yvonne was dressed more sensibly, in a long dress, but at least I could unbutton some of my shirt, whereas Yvonne was forced to maintain her dignity.

Once we had disembarked the bus, we couldn't quite believe that we were heading in the right direction, as the houses we passed kept getting larger with higher roofs and more windows, ever greener gardens and more and more warnings about their security systems. When we finally reached Neel and Elizabeth's house, if we had carried on walking past their front door for another thirty seconds, then we could have walked into Nicoll Bay. We hiked up their drive past Jaguars, Lincolns, other sports cars and Hummer-like beasts and wondered just who else was at this party.

Neel had promised a casual lunch, but we were still the dowdiest of all the guests. My uncle pressed a beer into my hand as I walked in, while Yvonne found one of the bathrooms in the house and returned looking as if she had just stepped into a fresh dress ('and I found you again without the use of a map,' she said pointedly, causing Neel to give her a wry smile). There were well over fifty guests in the house, and Neel and Elizabeth had hired outside caterers. All of our drinks, canapés and food for the rest of the afternoon were brought to us by waiters carrying ornate silver platters and heavy, starched napkins. I don't know how they didn't melt in their black uniforms and bow-ties.

I introduced Neel to Yvonne and they shook hands. While they made small talk, her eyes wheeled around his impressive open-plan living room, the paintings, the ornaments, the décor. I knew what she was thinking: there wasn't anyone else like us at the party.

'You know, I did enjoy living in California with Elizabeth, and we didn't need money per se, but I have to tell you,' and he winked at Yvonne, 'I don't mind being able to spend a bit of extra cash every now and then without having to worry about how I'll pay next month's bills.'

Yvonne maintained a straight face. 'If only millions of other people who can't afford their bills could feel the same way.'

Uncle Neel evaluated her for a few moments. 'Would it surprise you to know that we invest our personal savings in many start-up companies whose goal is social improvement? Robotics, disability programmes, inner city development.'

Yvonne pursed her lips. 'And I'm sure you make a good return out of them.'

'And Elizabeth spends most of her time running her own charitable foundation to help disadvantaged families?'

Yvonne shrugged. 'That's very good of her. But it doesn't take away from the fact that in Britain and America people live below the breadline while a few wealthy individuals enjoy overly privileged lives.'

Neel looked at her tolerantly. 'Yet here you are today, in our house in Long Island. My wife came from a wealthy family, yes, but I've worked hard for my own achievements.'

'And I applaud you for that. But it doesn't detract from my issue over this country's wealth inequality.'

Neel tapped his fingertip on his chin. He didn't look angry but I thought Yvonne had probably pushed her agenda far enough for today.

I coughed. 'You know, Uncle, when I revealed to Yvonne what Ajay and I were told about you when we were kids, she insisted how important it was that I meet you to understand the truth.'

Yvonne reached out and took my hand. 'Vik needs to learn about you from you, Neel, not from long-standing family myths.'

'I'm glad you think that,' my uncle said.

'Family is important, Neel.'

I looked at Yvonne, and for a second I saw her blinking back a tear.

Uncle Neel turned to me again. 'You know, Vik, you have a good woman here.'

'I know, Uncle Neel.'

'But she's a feisty one!'

'You haven't seen the half of it.'

'I bet.'

'I wouldn't get on the wrong side of her if you can help it.'

'I certainly won't!'

Yvonne leaned forwards and waved her hand between us. 'Hey, excuse me, I am still here you know.'

Elizabeth, looking elegant in what someone else later told me was a couture Calvin Klein dress, came over to greet us.

'Please,' Elizabeth said, after introductions had been made. 'You are welcome to stay as long as you like. Have some free drinks. Dance. Enjoy the champagne. All I ask is that you respect the other guests. The people here have quite traditional views on life.'

'How do you mean?' I asked.

'Oh, you know,' she said, glancing quickly at her husband. 'Don't get too drunk and, er, candid. They come from up-standing families, they feel they know what is right. But they're perfectly happy to put their hands in their pocket, for the right cause, and I am hoping that my foundation will be the recipient of some of their generosity!'

As Elizabeth had been talking, I had been aware that Yvonne was tensing up by my side. I could tell that her discussion about wealth with Neel still rankled with her, and now her powder keg of injustice had been relit. When Elizabeth finished, she took a step forwards towards my aunt.

'Well, I am very sorry if we don't fit your perfect clique that you have here. But I am afraid that we don't have any money ourselves that we can donate.'

Elizabeth looked shocked. 'That's not what I meant,' she started, but Yvonne interrupted her.

'Oh, I know what you meant. Have a drink, smile, be pleasant to the nice people and don't say anything which would upset them. Well don't worry, we won't, so you can get back to your friends. Because we won't be here for long.'

Elizabeth pursed her lips. 'You know, you remind me of one of my board members.'

'On your foundation? I hope not,' Yvonne said sharply.

'Actually, yes. A woman called Rochelle. And you know why? Because she was a single, homeless mother in her twenties, and she still doesn't own a house now. But I invited her on to my board because I wanted someone who knew what she was talking about, and not just a bunch of "rich shits", as Rochelle would say.'

'Elizabeth–' Neel and I said in unison.

'And every time,' Elizabeth continued, ignoring our intervention, 'I think I might be losing touch with why I actually hold these events, I talk to Rochelle, and she brings me right back down to earth.'

Yvonne stood her ground. 'She sounds like an excellent woman to have working for you.'

'She is.'

The two women regarded each other.

'Why don't I give you a guided tour of the house,' Elizabeth suggested, 'and you can tell me more about how you think I could help my beneficiaries.'

Yvonne gave a tiny shake of her head. 'Why not? I can do that.' She held out her arm, indicating that her host should lead the way. Instead, much to Yvonne's surprise, Elizabeth hooked her hands through Yvonne's elbow.

Neel and I exchanged a look of relief and followed them. Yvonne was a liability sometimes, even though I loved her for speaking her mind.

Elizabeth showed us around the four floors of their house, and once we were in their back garden we could see that we had been right about the Nicoll Bay – their garden backed on to the waterfront, and not only did it have the obligatory tennis court and swimming pool, but it also contained a small copse. They even had their own dock and a thirty-foot-plus cabin cruiser moored in it. Elizabeth then took Yvonne back to the party (with Yvonne glancing back at me and giving me a wink as she left, while I made a keep calm signal with my left hand) and passed me on to Neel who guided me towards his 'personal laboratory': a garage-sized room with workbenches and cupboards running all around the walls, crates of electronics and half-finished projects, diagrams and posters stuck on the backs of several doors and what looked like Meccano models hanging from the ceiling. It was remarkably clean. The windows sparkled, there wasn't a sign of any dust on the worktops, and although there was so much to look at, everything seemed to have its own place.

I spent a happy half hour with my uncle while he demonstrated some of his latest experiments, without seeming to mind that he was ignoring his important guests. As our discussion moved on to kitchen gadgets, he listened while I outlined my working experience and nodded when I explained how much I used to love cheffing in a proper kitchen.

'And your hand? That must have been so hard, losing the use of it.'

'Well, yes and no, seeing as I'm left-handed. The chef who attacked me didn't even notice that.'

Neel shook his head. 'The world is full of racist idiots.'

While Neel demonstrated his latest toy, I decided to put my request for help on the back burner. I knew I still had to ask my uncle if he could get me a job, or even lend me some money, but somehow I couldn't do it yet. Despite the fact we were talking about my work. It just felt wrong: Neel was being so welcoming to me, and to blurt out that I needed his help seemed inappropriate. But it didn't matter I consoled myself, I had the rest of the afternoon to find a more befitting moment.

I found Yvonne again after Neel was called in by Elizabeth. She was talking with, or rather, listening to a couple from Connecticut rave about their hedge fund. I think that afternoon at Elizabeth and Neel's house was one of the few times when Yvonne felt truly out of place; perhaps even daunted by the wealth and the glamour on show. Everyone seemed to be in finance or property management, or alternatively didn't appear to do anything except be chauffeured from one party to another. But not once did I hear Yvonne say anything scathing or disrespectful to any of the guests, or anything controversial whatsoever. She had, of course, promised me that she would be on her best behaviour but I had assumed that her 'best behaviour' would still involve taking some posh kingpins down a peg or two. Especially after her earlier denunciations of wealth towards my aunt and uncle. She barely said a word except to prompt a few people when they appeared to have finished talking. I think it must have been her way to ensure that she wouldn't say anything out of place.

It was nearly five o'clock when Elizabeth found Yvonne and me sitting together outside on a swing seat near the trees, lingering in the shade of the canopy and staring out at the bay, Yvonne with her head resting on my shoulder and both of us trying not to think about the return leg of what we expected to be an equally traumatic journey back to the Lower East Side. Elizabeth, with her brusque New York approach, told us to budge up and sat down beside me.

'Vik,' Elizabeth said coolly and took my hand, 'we have a problem. And I need your help.'

'Me, Auntie?'

'Oh, for God's sake, Vik,' Elizabeth snorted and squeezed my hand enough to make me jolt, 'I have told you not to call me that. I may be your aunt legally, but I am not some ageing, Victorian dowager.' She saw me grinning and tutted. 'Listen. I really do need to ask something of you.'

'Sure, go on.'

'The thing is, I have let some of the caterers go home already. I think some of them had auditions.' She let go of my hand and started fiddling with her necklace. 'But I may have been somewhat hasty. Because we still have the dessert to serve and, oh God, this is awkward…the chef has managed to slice open his hand and he bled everywhere, and now he's telling me he's not allowed to cook anything else because his injury means his insurance is invalidated. And I have fifty guests all waiting for a final course.' Her voice trailed away, and she looked back towards the house. I followed her gaze.

'And?' I prompted her.

She looked down at her feet. 'And...Neel told me all about what you had been doing in London, and yes, I know that you don't cook professionally now, but,' she turned back to me and looked me straight in the eyes. 'There is no one else I can ask. No one else here knows how to make the dessert from scratch, and if I don't serve it, then the party just won't be complete.'

I didn't say anything for a moment, and then I swallowed and turned to look at Yvonne, gave her my best help-me face. This I did not need. Elizabeth was entirely correct when she said I didn't cook professionally any more.

'I haven't put a foot into a professional kitchen since I lost my hand in the last one. You're asking me to cook in what amounts to a commercial environment. I can't do that. I don't want to do that.'

It scared the shit out of me that she was even asking me.

Yvonne laid a hand on my arm. 'What is the dessert which is so difficult, Elizabeth, that means no one else can do it?'

Elizabeth sighed. 'Chocolate profiteroles. I know, I know,' she added quickly as both Yvonne and I looked at her in surprise, 'they're not exactly haute cuisine are they. But – they're fun, right. And they're fucking delicious.'

Hearing Elizabeth swear about profiteroles in her broad New York accent, made Yvonne and I burst out laughing. My aunt looked puzzled. 'What's so funny, what's wrong? What have I said?'

'Nothing, Elizabeth, you've said nothing wrong,' Yvonne reassured her. 'It's just the way you said it.' She grinned. 'You sound like a bad advertising executive for the profiterole marketing board or something.'

For a moment, Elizabeth looked hurt, and then a smile cracked her face, and she laughed too. 'So, Vik,' she said once we had all calmed down, 'I'm glad you can find this funny, I really am, but I have to ask you again: please can you help? Please, can you make the profiteroles?'

She looked so distressed that I couldn't look directly at her. Instead, I looked back at Yvonne. 'Yvonne, I…tell her…'

Yvonne sat up straight and took my left hand in both of hers. She looked me in the eyes. 'Vik. I think you should do it.'

'What?' I shook my head and tried to pull my hand away, but Yvonne's grasp was too tight. 'No.'

'Yes.'

'I can't.'

'You can.'

'But… I only have one hand!'

'So.'

'So, I won't be able to do it.'

'You will.' Yvonne squeezed my one hand more kindly. 'You will, Vik, I know you will. You used to love making chocolate profiteroles at Le Jardin, remember? And they were fucking delicious.' She looked at Elizabeth. 'He even made savoury profiteroles at one of the restaurants he worked at.'

'Really?' Elizabeth said more calmly. 'I had no idea.'

Yvonne got to her feet. 'Come on, Vik. Let's do this!'

'But–'

'But nothing, come on. I'll even help you. I will be your second hand. I'll be your…pâtissier? Is that the right word?'

I looked up at her. Her body was half-silhouetted against the water, and the sun bouncing off her face and her smile made her look more beautiful than I could remember in months.

How could I say no?

Elizabeth led us into the house, avoiding the other guests, down a cool corridor at such a pace we were almost running to keep up. Yvonne held my hand all the way, and I tried not to shiver as I thought about what lay ahead of me. When we reached the open door to the kitchen, Elizabeth said, 'Well, this is it. I hope it's OK for you.'

I looked around. Her kitchen was larger than the Dog and Dragon's, and lighter: there were windows all along one side and the afternoon sunlight flooded in. A vast expanse of counter space rolled around the edge of the room, with machines and knives and crockery of all sorts laid out on it, and in the middle of the kitchen was an island the size of a snooker table. Above it hung multiple frying pans, saucepans, skillets, woks. In the corner, sitting on an old wooden chair, was a man in chef's whites with a sling around his left shoulder, looking very sorry for himself. It must have been one hell of an injury for him to have his arm in a sling. He met my eyes for an instant, glanced down at my right arm and then looked away, a bit embarrassed I thought.

'Vik, this is Frankie. Frankie, Vik.' Elizabeth waved at the chef and then me, and walked over to open a window. We nodded at each other. 'The good news is that Frankie had at least made the pastry before he cut himself. Is that right, Frankie?'

The chef nodded. 'It's in the fridge,' he said quietly and nodded at a massive, silver, double-doored behemoth.

'Frankie can talk you through the rest of the recipe,' Elizabeth continued and strolled back across the kitchen towards me. 'Are you ready, Vik?'

I looked nervously at my aunt, studied the kitchen once more, took a deep breath, and suddenly I felt a rush of adrenalin. I hovered where I was, half-closed my eyes to the sunlight, flexed my fingers on my left hand, noted a bird fly past the window as if in slow motion, and everything around me went quiet for an instant. Then I heard Elizabeth's voice again, and I jolted back to the present.

'Is there an apron I can use?' I asked abruptly, and I swear I felt the nerves at the end of my right arm tingle. I knew I didn't need any private chef who couldn't even hold a knife without cutting himself to tell me what to do. (It was a good thing, however, that Frankie had made the choux pastry as that would have been darned slow going.)

I went to work. I asked Yvonne to beat some eggs into the pastry until the mixture was smooth and glossy and had a soft dropping consistency. Then, with her help, I piped the batter into small balls in lines across a baking sheet, making sure I gently rubbed the top of each ball with a wet finger to make a crisper head. I slid the baking sheet into the pre-heated oven and started on the filling by lightly whipping double cream with a little orange zest until it firmed up and formed soft peaks. Once the profiteroles were golden-brown, I pricked the base of each profiterole with a skewer and returned them to the oven rack for five minutes. When the profiteroles were cold, Yvonne and I used a piping bag between us to insert the cream into the profiteroles. Then I made the chocolate sauce before finally placing the stuffed profiteroles into a series of large serving dishes and pouring the chocolate sauce over them.

I stood back and contemplated what I had just done. For forty-five minutes, I had been so engrossed in my cooking that I had almost forgotten where I was. Hell, if it hadn't been for the piping required, I would almost have forgotten that I only had one hand. I looked at what we had made, and slowly a smile appeared on my face. I had to hold the kitchen counter to steady myself.

Yvonne gave me a tight hug and kissed me hard on the lips. 'Well done, Vik, that was amazing. I am so proud of you.' Frankie appeared and slapped me on the back. 'Fuck me, man. If that is what you can do with one hand in an emergency in someone else's kitchen, then you must be a fuckin' ace in your own professional space.'

Elizabeth, Neel and Yvonne distributed the profiteroles to the guests while I stayed in the kitchen to gather my thoughts. Through the open window, I could hear oohs and aahs.

Neel paid for a taxi to take us back to our tiny apartment in the Lower East; I dread to think what it cost him. Yvonne and I barely spoke in the back of the cab, we didn't need to, we just held hands and watched the lights of Manhattan Island appear and grow brighter as we raced towards it. I hadn't got around to asking my uncle for money, but I didn't care. For the first time in months, I felt alive.

Twelve

October 1993

Two weeks after I had made the profiteroles at Elizabeth's, Uncle Neel called. 'There's something I want to talk to you about,' he said mysteriously. 'I'm going to be in Manhattan tomorrow, so I'll swing by and pick you up, and we can drive back to Long Island together.'

Which is why I found myself, the following day, watching the Long Island Expressway fly past me from the comfort of a Mercedes Benz. We pulled into his driveway less than an hour later, and Neel winked at me.

'You ready to see what I've commissioned? Come on, I'll show you.'

Neel got out of the car and led me into their kitchen. We walked over to a metal box that was sitting on the enormous island. The container was just about big enough for a pair of knee-high boots. My uncle placed his palm on top of it.

'Vik, I've been thinking how I can help you, and I want to give you something. I watched you cook the other night, and although I'm no Bobby Flay, even I can see how good you are, but clearly, you find it difficult with only one hand.' He paused and looked at me expectantly. I didn't know what to say, so I half-nodded, half-shrugged. Neel carried on.

'So I visited one of the robotics companies we have a significant investment in. I sat down with their engineers and discussed what I was thinking of, and between us, we came up with this prototype.' He patted the box in front of him. 'My idea, but it was created by the geniuses at the company, and they went way beyond what I had imagined. I think you'll be impressed.'

So saying, he opened the box, reached in and pulled out a metal contraption. He turned and held it up to me, and I literally took a step backwards.

'We'll need to make a cast of your arm so it's a perfect fit.'

Uncle Neel was holding what I assumed was a robotic hand, a cyber hand. It looked as if it had come straight out of *Terminator 2*, as created by the Cyberdyne Corp. Except that this one also had what looked like a long, metal gauntlet attached to the wrist part. Neel swivelled it around. 'What do you think?'

'I'm not sure what to think. Are you suggesting I have a robotic hand…surgically implanted on to me?'

Neel smiled. 'No! Although that might be possible one day. I'm sorry, maybe I should have warned you what I was doing, that would have been less of a shock. But I wanted to surprise you! It's a unique creation, something we designed and built from scratch.'

'And…what does it do exactly?'

Neel beckoned me towards him. 'Come. Let me show you.' I edged across the kitchen floor. He laughed. 'Vik, don't worry! It's meant to help you. But if you don't like it, then you don't have to keep it. At least let me show you.' I shuffled slowly towards my uncle. 'Here, give me your right arm.'

Neel slid the end of my arm into the gauntlet part of the device, so it covered most of my forearm. Then he pushed firmly around the edges of the top of the contraption, and I felt it close snuggly but not uncomfortably around my muscles. He gestured at me to lift my arm up. I did so, and looked at the robotic hand in front of my face, in the same way that Arnie does in *Terminator*, turning it around slowly. It was remarkably light.

'What is it made from?'

'Titanium.'

'Titanium?'

'Titanium, mostly, but we've drilled holes in it, so it weighs less and adapted it so that parts of it use an even lighter alloy.'

'Oh. Wow.'

'Wow indeed. Now. Let me explain how it works. Do you know what myoelectric means?'

'My-o what?'

'I assume that's no, then.' Neel smiled. 'It refers to the electric impulses of muscles. And this is a myoelectric-controlled prosthetic hand. Which means that you control and direct it with the electrical signals generated innately by your own muscles.'

'I'm sorry, I don't fully understand.'

Neel tapped the robotic hand. 'In this hand are multiple sensors which are programmed to receive electric signals when you engage specific muscles in the rest of your arm. That is translated into commands for the electric motors built into the prosthetic, which subsequently moves your joints.'

'You mean,' I said incredulously, 'that if I just move my arm, my hand will react to that?' Neel nodded. 'Holy shit! That's incredible.'

'It is, isn't it. The concept has been around since the eighties, and our company has been experimenting with the technology in a similar area for the last three years, but this is our first device to put all our research into practice.'

'Like the six million dollar man!'

Neel grinned. 'Shall we see how it works?'

He slid open a drawer in the island and pulled out a carrot, a cucumber and several cherry tomatoes. He put them all down on the counter in front of me.

The prosthetic hand I had been offered at the hospital was a passive, skin-coloured thing that didn't do much – mainly just saved other people from having to deal with an amputee. But this piece of technology already felt like it could become an extension of me.

Neel pointed at the hand again. 'If you look carefully at the fingers, you will see hundreds of small pin-point circles. They are more sensors. So not only can the hand grip say, a carrot, but it knows when to stop applying pressure when it feels the carrot, and therefore it doesn't grip it too hard. Go on, try it.'

Uncle Neel looked like an excited child. I raised up my new hand, flexed my elbow and the hand revolved automatically to the right. I couldn't believe it. I flexed a different way and it moved left. I grinned idiotically.

'It's amazing, Uncle.'

For the next few minutes, Uncle Neel showed me how to make the hand do different things depending on which muscles I flexed in my arm, how that changed if I varied my muscle intensity, and ultimately how I could pick things up.

I pushed the carrot into the middle of the counter and, after a couple of attempts, the hand picked it up. I shook it gently. The carrot slipped slightly but didn't fall out of my grasp. Then I held the arm over the counter, and dropped the vegetable on to the table top.

I puffed out a breath. 'Uncle Neel, that is bloody amazing.'

My uncle clasped his hands together. 'It is, isn't it. Even if I say so myself. I know it buzzes a bit when it contracts and expands, but we're working on that. Now go on, try the other vegetables.'

I spent the next ten minutes picking up and putting down vegetables, working out where I could hold them so I could slice with my other hand. The tomatoes were the hardest, and I squashed a few during my first attempts, but more because I didn't position the hand properly rather than the hand squashing them itself. We also worked out that if I wanted to chop something quickly, then I could use the robot more like a prosthetic hand, holding the vegetable and sliding it backwards slowly.

'Mind you, if that's what you want to do,' Neel said thoughtfully, 'then we could add some material where your knuckles would be and that will make it glide better over the veggies without so much friction.'

We discussed various further improvements and adaptations Neel's engineers could make and then I said I had better take it off.

Uncle Neel said brightly, 'Oh you can't take it off, Vik, it's attached to you for life now. Didn't I say?'

I raised my robot arm. 'Hey, I can use this as a weapon too, you know, so be careful what you say.'

Neel winked. He showed me how to release the whole hand, and I slid it off. I rubbed the end of my right arm; it didn't hurt, but it felt slightly sore.

'I'll get a cast made and we can adjust it for you so it fits perfectly.'

I looked at my uncle. 'I don't know how to thank you.'

Uncle Neel smiled. 'It's I who should thank you. I've been waiting so long to hear from another member of the family. After you called me I felt so happy.'

I nodded, shaking off the guilt I felt. Although I'd contacted Uncle Neel because I needed a job, I really liked him.

'You've been so kind,' I said.

He waved away my words. 'Now,' Uncle Neel said decisively, 'Elizabeth would also like to see you. Come with me.'

I followed my uncle into one of the lounges. (The smallest of the reception rooms, Neel assured me, but it was still half the size of a tennis court.) Elizabeth was waiting for us on a sofa, wearing a long white dress. She looked up when she heard us come in and put down the book she had been reading.

'So, how do you like Neel's present, Vik? Does it work?'

'It's incredible. Really. I didn't want the hand the London hospital was offering – it didn't do anything – but this is almost as good as the real thing.'

'Good. I don't know what we would have done without you last month. Everyone said how wonderful your profiteroles were. Consider it a thank you gift.' She patted the sofa beside her, and I sat down, thinking hard.

'You know…if you ever needed me again, to chef that is, I'd be happy to give it a go,' I said. 'This hand would make all the difference for me in a kitchen.'

Elizabeth nodded slowly. 'We currently do a lot of entertaining.' She steepled her fingers. 'In a couple of weeks, I am having another event, but this is a more formal dinner party with some very important investors. Only six or eight guests. I have a couple of chefs I was planning to use. It's a full meal and it would be a big responsibility. I'm not sure, could you handle that?'

'A few weeks ago, I would have said no. I wouldn't even have wanted to. But now? I know I could do it. Especially with Uncle Neel's new hand.'

Elizabeth held her arms out and embraced me. 'It's not just the hand, is it? I knew that fire was still in you. And don't tell me you didn't enjoy cooking when you were here. I saw it in your eyes while you were working.'

I agreed that it had been quite fun.

'Good. So you'll do it then?' said Uncle Neel.

Perhaps it was the note in my uncle's voice that said mission accomplished, or my aunt's warm embrace. Had I offered to chef or had they manipulated me into it?

'There is one problem,' I said. 'I don't currently have a job, and so if I do get any work before your meal, then I wouldn't be able to cook for you.'

'We will pay you for this work,' said Elizabeth quickly. 'I would have paid another chef if I'd employed them, so that's only right.'

'Oh, right. Well in that case.'

'You deserve this, Vik. Your food is amazing, everyone said so last month.'

'Everyone?'

She laughed. 'Of course. And you saved the day.'

We discussed a menu and then Elizabeth kissed me on the cheek and Uncle Neel drove me back to Manhattan. It seemed that at least in the short-term I would now be earning something.

After a cast had been made of my arm, and the hand was ready for me to use, I showed it to Yvonne who was initially astounded, then somewhat dismissive, almost indignant, that my rich uncle thought that creating such an invention was a worthwhile use of his money, when he could instead be putting his skills and investments into helping children who really needed prosthetics.

'But you said family was important when we were at the party,' I said. 'Why is it such a bad thing for Uncle Neel to do this for me?'

Yvonne grimaced. 'Vik, it's understandable that your uncle wants to help you. But it shouldn't have to mean that only the privileged get such benefits. Family doesn't have to mean nepotism.'

'Jeez, Yvonne, I hardly think Neel giving me a new hand is nepotistic. It's a present. And a prototype. And you know what – if I can show the benefit of it, then his company will be able to start marketing it and help other people.'

'Who can afford it,' Yvonne added sharply.

I held her gaze. 'Let me show you how it works.'

She recanted once she saw me use the robot and realised just what it could do, and how happy it made me, but her lack of encouragement still rankled. But I didn't let it bother me any further; I was already looking forwards to using it at Elizabeth's dinner party.

Despite her grudging approval of my robot hand, Yvonne refused to come to Neel and Elizabeth's meal even though she was invited.

'You go and play with your rich friends,' she said the second time I asked her to change her mind, 'but I won't join you.'

'It's not about Elizabeth's friends,' I protested, 'it's an opportunity for me to cook again, something I haven't wanted to do for ages, and to help out my aunt and uncle. Why can't you see that?'

Yvonne took my face in her hands. 'Vik, I know you want to be cooking again, and that is so wonderful. Really it is. But if you choose to do this by pandering to a bunch of moneyed, egotistical, upper-class buffoons, then that is your choice, but do not expect me to be part of it.'

'But –'

'I mean, can you really imagine me sitting there with six or seven snobby parasites and keeping ma mouth shut as they discuss their wee holiday cottages in the Hamptons and how terrible the Democrats are? I wouldn't get past the hors d'oeuvre before I slammed one of their bastart faces in the soup or shoved my serviette in their gob. Would I?'

I had to agree. Although I added that I had never heard her say hors d'oeuvre before and it sounded very sexy in her angry Scottish accent. She tried not to smile at that but failed.

I couldn't really blame her for not wanting to traipse out to Long Island. Yvonne was now fully immersed in *Boon!*, regularly rehearsing at a studio, or spending time with other cast members going over specific parts of the script, or being invited out by Wilton Stratford Pine in the evening to meet some new people.

I gave Elizabeth the list of ingredients I needed a week before the meal. On the day, I arrived early in the afternoon and started my mise en place in their oversized, wonderfully light kitchen. As the guests arrived, Elizabeth brought each one in to meet me while I was working and introduced me proudly as her nephew.

One of the guests was a middle-aged woman called Myra Michl, who came in with a happy face, long dark hair and a bit of a swagger.

'Myra's a native New Yorker who has been working in Chicago for the last ten years,' my aunt said.

'But I've just moved back to my home city,' Myra Michl confirmed. 'Elizabeth's told me all about you and your amazing new hand. Although she didn't tell me how you lost your real hand.'

'I asked her not to.'

'And you can't tell me now?'

'I'd rather not.' I was getting frustrated at this new guest's probing, I had a lot of work to do.

'Do you wear it all the time?' Myra Michl continued.

'Not yet. My arm still gets quite sore if I wear it for a long time. Maybe I will one day.'

Myra gazed at my hand while I picked up some ingredients. 'Can I watch you work for a while?'

'Of course. But if you don't mind keeping to one side, so I can do all my prep.'

She looked a little taken aback by my last few words, but recovered her composure in the blink of an eye, gave me a wicked smile and propped herself up, wine glass in hand, against one of the counters on the other side of the room and observed my work without saying a word. When I turned around fifteen minutes later to look for her, she had already slipped out.

I had decided to serve Salmorejo – 'gazpacho's richer, deeper cousin' as Chef Michel had described it to me – as the first course. I had learned to make this soup at Le Jardin and even though summer was pretty much over, I thought it would provide a refreshing starter for the meal. Although the dinner was a formal sit-down affair, Elizabeth wanted to keep it 'less stuffy' and so she insisted that she and Neel help me bring the food through from the kitchen to the dining room. We served the Salmorejo between us and I left the guests to experience it. I was still getting used to my new robot hand but it was feeling more and more a part of me. I could imagine a time when I would be able to wear it every day, but to begin with I only wore it for cooking.

I then pulled together my amuse-bouche to serve after the soup: scallop, salmon roe, basil accompanied with a basil flower.

At the last minute, I realised that I had made a fundamental oversight as I hadn't considered how I was going to serve it; I couldn't put the dish on a large plate or in a bowl, and I started searching all the cupboards for inspiration. There was nothing. Just as I was resigning myself to using a set of china bowls after all, I opened a drawer and I found a collection of large white spoons. I slipped my first scallop on to the bowl area and it fitted perfectly. I dressed the rest of them and they looked delicate and enticing.

For the main course, I cooked coq au vin, and for dessert, lemon mousse. Elizabeth then insisted I join her guests for coffee and digestifs. I removed my apron and my robotic hand (my wrist was quite sore by now) and walked down the corridor into the dining room.

I sat beside Neel, and he slapped me on the back and told me how awesome the meal had been. I laughed; Neel hadn't picked up an American accent despite living in the States for over twenty years, so 'awesome' didn't sound quite right coming from him. Several of the other guests also told me that they had loved the food. Elizabeth came over to my chair, Myra Michl following behind her. 'Vik, that was wonderful. You excelled yourself.'

'Thank you, Elizabeth.'

'We especially liked the way you served the scallop and salmon, didn't we, Myra.'

'We certainly did,' her guest agreed. 'In fact, I'd love to talk to you about your cooking. Can I borrow your nephew?'

Elizabeth put her hand on my shoulder. 'Vik, go and have a chat with Myra while I serve coffee.' She indicated the door to the lounge next door. I followed Myra through, she sat on a sofa and I took one of the armchairs.

'Vik, I'm guessing you don't know who I am, do you?' she started.

'Um, no. Should I?'

Myra Michl gave me a warm smile. 'You don't know how refreshing it is to hear that someone doesn't recognise me. Unless I'm wearing one of my disguises, that is.'

'I'm sorry,' I stuttered. 'If I should know you then I apologise. I haven't been in New York very long.'

'It's fine, Vik. As I said, I'm thrilled you don't know me. It means you were perfectly natural with all your cooking and you didn't try to play up to me.'

I considered Myra's words. 'Are you a chef? I didn't realise.'

'I was a chef, yes, when I lived in California. That's where I met your aunt. Now I'm a restaurant critic. I was the restaurant editor for the *Chicago Tribune*, and I've just returned to New York to become the food editor for the *New York Times*. When Elizabeth heard I was coming home, she invited me here tonight.'

My mind started spinning. 'I've just cooked for a restaurant critic?'

'Relax, Vik. We didn't tell you because we didn't want to faze you.' Myra Michl sat back on the sofa. 'I thought it was some of the best food I have had in years.'

I couldn't find any words to respond to that, and for several minutes I just listened as Myra praised the meal and told me what she had especially enjoyed about it. She also criticised what she didn't like, which I found more reassuring. It made me feel she was open and genuine.

'Elizabeth was also telling me,' she said, 'about how you have been cooking Indian and Jewish fusion food.'

'Well, I've tried to, but I haven't been that successful.'

'That's not what I've heard.'

'Oh. Well, I…don't think it's restaurant quality yet.'

'Chefs can be their own harshest critics sometimes,' Myra said. She sat forwards. 'Vik, I don't mess around. Let's cut to the chase. I think that fusion is going to be one of the up and coming food trends and I would like to give you the opportunity to be part of that.'

'Me?'

'You. And that's why I want to propose something. I'm planning to open a restaurant in Manhattan. I've been considering fusion for a long time, but not the Jewish-Indian combination. But now I can see it has so many rich possibilities and it excites me. So listen. I have an opening for a head chef at my new venture and I'd like you to come along for an interview so you can show me some of your dishes. Although on the basis of what I've eaten just now, you'll be one of the front runners.'

For a moment, I thought I hadn't heard her correctly. 'Well, what do you say, Vik? Are you ready to become the next great chef in New York? It's a huge commitment, you know.'

I turned back towards the dining room. Neel was leaning against the doorframe. He held up his glass of brandy.

'I, ah…but I haven't even got a working visa,' I blurted out.

Myra swatted that away. 'Oh, I can fix that in no time. Trust me. If you're successful – and don't forget you haven't got the position yet – I'll take care of everything else.'

'You can do that?'

'Vik. Let me deal with that as and when I need to.' Myra continued to scrutinise me. 'Do you want to be considered for the head chef position in my new restaurant or not? There's a shortlist already, I have to warn you. You'll have to be better than all the rest.'

I looked at my uncle and aunt and then at Myra Michl. I took a deep breath.

'Um, yes,' I said. 'Yes, please.'

Myra smiled broadly, Uncle Neel shook my hand and Elizabeth gave me a tight hug.

'What are you calling your new restaurant?' Neel asked Myra Michl.

Myra shrugged. 'I don't know yet. It needs to reflect the type of food. I did have some ideas but now I'm thinking something different. And I really like the idea of Jewish Indian fusion. What a brilliant combination. Thank you Vik. Everyone in New York loves a kosher deli after all. So something which will show that's what it is.'

'The Jewish Deli?' Elizabeth suggested. 'But aren't there dozens of places called that already?'

'OK, so, how about Not the Jewish Deli,' Neel joked. 'Not Just Another Kosher Deli. NJAKD for short. Acronyms are in, right?'

I looked at Neel, and then I thought of something. 'Actually, Uncle, you are nearly there, but I think I have it.' I saw a pen lying on a coffee table and scribbled on a copy of the *New York Times* lying beside it. I held it up. 'What do you think?'

Myra read it out. 'The Kosher Delhi.' She shook her head. 'Vik, I like that, I think it could work. The Kosher Delhi.' She raised her empty coffee cup, and Neel held up his brandy glass.

'The Kosher Delhi!' repeated Elizabeth. 'May all her food be fucking delicious.'

Thirteen

November 1993

I barely saw Yvonne the week before *Boon!* opened, so busy was she with last minute rehearsals. There was an eleventh-hour potential disaster when the owners of the theatre told Wilton Stratford Pine that they hadn't been paid for the entire run, and he and his primary business partner had to scrabble around for twenty-four hours to find the last few dollars they owed.

And just days before opening, two representatives from the US Department of Arts and Culture suddenly appeared at rehearsals to warn the show's director that they had heard there were several explicit scenes in the performance, and if they weren't cut, or at least cut back on, then the show would be shut down. Yvonne said that it was true that there was one scene where the President appears to be receiving a blow job in the Oval Office, but it wasn't actually happening. The problem was that one of *Boon!'s* key selling points was its anti-establishment stance and not giving a flying beep for what New York's reviewers thought. In the end, the other two scenes which the USDAC had complained about were deemed to be on the edge but acceptable, but they had to lighten up the blow job scene. The notion amused me, that anyone would think for a moment that the President of the United States would be idiotic enough to be caught out like that.

I had never seen Yvonne in the least bit tense when she was singing with The Libertine Dolls, I would have said that she thrived on nervous energy. But it seemed that performing in *Boon!* was 'just not the same'. Three days before the opening night, I got a late-night call at our apartment from Yvonne telling me that she was panicking ('shitting bricks' to use her specific vocabulary) and couldn't carry on and what was she to do? As I was trying to get her to calm down, I heard Wilton Stratford Pine's voice in the background telling me not to worry, he was there with Yvonne, and he would look after her. He and the director would ensure she was all right. But it might take a few hours and not to worry. Then he rang off.

Of course, I did worry. It was only because I had no idea where in Manhattan she was calling from that I didn't go straight out and find her.

I finally went to bed at about 2 a.m. but barely slept, and when Yvonne eventually came home at eight o'clock the following morning, I was so wired and whacked out and worried, that I was just relieved that she was back. Yvonne went straight to bed without even getting undressed. I watched her sleeping and decided that I would talk to her about this, her nerves and her night out, the next morning if she raised the subject herself.

She didn't.

Boon! opened on 5 November. I went to the opening night with Wilton Stratford Pine. It was almost like a rock gig, with lighting to match. I don't know how Yvonne and the cast managed to see anything past row one. The best song in the show was definitely Yvonne's solo number, 'Apocalyptic President', which started slow and built up bar after bar, before becoming a pounding, pile-driver of a song which ended with Yvonne collapsing under the spotlight in front of a tank which rolled on stage. The audience was on their feet when she finished that.

The after-show party was the first time since London that I had seen Yvonne immersed in a group of artists, and despite her earlier protestations of how seedy and cheesy the show was, she was clearly loving it. She was once again the central focus and I could hardly get near her because of the attention she received from the other actors, the back-stage crew, random hangers-on and Wilton Stratford Pine.

I finally managed to press my way through a small group of cast members and called out her name loud enough so that she could hear me. She turned and saw me, and held out her arms. We managed to embrace.

'Vik! Vik! What did you think? Did you like it?'

'It was great, Yvonne, really great.'

'Really?'

'Really. And you were wonderful.'

'I was?'

'You know you were. I'm sure everyone is telling you that.'

'Yes, but it means so much more coming from you,' she said into my ear.

She gave me a big kiss and I closed my eyes to soak up the moment. It seemed an age since we had kissed like that. I felt her suddenly pull away and I opened my eyes to see a woman dressed in an outrageously sequined green dress yanking at Yvonne's arm. Yvonne laughed and mouthed 'sorry' at me and swivelled her hand in a 'get me a drink' motion before disappearing into the hubbub again.

When I returned five minutes later with two bottles of Bud, I finally caught sight of her standing among a group of the actors, holding court and laughing with more happiness than I had seen for weeks. Wilton Stratford Pine was beside her. I took a step towards them and then I saw that Wilton had his left hand resting lightly on Yvonne's bottom.

She wasn't asking him to move it.

For the following few weeks, I tore myself apart wondering if I should say something to Yvonne about what I had witnessed at the theatre. Part of me wanted to confront her, to ask her what she was doing, to force it out of her and make her admit if she was having an affair; and, of course, to find out that she didn't want me any more if all that was true. I came so close to doing that but I didn't. Whenever I thought about the possible consequences of such a confrontation, I chickened out.

I didn't want to not be with Yvonne.

And we were both so busy. She with *Boon!*, while I was spending most of my time preparing for my interview at Myra's new restaurant. When the day came, I worked harder than I'd done in my life preparing three courses which I felt did justice to my food. Myra phoned me at our apartment the following morning, just before I was due to meet Neel and Elizabeth for lunch in Greenwich Village.

'Vik, it's Myra Michl.'

'Myra…hello.' I gripped the receiver.

'Thank you for coming in yesterday. You know we had a lot of excellent chefs going for the job.'

My heart sank. 'Yes, I appreciate that.'

There was a few seconds of silence on the line. 'But I'm pleased to tell you that you were the best and you've got the position. If you still want it.'

'If I…of course! Thank you.'

Myra laughed. 'Welcome to The Kosher Delhi, Vik. You are our Head Chef. The hard work starts now!'

I yelped a series of thank yous down the phone, put down the receiver and punched the air.

'Congratulations, Vik!' Neel said to me half an hour later. 'I knew you would get it.'

'I can't believe it, Uncle. My own restaurant.'

'You deserve it,' Elizabeth echoed. 'I can't wait to taste your food.'

It was wonderful to celebrate with Neel and Elizabeth, even though Yvonne was too busy working. She was performing six nights a week in *Boon!*, and therefore sleeping half the daytime. Our waking lives barely coincided with each other. We did still spend time together, especially on the days when Yvonne didn't have a performance, but on such days, she was either too tired to go anywhere, or Wilton had got 'something else planned' for her, such as an interview with a magazine or a TV appearance – or so she said.

I was soon spending twelve or fourteen hours a day at The Kosher Delhi. Having offered me the position, Myra had phoned me the following day to tell me that she intended to open the restaurant in less than ten weeks' time. I told her that there was no way we could do it that quickly; most restaurants would take six months or more, and that was with a team of experts.

'Vik, you worry too much,' Myra snorted down the phone. 'I've bought an existing restaurant, although I would hardly call it that myself from the way it looks. So we don't need to apply for any change of business licence, worry about local planning laws and so on, and it already has a kitchen. OK, we'll probably need to gut it and redecorate and bring it up to a contemporary standard but leave that to me.'

'But Myra –'

She sighed down the phone. 'Vik, you're aware of Richard Branson?'

'The man who owns Virgin? You know him?'

'Yes, I do, but that's not the point. The point is that when Richard started his Virgin Atlantic airline, he was told he couldn't start such a service in under eighteen months, and he did it in three.'

'Is that true?'

'Who cares if it's true! I'm telling you that we will open in the middle of January. All you have to do is design the menu and help me interview some of your key staff when we get to that stage. OK?'

The next ten weeks were a crazy time. Myra discussed kitchen and front of house layouts with me and sourced equipment and furniture, redecorated the premises and launched a marketing campaign. And she helped me acquire a working visa. Myra initially sent the application form to me, which I filled in and sent to the United States Citizenship and Immigration Services. I then attended an interview at their Brooklyn office, where I was told that I might have to leave the country even if I was to get a permit, especially as my tourist visa was about to expire. They quizzed me for a long time as to what I had been doing in America for the three months I'd been here; I said I was here visiting my aunt and uncle, and living with Yvonne who was singing off-Broadway. I wasn't sure they believed me. So when I received a letter soon after, confirming my visa application had been successful, I was astonished and delighted. I'm sure Myra must have had a hand in the process.

Myra also hired an agency to create a website for The Kosher Delhi, which was one of very few such examples of 'online marketing' which you could find in late 1993. I'm not sure if it led many customers to our door in its own right, but it caused a bit of a stir among the traditional press that a small, start-up restaurant could have its own website.

She had been right that the premises needed a bit of an overhaul. The building was a restaurant already, but it hadn't received much love and care over recent years: the tables were old and rickety, some of the chairs were a public health hazard waiting to happen, and the décor was stuck somewhere between the 1970s and the 1980s, with neither decade winning. Dowdy was too generous a word to describe it. The kitchen was in a somewhat better state, and we managed to incorporate parts of it in the new design, but Myra still had to invest in new ovens, boiling rings, sinks and appliances. I refused to have a meat grinder and insisted that the staff slice up all the meat by hand. Myra accepted this after I told her all about Kevin Tyndall. I didn't tell the staff. They often moaned about the manual process but I didn't care. We used it to our benefit by promoting the restaurant as following artisan practices.

As for me, I did what Myra told me to do: concentrated on the food and the key staff. Myra barely questioned my menu during this time although there were a few occasions when, after I had suggested a particularly obscure fusion option, that she returned the next day to politely enquire whether I was quite sure that such a dish would work or was appropriate. I persuaded Myra that the menu should have three parts to it: traditional Indian dishes, Jewish food and fusion. So, we had puri, chana masala, daal, two different chicken curries, sitting alongside knish, kugel and kneidlach; and fusion dishes such as curried lamb brisket, gefilte fish curry, savoury kosher/Indian profiteroles. We refined the menu over the weeks after we opened, as we discovered what was selling better and what was less popular, and as we started to define the gastronomy of The Kosher Delhi.

Our staff recruitment was an equally speedy process although we were extremely vigilant about our selections for the key roles of sous chef and head waiter. Vigilance, however, did not mean playing safe and by the time we were ready for our opening night, The Kosher Delhi was entirely 'rojak', a word I learned from our head waiter's Malaysian boyfriend, meaning 'eclectic mix'. It summed up our staff perfectly: Gina, my sous chef, native of Brooklyn, white lesbian, tattoos all over her body, a stud in her tongue (among other piercings), and a foul mouth when she was angry – she told me she had learned to cook in the East Jersey Penitentiary, which I had assumed was a trendy restaurant until I realised it was what it said on the tin; two straight assistant chefs from Puerto Rico and Detroit complemented her. Jack became my head waiter, a gay, black man, originally from Senegal. Our waiters and waitresses lived in the neighbourhood and hailed from all over, from Queens to the West Coast.

We couldn't have been further removed from the traditional world of Neel and Elizabeth's upper-class patrons if we had tried.

New York in winter is freezing. That December, the temperature rarely got above five degrees centigrade during the day and dipped below zero every night, with the nadir being 27 December when it reached minus fifteen centigrade. It steadily snowed from the middle of December through to January. In another time, Yvonne and I might have found it exciting and romantic but not this year. We were both so fatigued from our respective employments, that although we still had sex when we could, it wasn't with the same passion that we used to have. I couldn't bring myself to believe that she could be sleeping with Wilton Stratford Pine as well.

Boon! came to an end in the middle of December, just as the weather was becoming atrocious, so bad that work almost ground to a halt on The Kosher Delhi makeover when contractors couldn't even travel into the Village. Fortunately, most of the remaining work was indoors. It also meant that I got to spend more time at the apartment with Yvonne.

I went with her to the Last Night Party of *Boon!* after its six-week run, and spent most of the time either clinging to her side when I could, or jealously watching how she interacted with Wilton Stratford Pine. Either I was wrong, and they weren't sleeping together, or they were being more careful in public to prevent anyone from guessing. I knew where my money lay.

I got spectacularly drunk at the party. So much so that I threw up, fell asleep in the corner and Yvonne put me in a taxi to take me home. It was the only reason I didn't challenge her there and then to tell me what was happening between her and Pine. By the following day, I had retreated into my shell and didn't even want to consider it. It was easier to pretend that it couldn't possibly be true.

Wilton Stratford Pine also made a 'thrilling announcement' that evening. *Boon!* had developed into something of a cult hit, and as the production was coming to the end, there was interest from other theatres on the East Coast. Pine and his co-investor decided that they should take the show on the road, with Pine himself as their 'road manager'. They declared that they had lined up 'a series of special nights' in a chain of towns in New England, starting immediately after New Year and including several evenings in Boston. The news was greeted with wild cheers by everyone at the party. Except me.

Unsurprisingly, Yvonne was uncontrollable. To be fair to her, she would have been that way regardless of whether she was sleeping with the producer of the show or not. But the announcement didn't help my demeanour, and vindicated my subsequent drunkenness for the rest of the evening. When I woke up at five the following morning, shivering, with the king of hangovers and a tongue made of sandpaper, I was lying on our apartment floor with just a thin blanket covering me, while Yvonne was fast asleep and tucked up in bed. That had never happened before.

Pine invited us both to his house for Christmas, but Yvonne declined on the grounds that she wanted a break from everyone involved with the show before they reformed again in January. I assumed this was further proof that they were having an affair, as even Yvonne must have seen the foolhardiness in spending Christmas with her partner and her lover at her lover's abode.

Our apartment in the Lower East Side was not only small, but it would never truly warm up, and we often spent the early winter mornings, when both of us were in bed, huddled together under layers of blankets. Having turned down Pine's proposition, our chilly apartment was probably the one reason why Yvonne agreed to spend Christmas Day at Neel and Elizabeth's on Long Island. Even though Yvonne knew it would 'inevitably look like something out of a Hollywood movie with an oversized Christmas tree, mistletoe everywhere, snow on the ground and a fake bloody robin on the porch'. However, she also recognised it would undoubtedly be warm. Plus we both reasoned that there would be so many people there that we could get lost in one of their rooms and just drink mulled wine and ignore everyone else.

We travelled out to their house on Christmas Eve, courtesy of a limousine which Neel sent for us and which Yvonne didn't decline as we knew how long and cold a journey it would be via public transport. We spent the evening there, during which Yvonne managed to fake a severe headache, and then made it through Christmas Day itself thanks to a combination of alcohol and playing hide-and-seek in far-flung rooms of the mansion. Yvonne had agreed that we should bring presents for Neel and Elizabeth out of courtesy ('even though they obviously don't need a single bloody thing'), and so I handmade some handmade chocolates and Yvonne bought them a CD of *Donnerstag aus Licht*, an opera which she said she had been told about by one of the actors in *Boon!*, but which in my opinion reeked of Wilton Stratford Pine's influence.

Neel and Elizabeth bought us 'his and her' sweaters, without any irony. I did enjoy seeing Yvonne have to smile through gritted teeth, and I forced her to wear hers all of Christmas Day. It was in a Thrift Store before New Year.

If Christmas had been tense, our New Year's Eve celebrations were thankfully a wonderful relief. Brad, Yvonne's leading man from *Boon!*, had invited us to his attic apartment in downtown Manhattan, along with a bunch of other actors, artists and even a chef or two (and no Wilton Stratford Pine). We walked there through the snow-laden streets of New York and had a rowdy, drunken and extremely merry New Year.

I think it was probably the last time that Yvonne and I were happy together.

Two days after New Year, I returned to The Kosher Delhi to finalise preparations for the opening night. And a few days after that, Yvonne went away to New England, packed into a tour bus with Wilton Stratford Pine and the cast of *Boon!*. It reminded me of The Libertine Dolls' tour, but the contrast of being driven around England by Terry in a battered old van compared to the luxury coach that Wilton Pine laid on was not missed by either of us.

She would be away for five weeks, the longest we had been apart. Yvonne would also miss the opening night of The Kosher Delhi. I knew she couldn't do anything about it because her tour was so important for her, but that didn't make it hurt any less.

I overslept on the morning of her departure, and had to rush round our apartment getting my stuff together in order to attend a meeting with Myra at the restaurant, while Yvonne sat up in bed with a sheet wrapped around her, hugging her knees, watching me chase my tail around the room. When the moment came to say our farewells, we hugged, kissed, whispered that we would miss each other, Yvonne touched my cheek and then I disappeared out of the door. When I got home late that evening, Yvonne was halfway to Connecticut. I lay in bed and tormented myself, wondering whether she would be sleeping alone tonight as well.

Fourteen

January 1994

On Friday 14 January 1994, US President, Bill Clinton, and Russian President, Boris Yeltsin, signed the Kremlin Accords, which stopped the preprogrammed aiming of nuclear missiles at any nation; Russian athlete, Inna Lasovskaya leapt to a new triple-jump world record of 14.61 metres; and in England, the Duchess of Kent converted to Catholicism, the first member of the Royal Family to do so in more than three hundred years.

In Greenwich Village, New York, The Kosher Delhi opened its doors to the public for the first time.

The restaurant looked terrific: Myra's team had done an incredible job, converting what had been an old, unloved eatery into a smart but somehow still cosy, local restaurant. The walls had been stripped of their 1980s wallpaper and were painted a pure magnolia, other than one feature wall where the brickwork was left exposed, and adorned with black and white photographs of Manhattan buildings and people, taken over the years since the 1950s. Similarly, the beautiful old floorboards had been restored. The tables reminded me more of a London gastropub, and Myra had deliberately bought non-matching chairs to provide a homelier environment. We let the light flood in as much as possible. The steam-cleaned kitchen could not have been fresher if a team of FBI agents had scoured it for a President's visit. The restaurant was completed by a small bar area displaying a rainbow of liquors and exotic drinks, half of which I hadn't even heard of.

Despite the still cold January weather, the restaurant was full and the clientele that first night was as diverse as the staff: Elizabeth had, of course, brought a number of her more liberal friends, and Myra had invited several restaurant critics, but we had deliberately left half the covers open for local residents. My aunt had also, incredibly generously, offered to fly over my mother and father for the opening and put them up in a hotel for a week. I had written to my parents telling them about The Kosher Delhi, and how I had met Uncle Neel, but they didn't refer to him in any of their replies. I couldn't bring myself to talk this through with Neel in case I upset him. As much as I would have loved my parents to have seen what I was doing with my life, I realised that a reunion between estranged brother and sister needed a bit more thought and care.

I wished Yvonne could have been there.

The evening went as well as we could have hoped, with only one minor disaster when one of Neel's Jewish friends discovered a prawn in his dish. Fortunately, he found the detection more amusing than disturbing, and it led him to tell a long, Jewish joke about a rabbi who wanted to taste pork before he died. Which subsequently led to a loud and raucous thirty minutes when every other Jewish man in the restaurant wanted to stand up and tell his favourite Jewish joke. It was a half hour of spontaneous hilarity that no one present that evening would forget.

In the kitchen, Gina and I and our assistants turned out plate after plate, so that we soon ran out of curried lamb brisket and only just met the demand for the gefilte fish curry. I was, of course, using Neel's robot hand and I had reached the point where there were times when I almost forgot that it wasn't my own metacarpus still attached to my right arm. The first time that Gina had seen my hand in action, she had, in her inimitable style, taken one look at my personal appliance, watched me slice a leek and a half head of garlic with it, declared it to be the 'scariest mother-fucker of a hand' she had ever seen and, apart from telling me that she would like to use it on her girlfriend sometime, never mentioned it again.

My hand was also a key part of Myra's PR machine. Although she could have got a fair degree of press coverage just with the contacts she had, she knew that something as unique as my robotic hand would ensure that it gained extra space on the pages of New York's magazines and newspapers. The food would keep the restaurant in the spotlight if the food we served was any good, but my hand would give us an angle. She arranged for photographers from several dailies and glossy mags to come round to the restaurant the day before it opened to snap my hand and me. I lost count of the number of poses I was asked to hold: simply cutting a carrot; gripping a single strand of spaghetti as it dangled over a pot; holding a knife across my chest, crossed arms, James Bond 007 style; and more.

Several of the journalists tried to pump me for information on how I lost my hand.

'Come on, Vik, tell us what happened.'

'I can't, I've already told you that.'

'Was it an accident?'

'Yes, I've said. It happened when I was living in London. That's all I can say.'

'In a restaurant?'

'I can't tell you.'

'It all sounds highly suspicious. Was someone else involved?'

At which point, Myra cut in and told them we were only going to answer further questions about The Kosher Delhi. As much as I wanted to name and shame Chef Kevin, Neel had been at pains to remind me that I was now living in the land of litigation, even if the accused wasn't living here himself, plus Kevin Tyndall had never been charged with a crime. I knew I had better watch my step.

By the end of service, we had started to come together as a team – the kitchen staff and the crew in the front of house. There were lots of things we needed to fine tune, but we hadn't let anyone down (apart from Neel's Jewish friend maybe…), and no one had complained. In fact, we had constantly received feedback via the waiters as to how much the customers were complimenting the food. But it had been tough going, and we were all exhausted.

After the last guest had left, Myra cracked open two bottles of Moët for the staff, and we toasted the success of The Kosher Delhi. Gina, Jack, the waiters and cooks cheered and discussed where they should carry on the party. I loved what was happening, I loved it all. I couldn't quite believe that I really was the head chef at a hot new restaurant in New York, that my apprenticeships at the Dog and Dragon, Restaurant Le Jardin and even The Three Rs had led me here to Greenwich Village, to be able to cook the food I adored for people who also seemed to appreciate it. What more could I ask?

I couldn't wait for Yvonne to come back so that I could share it all with her.

Following our opening night, the next few weeks were frantic. The first reviews of The Kosher Delhi were all positive, and we began to take bookings for days and then weeks ahead. We decided we would always keep a selection of tables available for walk-ins which had the upside of creating a queue outside the entrance and down the sidewalk. We started putting up signs outside the restaurant saying '30 minutes from here to eat', '60 minutes from here to eat' and so on. On some evenings, Gina and some of the crew would cook Babka (cinnamon and chopped nuts or chocolate, swirled into a challah cake) or a selection of Chaat (Indian vegetarian street food), or just whip up a batch of hot chocolate, and feed those waiting in line for free.

Being in New York, and being in the heart of the Village, meant that our clientele was an esoteric mixture, which I loved. We had young, old, white, black, Latino, Indian, Jewish, jew-ish, straight, gay, the well-off and the downright weird, as well as conformist, middle-class New Yorkers. There was a definite trend towards young, non-conformist customers and, in particular, a constant stream of happy, gay patrons who felt comfortable no matter who else was in the restaurant.

I celebrated my twenty-fourth birthday with a small party in the KD, but because Yvonne was still on tour, it felt flat to me no matter how much I tried to smile. The glimpse I'd had of her standing so close to Wilton Stratford Pine at that last night party continued to haunt me.

Fifteen

February 1994

As February marched on and the weather improved very, very slowly, I started to count the days before Yvonne would return to Manhattan. We had managed to exchange a few words with occasional phone calls during the time she had been on tour, but such conversations had not been easy to arrange. I was working all hours, and although Yvonne only performed in the evenings, she was travelling for much of the daytime, and when she did call me, often at the restaurant, I barely had time to say hello. We managed two extended conversations but both of us found it an effort.

I followed her tour as much as I could by reading reviews of the shows. This only happened when I could find a regional New England newspaper on a Manhattan newsstand, but often that just reminded me how much I was missing her. Consequently, I would throw myself back into my work in the KD kitchen and cook with even more determination, and wind up back at our apartment in the wee hours of the morning, exhilarated but exhausted.

Two days before she was due to return, Yvonne phoned, and I suggested I met her off the bus when they got in to New York, but she said that it was difficult to predict exactly what hour they would arrive so it would be easier if she got a cab back to our apartment and I could meet her there. I reluctantly agreed and arranged to have the day off work unless any emergencies cropped up. It was the first time that I would not be at a shift in the restaurant, and I think Gina was happy that I was giving her the responsibility to run the pass.

On the day of Yvonne's return, I knew the earliest that she could arrive would be after noon and so I spent the entire morning biting my fingernails, looking in the mirror, plumping up pillows and wiping down surfaces in the apartment. By two o'clock I was pacing round the lounge like a caged animal and I'm surprised that the people who lived below didn't knock to tell me to sit the hell down.

Just before three, I heard a key turn in the lock, and I pulled the door open so fast that Yvonne stumbled into me.

'Sorry! Sorry,' I stammered. She looked up at me and smiled and let me pull her into my embrace. She was wearing a blue duffle coat, leggings and knee-high boots and she looked fantastic. I kissed her hard.

'All right, Vik, for God's sake, you dinna have to squash me that much. I'm no going to collapse.'

'Sorry,' I said again, letting her go and grabbing her bag from where she had left it outside the door. 'Come in! Are you all right? How was the tour? How did it all go?'

'Vik. Give me a minute to get my feet in the door.' She walked slowly into the room. 'A cup of something would be great.'

'Tea?'

I edged nervously across to our small kitchen area and put the kettle on the hob to boil. I turned around to face my girlfriend. She was sitting on the sofa now, duffle coat removed, gazing at me intently.

'I've, ah, I've changed the sheets,' I started cautiously, 'for when we, when you're, you know...'

Yvonne ran a hand through her hair. 'I don't know Vik, I think I'll just crash tonight, I'm so tired.' She patted the seat beside her on the sofa. 'Why don't you just come and sit here for a while.'

I nodded and sat down beside her. Yvonne took my hand in hers and stroked it. 'How is your arm?' she asked with a sad smile. 'While I was away I thought about it, about you, such a lot.'

I let out a deep sigh. 'I did too! I mean, thought about you.'

'I should hope so!'

'I've missed you so much.'

Yvonne flicked her eyes down. 'And yes, to answer your earlier question, the tour was amazing, thank you for asking, and yes, it went better than any of us could have hoped. Wilton…Wilton says that some of us are bound to get offers for other shows now.'

'Did he,' I said coldly.

'Yes.'

'How is Wilton?'

'Good…' Yvonne looked down at her knees.

'Yvonne–'

The kettle whistled and I jumped up and made her tea. I put it on the table and sat down beside her again. Yvonne was still staring at her feet, rubbing her thumb hard into her other palm. We exchanged a few words about the apartment and the weather, before lapsing into silence.

'Yvonne.'

She looked up at me.

'Yvonne, we need to talk about something.'

'Look, Vik–'

I turned my body to face her. 'I have thought about you all the time you've been away. But I can't stop myself also wondering about…Wilton.'

'Wilton? Why?'

'Because I knew you would be spending so much time together.'

Yvonne tilted her head. 'So?'

'And that worried me.'

'Why? He was our tour manager. Of course we would be seeing a lot of each other. So what?'

'Yes, I know, but…'

'Vik?'

'I saw you at the *Boon!* last night party.' I rushed my words. 'I saw you standing together. I saw him…touching you.'

'Vik–'

'Tell me, Yvonne. Did anything happen when you were on tour?'

She blanched. 'Like what?'

'You know what. Just tell me. I need to know.'

Yvonne pushed her tea away and stared out of our window. Closing her eyes, she shook her head, and for a moment I thought I was wrong. Then she opened them again and looked at me.

'I never thought it would happen. I didn't mean it to happen, but…it did.'

'Uh-huh.'

'And, well…oh, look, Vik. You must have noticed that things haven't been, I mean, weren't going so well between us before I left for New England.'

'Oh.' My body tensed up. Now I knew where this was going.

'I mean, it wasn't your fault. It wasn't my fault, either, really. We just, I don't know, we didn't seem to be connecting, did we?'

'*I* didn't feel like that,' I snapped. 'I thought we were both just tired all the time. Working too hard.'

'Well, yes, we were.' Yvonne stood up. 'But even when we were working in London, even when I was gigging all the time with the Dolls, and you were working in the restaurants, we still found time for each other then, didn't we. We still had that spark.'

'I know.'

'But when Wilton started to…show an interest in me, well, I was flattered.'

'Flattered?'

'Yes.'

'By Wilton?'

'Yes!' Yvonne stamped her foot. 'Yes, by Wilton. Is that so hard to believe?'

Now it was my turn to look away. 'No,' I said, clenching my fists, 'I always thought you would find him attractive. I was always worried about that.'

And then it all came tumbling out of Yvonne's mouth. They hadn't meant to get together (yeah, right), or to start an affair (her first actual admission), it had just happened; it was understandable, natural, so normal, considering they were all living hand-in-hand twenty-four hours a day. What else did people do when they were in each other's pockets on tour? And after it had happened the first time…

'"It"?' I asked perniciously.

'You know,' Yvonne said.

'No,' I replied coldly.

Yvonne stared directly at me. 'When Wilton and I had sex the first time.'

I clenched my teeth and looked away.

… Yvonne decided that she wouldn't ever do it again, but then, she said, she found she wanted to do it again, and so she did. And so, yes, she and Wilton Stratford Pine had begun what was at first a fleeting affair, but had already, apparently, developed into something much deeper and much more meaningful, and so she was intending to stay with him.

'So you're leaving me for that manipulative tosser?'

'He's nae that, Vik.'

'He's a conniving thief.'

'He cares about me.'

'And I don't?'

I think at that point I started shouting and Yvonne shouted back, and then I picked up a mug and smashed it on the floor and Yvonne screamed. I kicked the coffee table and the tea went flying. Yvonne started to cry and to say that she hadn't wanted to hurt me and I used a lot of swear words (and the downstairs neighbours banged on their ceiling), and finally I grabbed some cash and my keys, tugged one arm into my coat, and with Yvonne still calling out to me to come back and talk, I slammed the front door behind me and ran down the stairs of our block and on to the Manhattan streets.

I have no idea to this day exactly where I walked – I know I went to several bars, and I ended up in a club on the outskirts of the Meatpacking District which was a terrible idea as the area was a hotbed for drug dealing, prostitution and underground sex clubs. But there is a god of drunks who sometimes looks over us, and even though I was weaving along streets where I could easily have been mugged or knifed, I simply received perplexed looks from passers-by and just got very, very cold, and ended up following another drunk couple into the lobby of their apartment block somewhere on Washington Street. There, I lay down, shivering under the stairs until a cleaner found me in the early hours and kicked me out.

I walked home in daylight, sobering up in the freezing cold morning air, took a deep breath and stepped back into our apartment. Yvonne wasn't there, unsurprisingly, but her bag was still on the floor, unopened, where I had dropped it. I found my old rucksack, stuffed a few clothes into it and then wrote a message on a scrap of paper I tore off from a copy of the *Boon!* manuscript. I explained I was moving out and that she shouldn't worry about me, and if she needed to return anything to me, then she could either contact Neel or have it sent to The Kosher Delhi. And then I walked out. Again.

I didn't know where to go. I toyed with the idea of crashing at the KD, but I didn't want my staff knowing my business. I could have checked in to a decent hotel but I didn't want 'nice', and I coveted a place where I could remain anonymous.

The Sunshine Hotel was a last resort for many men in New York; it accommodated one hundred and twenty-five men (only men) in cubicles measuring four feet by six with no windows and chicken wire ceilings. Most of the other residents were drug addicts, alcoholics or had just fallen on hard times. You were welcomed by the manager who sat in a metal cage at the front desk, answering the phone and doling out toilet paper for a few cents.

One more lost and bewildered man with one hand fitted in fine. I crashed out for the day and welcomed the oblivion.

I worked that evening at The Kosher Delhi, and although I think Gina knew something was up when I responded monosyllabically to her enquiries about Yvonne, she didn't ask any further questions. When my staff asked me how I was, I said I was getting over a cold.

During my second night at the Sunshine Hotel, I was awake for most of the night, torturing myself with imaginings about Yvonne and Wilton Stratford Pine. I felt as if I'd hit rock bottom. Why was I here? If Yvonne was going to stay in our apartment, how would I manage Myra's restaurant if I was living in a flophouse? I considered asking Uncle Neel for help but I couldn't face the humiliation. And what would Myra think if she knew where I was staying? There were plenty of other chefs in New York who would be more than happy to take my place in the restaurant. It was that thought that forced me to make the call.

My aunt turned up at The Kosher Delhi and insisted on taking me out for a coffee down the street. It took her ten minutes to get the full story out of me. (I've rarely seen anyone look so horrified).

'Elizabeth, you and Neel are the only other people I know here. Is there any way I could stay in Long Island with you, just until I get myself another place?'

Elizabeth looked doubtful. 'I hardly think that's going to work, commuting from there to Manhattan every day.'

I hadn't thought of that.

'We do have our apartment in Manhattan,' she continued. 'No one's there at the moment.'

'That would be amazing.'

'But we have friends coming to stay next month. We had promised them they could use it.'

'I only need it until I find somewhere else.'

She paused. 'I'm not sure, Vik. You might need it for longer than a few weeks, and I've already committed to lending it.'

'Elizabeth, please. I'll be no trouble. I'll move out when your friends come. I'll chef your private parties, whatever you want.'

'It's only a one bedroom apartment, not very glamorous,' Elizabeth said in a matter of fact way. 'Just east of the Village, off Lafayette Street.'

'That's more than enough for me. And I'd be so grateful if you would let me use it just for now. I can pay you of course.'

Elizabeth sat back in her chair. 'Don't be silly, Vik, you're our nephew.' She smiled. 'It would be my pleasure to help you.'

My aunt slipped a key off her keyring and handed it over to me. I moved in the same day. It might not have been very glamorous to her, but compared to the Sunshine Hotel, it was like moving into a plush flat in Mayfair.

Neel and Elizabeth ended up inviting their friends to stay with them in Long Island, and I stayed in their apartment for the rest of the time I lived in New York.

The first few days after Yvonne confirmed her affair with Wilton were painful and distressing. I was shocked, angry, distraught, but mostly I just felt like shit. I couldn't quite believe that only six months ago, I had felt so happy and carefree, and I could never have imagined doing anything in my life that didn't somehow involve Yvonne. I thought that she had felt that way too. Maybe she had for a while. Clearly, something dramatic had changed in her psyche if that was the case. Maybe my involvement with my American aunt and uncle had changed her feelings towards me, I'm sure her association with Wilton Stratford Pine and *Boon!* had changed her. Hell, New York had changed her.

I carried on going to the KD every day, enjoying cooking, even appreciating the banter of the kitchen, but at the same time I knew deep inside I was faking it. What did it matter if I cooked or not? Why should I care if the food was any good or if the customers liked it? I didn't go out after work with the other staff, I didn't do anything on my days off except lie on the sofa and watch daytime TV, and only when my stomach forced me to did I venture downstairs to find a deli, a real deli, or a grocery store to buy some cans and a bottle of wine.

Two weeks after we split up, Yvonne left me a message at the restaurant saying that there were a few of my things at our old apartment and I could pick them up if I wanted to. She was still living there. I screwed up her note and chucked it straight in the bin.

Sixteen

April – July 1994

While I was still coming to terms with Yvonne and Wilton Stratford Pine, Gina and Jack held the restaurant together: when I was staring out of a window, or dropping things from my robot hand; or dicing up a carrot into such minuscule pieces that one of them had to gently touch my arm to get me to stop.

In April, we had our best month to date: we did more covers, had longer queues outside, and we received more write-ups and recommendations in the mainstream newspapers, as well as obscure, speciality magazines. We even began to attract a few C list celebrities, although I stayed cooking at my station while the other chefs peeped through the kitchen door to ogle whoever had come in.

I did one interview with a magazine called *New York Encounters,* noteworthy because it was one of the few articles written about the KD that concentrated more on our staff and clientele than our food. The journalist seemed to be very interested in my colleagues, and quizzed me intensely. I was happy to talk about the diverse backgrounds of Gina, Jack, and our various waiting and kitchen staff.

'Was that something you had expressly aimed to achieve?' she asked.

'No, it just happened that way,' I replied. 'It doesn't matter a hoot to me if someone's gay, straight, white, Latino, Jewish, whatever. If they're the best person for the job, or even if they just show suitable promise and enough enthusiasm, then their sexual slant or ethnic background isn't an issue.'

As Gina passed our corner table she raised an eyebrow.

'But you do have a lot of gay employees, don't you,' the journalist persisted.

'It's not something I've given any thought to,' I retorted.

'And what about the clientele? You have more than your fair share of gay customers.'

'Again, that is not something I set out to do,' I said. 'I'm happy that we have any customers, and if the gay community enjoy coming to our restaurant, then I'm delighted to invite them in. As I am with straight customers,' I added. 'We've never even had as much as a raised voice from a diner.' (I didn't mention the old Jewish men telling jokes on our opening night; I wasn't in the mood to explain the inadvertent prawn.)

At that point, the journalist abruptly switched her attention to the history of my hand, and I was back on more solid ground, telling her all about Uncle Neel's invention. I was tempted to talk about what had really happened in The Three Rs, but I knew that I wanted the story, if it ever broke, to be on my terms. There was something about this journalist that I didn't like or trust.

When the article was published, it caused a bit of a stir for a day or two because the journalist had ignored all my explanations about how we had recruited our staff, and instead made us out to be deliberately anti-establishment, discouraging nice middle-class New Yorkers from dining there. Along with my own racial background and my robotic hand, the piece portrayed us more as a bunch of kooks than cooks. A few of our regular customers told us that one or two of the AM radio stations in New York had picked up on the story, and there had been a couple of phone-ins where some of the callers had been quick to pronounce us 'fag lovers' and 'serving food for kikes and dykes'. Fortunately, Gina and Jack seemed to find the *New York Encounters'* article amusing rather than insulting, and I think they were proud to be associated with a restaurant which wasn't mainstream. But their laissez-faire attitude didn't stop them from tearing out a photo of the journalist and pinning it to the kitchen wall, where it became a target for fish innards and rotten vegetables for a few days.

Although I hadn't heard anything more from Yvonne, I had heard a lot more about her. This was because she was causing quite a stir in the alternative music scene in New York. Wilton Stratford Pine had released one of her songs from *Boon!* – 'Apocalyptic President' - as a single, with Yvonne billed as 'England's own Libertine Dolls star', and the track was working its way up the Billboard charts. He had also delivered the obligatory MTV video, which was a combination of Yvonne singing 'live' on stage to an adoring audience with bright lights and firecrackers, Yvonne singing in some sort of dystopian wasteland, and an animated version of Yvonne singing to a character with a remarkable resemblance to the then President of the United States, Bill Clinton.

Consequently, I was able to follow Yvonne's movements from afar, if I wanted to. I didn't want to, but of course, I did. It wasn't quite as simple as turning off all my emotions and ignoring the last three years of my life. In some ways, seeing her on a video, or hearing her speak during a radio interview, was worse than being with her, because Media Yvonne always looked stunning, always said the right thing, always had a twinkle in her eye which suggested that you – yes, you – could be the next man she wanted to take to her bedroom. That I had been that man made it feel worse.

During May and into June, not only did Yvonne's song climb up the Billboard charts, not only did I see her on MTV, and not only did she therefore force her way into my mind (night and day), but everyone who knew we had been together persisted in telling me how amazing she/her song/her video was. She even appeared on the front cover of *New York Encounters*. I'm sure they knew that Yvonne and I had been in a relationship. I refused to read the interview but my staff did, and although none of them said anything to me, there were a few glances in my direction which made me think that Yvonne hadn't been exactly complimentary. I consoled myself with the knowledge that as the magazine had twisted my words, then it was equally possible that they had done the same in Yvonne's article. Plus, she had Wilton Stratford Pine to add venom wherever they needed it.

The Kosher Delhi continued to get busier in June. We introduced new dishes, added tables outside the restaurant and took on new staff to cope with the additional trade. We were nominated in an East Coast food award. Temperatures in New York City escalated at the same pace, and by the start of July, we saw the thermometer reach the mid-eighties every day. The diners were cool enough at their tables, but in the KD kitchen, we sweated our way through services, drinking gallons of water, and not without the odd affray as tempers reached breaking points. I re-introduced my Salmorejo with added spices as a cold starter, and it instantly became our best seller.

Conversely, as June progressed into July, Yvonne's public appearances suddenly dwindled. Her single dropped out of the charts, her video was rarely broadcast on MTV any more, and I heard that at one gig where she was booked to sing, she didn't turn up, and the crowd booed and shouted aggressive chants against her. On the one hand, it wasn't surprising – in music and fashion, what's in one minute can be out in the blink of an eye, but all the same, it was a precipitous fall from fame. The newspapers published photos of her coming out of a club late at night, looking haggard with bloodshot eyes, her short dress ripped, apparently taking a swing at a photographer and only just avoiding arrest. It was so far removed from the Yvonne that I had known, who even in her most intoxicated moments had always been fundamentally in control of herself. Part of me couldn't help but feel a degree of smugness, but there was another, deeper constituent of my psyche that felt depressed and disturbed.

The end of June also heralded New York's annual Gay Pride March, and 1994's parade was especially poignant as it marked the twenty-fifth anniversary of the Stonewall Inn riots. Activists carried a mile-long rainbow banner to Central Park and hundreds of thousands lined the streets. But at the same time, the event was a catalyst for the homophobes and bigots to spout their vitriol. This could be witnessed every day on the streets at any time, but it also emanated from public figures; Senator Jesse Helms, the Senate Foreign Relations Committee chairman, well known for his public opposition to the 'homosexual lifestyle' was interviewed by *Newsweek* and referred to 'such people' as 'degenerates' and 'weak, morally sick wretches'. He had support from many quarters. In some people's minds, Pride justified the antagonism the gay community received.

Thursday 14 July started out as any ordinary day. Gina and I arrived early to do our prep, we opened the restaurant at lunchtime and carried on serving through the day. We each took breaks in the afternoon, but by five o'clock, we were both in the restaurant again, back in the kitchen, cracking out dish after dish. Sometime after six, I recognised a group of our regular customers, seven or eight of them taking a table in the corner, adding a splash of colour. I went out to greet them, a quirky and flamboyant New York combination of gay men and women, one transgender man, and a couple who may have been straight. They immediately ordered several bottles of wine.

Jack staggered into the kitchen soon after that to tell us that the line outside the restaurant was as long as he had ever seen it, and if we could make some cold drinks to refresh those in the line, then that would be awesome. I considered whether I should do that myself to take a quick break from the pressure of cooking all the meals, but one look from Gina cancelled out that idea. I assigned Ravi, one of our Indian commis chefs, to do the job, and told him to help one of the waiters when it was ready and hand out as many drinks as they could.

I can recount what happened in the remainder of that evening partly because of what I saw, but also from other witnesses who came forwards later.

When I heard the first scream, preceded by the blaring of car horns, I knew it came from outside the restaurant and I barely gave it a second thought; this was New York and it was a hot summer evening, and screams (and car horns) were not uncommon, whether they came from an annoyed girlfriend or a sadly disturbed homeless man. But when those screams didn't desist, I realised that something out of the ordinary was occurring. I was just wondering whether we should investigate when I heard the first gunshot. I instantly dropped the tomato I was holding (I can remember how vividly it splatted across the floor) and sprang towards the door leading into the restaurant. I could hear Gina shouting behind me, but I couldn't make out what she was saying. I pushed open the swing door, and as I took my first step into the dining area, all hell broke loose.

Outside, I could hear screams of pure terror as people ran away from the restaurant. It was mayhem on the sidewalk with people pushing past each other to get away, accidentally knocking over others who were, in turn, being trodden on as they struggled to stand up. At the same time, people were rushing *into* The Kosher Delhi, sending empty chairs flying, jumping over and under tables, regardless of whether anyone was sitting there. I saw one of my waitresses who was carrying a tray of drinks get slammed in the back and spin, sprawling on to her knees, the tray crashing to the floor, shattering glass and liquid all around her. Customers already in the restaurant were either watching in horror or standing up to try to see what was happening. This was when I first heard the shouts of 'Gun, gun! He's got a gun! Get away!' I watched as more customers dived under tables. From the kitchen I heard Gina calling out, and I saw her beckoning people to come to her. The back door led out of the cooks' room into an alley, and I realised that was the best escape route from whoever was outside.

That's when I snapped out of my shock and started tugging at people's arms and shirts, repeating Gina's instructions to get the hell out the back. Some didn't move, seemingly frozen, but others heard me and charged towards the kitchen. Out of the corner of my eye, I saw a man lurch out of the restroom, his belt flapping around his waist, staring wide-eyed at the commotion in front of him.

Moments later, I heard the second gunshot. It sounded as if it was just outside our front door. It was followed by more shrieks and more people inside the KD pushing and shoving each other, but because no one really knew what was happening, no one knew where to run. I called out again, trying to get more people to head towards the kitchen. I glanced behind me for a moment to see if Gina was still herding customers out, and then I looked back, towards the restaurant entrance, and at that moment, I got my first look at the gunman.

He stood in the doorway of The Kosher Delhi. He was in many ways an average-looking man: no taller than myself, short cropped hair, wearing blue jeans and a short-sleeved red T-shirt with 'enjoy cocaine' printed on it in the classic Coca-Cola style. At first sight, he looked Caucasian, but when I was to see his body later, I could tell that there was some darker pigment to his skin too. I could tell that he had tattoos on his arm, but I wasn't close enough yet to see that they were eagles and swastikas.

He was chewing on a matchstick and wielding a pistol.

For a moment, he stood stock still and slowly turned his head from left to right as if scanning the pandemonium in front of him. Then his eyes rested on me, and his lips curled up very slowly into a smile. Then, unbelievably, he nodded at me as someone would when acknowledging an acquaintance. He raised his gun again but rather than point it at me, he looked back into the centre of the room and fired two shots in the direction of the corner table where the group I had greeted earlier were sitting. Everyone seemed to be screaming, and I couldn't tell if he had hit anyone.

Then he began to shout and curse, some phrases repeated over and over again: 'motherfuckin' faggots', 'goddamn motherfuckin' queers', 'fucking half-caste fucking bunch of brownies', interspersed with derivatives and variations.

I didn't know what I should do. My body and most of my mind were telling me to turn tail and run and get out the back with everyone else heading that way. But the Head Chef in me told me to stay. Maybe this was how teachers felt towards their pupils when gunmen lurched into their classrooms. My customers were my responsibility, and I had to help them. Incredibly, I found myself thinking, what would Yvonne do? For once, I didn't have an answer.

Just as I was wondering if I should rush him, the gunman suddenly let out a wolf howl and jumped from a standing position straight on to one of the tables, sending plates and glasses crashing to the floor, pointed his gun at the ceiling and shot off another two or three rounds, screaming as he did so. Everyone who was still in the dining area covered their heads with their hands and shrieked in unison.

To this day, I don't know why he didn't continue to shoot. Instead, he remained on the table, and for what must have been nearly two minutes, he turned slowly round and round on the spot, occasionally holding out his arms to balance himself, grinning, looking down at everyone who was still cowering on the floor.

'Fucking faggots and niggers,' he spat, waving his gun in their direction. At one point, he peered at our list of specials on the wall, and he frowned and read it for several seconds before spitting on the floor and resuming his circling movement again. By now, anyone who was left in the restaurant didn't dare move, and there was no sound apart from quiet sobbing. Outside, it also seemed more subdued. I guessed that anyone with any sense had fled or run indoors into whatever shop or building they could access. I was still a few feet from the kitchen door, half crouched in the same position I had been when he shot his last round. But very, very slowly I was starting to stand up straight. I wondered if there was any way I could grab his gun…

Behind me, I heard a pot being knocked in the kitchen, and the gunman turned, and, still on the table, looked straight at me. He raised his pistol again. Then he raised his left arm, and I thought he was going to give a Nazi salute, but instead he waggled his fingers at me, and I realised, incredulously, that he was waving. I knew what I should do: drop to the floor, run, leap sideways, stoop, anything except remain as I was, a sitting duck. But I didn't move; I couldn't.

And then he pulled his trigger.

I don't know how he missed me. He can't have been more than thirty feet away. One of the other customers lying on the floor later said that he saw the table the gunman was standing on rock slightly just as he fired, so maybe that small movement affected his aim and saved my life. Thank God for restaurant tables with unlevel legs.

Then I heard another gunshot and this time I did duck instinctively, although if it had been the gunman firing again, I don't think that would have saved me. In the following seconds, as I realised that I hadn't been hit and that he wasn't shouting any more, I slowly raised my head and saw that our assailant was now lying on his back on the table, his arms flung out on either side. I watched as he slowly slid off the top, his head hit the floor, and his legs crumpled. Blood began to seep out from under his body. An NYPD police officer was advancing slowly, silently into the room, his own gun still raised at arm's length as he approached the body. The policeman looked down at our attacker, let out a deep breath and lowered his weapon.

'OK, folks. He's incapacitated. You're all going to be all right.'

They were the best words I ever heard a policeman say.

The whole episode with the gunman – a loner by the name of Aaron J Stoats – must have lasted no more than four or five minutes, but the aftermath stretched out for weeks. Ironically, the immediate few minutes after Officer Martin had shot Stoats are the blurriest in my mind. I remember a moment's silence, and then I heard crying and saw Officer Martin speak into his shoulder radio, and go around the room checking if anyone was hurt, while I just crumpled to my knees. Someone put their arm around me, and I rested my head on their shoulder.

'It's OK to cry,' they said.

But I knew I wasn't crying, and it was only then that I realised I was sweating so much that perspiration was running down my face.

Stoats was shot at 7.01 in the evening and by 7.08, there were more police officers inside The Kosher Delhi than I had seen in an entire series of *Hill Street Blues*. Outside, the whole street was a mass of flashing blue and red lights; I don't think they could have jammed in another police car or ambulance if they had tried. I sat in a chair near the bar and watched as the police and paramedics began to lead customers out of the restaurant. Whenever I saw one of my staff being led away, I tried to say a few words to each of them. Some just stared at me with blank looks or patted my back as tears streamed down their cheeks.

I must have been sitting in the chair for another fifteen minutes before I became fully aware of the blankets laid out on the far side of the restaurant. Until then, there were so many people in the room that I could barely see past the legs that rushed by me. Eventually, enough people left so that I could see Stoats' body surrounded by a mass of medical staff, and I presumed that he must not be dead, that they were trying to save his life. It was only when I saw two further blankets laid out on the floor with the shape of bodies underneath them, their faces fully covered, that I knew that Stoats had killed two people.

No one was paying any attention to me yet, so I pushed myself up and weaved my way over to where the bodies lay. I looked down at them. They were lying in the corner of the restaurant where my group of regular customers had been eating. I didn't know any of them well but the guilt and pain I felt at that moment that they had been killed in my restaurant, under my watch – my patronage – made me feel sick to the stomach, and I squeezed my eyes tight and reached out to a chair to balance myself.

I felt someone touch my elbow and opened my eyes to see a police officer asking me to move away from this area. I nodded and backed away. An hour or so later, I was asked to go with a Detective Harris to the police station to make my statement. I got back to the apartment in the early hours. I was grateful to find Elizabeth and Neel there, and we hugged each other until our arms hurt.

Detective Harris visited my apartment the following afternoon, by which time my uncle and aunt had returned to Long Island. He sat opposite me on one of the sofas, and told me everything he knew about the shooting.

'I want to know what's happened to Ravi,' I said, referring to my commis chef. 'I don't remember seeing him in the restaurant after Stoats was overpowered.'

Harris nodded with a professionally blank expression, and I knew what he had to tell me wasn't going to be good.

'Ravi Laghari, and one of your waitresses, Elena Vialli were outside the restaurant, when Elena noticed Aaron J Stoats walking down the street towards the restaurant.'

I felt terrible. 'I sent them there. I asked them to hand out fruit cocktails and sweet lassis to the people waiting in the line,' I murmured.

Harris explained further: 'Your waitress says she noticed him because he was walking in the middle of the road and several cars behind him were blaring their horns, but he was ignoring them, just walking purposefully towards The Kosher Delhi.'

'So, they were the horns I heard.'

Harris continued. 'When Stoats reached where they were standing, serving the drinks, Ms Vialli said he took one look at them and reached behind his back for a gun. A Heckler & Koch MK23 semi-automatic, large frame pistol,' the detective added coldly, reading from his notebook. Elena had screamed, and as Stoats waved his gun around, the people waiting in line outside the KD scattered in every direction. Ravi dropped the tray of drinks, turned and started to run. At the same time, Stoats pulled his trigger and shot Ravi in his thigh.

'Your waitress reported that Ravi dropped like a stone on to the sidewalk. She remembers the sound of the tray dropping and the glasses smashing. We think Stoats must have thought he had killed your chef, because apparently he just stepped over him and moved towards the front door of the restaurant.'

'So Ravi's...dead?'

'Actually Ravi was the reason we were called so promptly,' the detective said. 'With the help of Elena and a couple who had been in the queue, he managed to clamber to his feet and they pulled him into a nearby shop. It was Ravi who ordered the shopkeeper to call 911 – if he hadn't done so, it might have been several more minutes before anyone else had phoned the emergency services and God only knows what Stoats might have done by then.'

'So Ravi's OK?' I blurted out.

Detective Harris smiled. 'Yes. Paramedics from the first ambulance to arrive took care of him. But I understand there might be some long-term implications for Ravi's leg; you can ask him yourself.'

'OK,' I said, staring at my knees. I still felt like shit. Here I was, unscathed, while one of my waiters had quite literally taken a bullet for me. Ravi wasn't the one who'd done the interview with *New York Encounters*, the piece that had, more than likely, brought the restaurant to Stoats' attention. In all probability, I owed Ravi my life.

I got Harris to give me the details of the hospital where Ravi was, and before the detective resumed his account, I phoned Myra to update her about our waiter. She immediately said she would visit him and ensure he had all he needed.

Detective Harris finished his report: Officer Martin had only been a few blocks away when he received the alert, so had been able to get to the restaurant before the rest of the force. He heard the commotion, managed to creep up to the restaurant and make it to the front door in the nick of time to see Stoats point his gun at me, and that was when the NYPD policeman had shot him.

'The officer hit Stoats in the shoulder, and despite the loss of blood, we now think it is likely that Stoats will survive. So we can charge the perp and bring him to justice anyway.' Harris almost spat the words. I got the feeling he would have been perfectly happy if his officer had killed Stoats.

Detective Harris moved on to tell me that the NYPD had raided Stoats' apartment this morning and they had discovered hordes of leaflets and posters and magazine articles, all containing violently homophobic and extreme racist material. Their database confirmed that he had a history of petty theft and illegal possession of arms. He was also mentally ill, and it hadn't taken much for him to transition from passive racist to actively wanting to kill. According to Detective Harris, the Gay Pride March, Senator Jesse Helms' remarks about gay people, and the radio phone-ins which had portrayed The Kosher Delhi as a den of vice, had combined to push him over the edge.

'I can also confirm,' Harris said, fingering his shirt collar and flexing his neck muscles, 'that we talked to the friends of the two deceased men and they are both recognised as part of the gay community. It seems that Stoats specifically targeted them because they were gay.'

I sighed and waited for the detective to continue, but it seemed he was expecting me to respond. But I didn't know what to say.

I indicated for him to resume.

Detective Harris cleared his throat. 'There is one more thing, Mr Cohen. As you might imagine, the press has been clamouring for information from us. We can tell them all the facts, but I know they would like you to make a statement too. Tell them your side of the story.' He lowered his voice. 'It's your chance to say what you think about Aaron Stoats.'

I nodded. 'Of course, I'd be happy to.'

I thought of the times that Yvonne had urged me to be angrier, to fight back, to care more about injustice. But she wasn't in my life any more to give me her opinion. This time it was up to me.

Which is why, three hours later, I was sitting in a police precinct in a classic 'meet the victim' press call, in front of dozens of journalists, being blinded by camera flashes, wondering why I had said I was happy to do this. It had just seemed the natural response to say yes when Detective Harris had asked, but now I was here, what was I going to say? What were they expecting me to declare? Did they want me to just state how sick Aaron Stoats was, how much I hated him, and to tell them all how sorry I was that people I knew had been killed? What was the point of that? I looked around at the throng of dictaphones and notebooks and cameras and waited while Detective Harris, sitting beside me, talked into the microphone placed on the table in front of him, outlining his account of the facts.

I leaned on my left hand and closed my eyes. I had gone so many years not speaking out against racism, homophobia, bigotry, never concerned myself enough about these serious issues, that I wondered how I could now say anything of meaning. Then I had met Yvonne, whose life usually revolved around a fight for fairness and equality. If she had taught me anything, then it was that we do need to speak out when the time is right. And it seemed that now was my time.

I realised that Harris had stopped talking and I opened my eyes to find everyone was looking at me. I glanced at the detective.

'Take your time, Mr Cohen.' Detective Harris flicked a switch on the mic in front of me. I nodded, focused on a spot on the back wall as he had recommended earlier, paused for a moment and started to speak. My voice sounded creaky.

'I was listening to the radio the other morning when I was at work at The Kosher Delhi. It was another phone-in about homicides in the US, and the presenter was saying that last year, in 1993, there were over fourteen thousand deaths caused by guns in the US, the highest figure ever recorded. I remember that because I was so shocked by the number that I almost sliced into my finger. Well, my robotic finger which is now half famous, so at least it wouldn't have bled.' I heard a few polite chuckles and took a deep breath before continuing.

'Unfortunately, when a bullet hits you, you do bleed. It does destroy. So when Aaron Stoats came into my restaurant and fired a gun at two gay men who were simply eating dinner, they were killed. Murdered. Just because, it turns out, that their sexual preference was for other men. That seems…bizarre to me. And incredibly sad. That a young man with mental health issues could get hold of a pistol so easily, that's stupid enough, isn't it? And that he had been persuaded because of the vitriol and lies that he had heard spouted for years on radio shows, on TV, on the streets where he lived, to take that gun and go down to a restaurant he knew nothing about to kill some customers because of their sexuality. We should be ashamed as a society that this could happen.'

Several flashes went off as cameras clicked. I was wearing a polo neck T-shirt, so the stub at the end of my arm was clearly visible. I could see the photographers zooming in. Without thinking it through, I held up my right arm.

'I suspect that many of you already know that I lost my right hand in an accident when I was living in London. Well, that's only part of the story. It happened in a restaurant I was working in, but it wasn't an accident – it was actually a racist attack that left me this way.'

There was a murmur of interest from the press, and two or three journalists asked questions as the camera flashes intensified, but I held up my left hand to silence them.

'I accepted compensation from the restaurant for the attack,' I said more loudly, 'but the British police didn't care enough to investigate it properly, so no one was ever charged. The man that did this to me got away scot-free and he's still working. I'm glad that Aaron Stoats was caught and I'm glad that the NYPD were able to stop him without killing him. I don't see the point in that. If we're going to see justice, if we are going to help people understand why such attacks are wrong and pointless, then men like Stoats need help, not persecution. And we have to ask what caused him to feel such hatred for his victims in the first place, and address that to stop others from doing a similar thing in the future.'

Several more journalists shouted out questions, but I waited for them to quieten down before continuing.

'I have spent a long time, too long, not speaking out against racists and bigots because I didn't see the point, I didn't think that would change anything. What had it got to do with me? Someone has tried to persuade me otherwise over the last few years, and I think I finally understand now what she was getting at. Now I see the point. Now I see the need.'

I stopped talking, and for a few seconds, there was silence while the journalists waited to see if I was going to say anything more. I didn't know either. When we all realised I had said all I was going to for now, the hush was broken by the rush of a hundred questions all directed at me. The noise was like the floor of the London Stock Exchange. I leaned backwards, bemused by the furore and looked sideways at Detective Harris. He asked me if I wanted to take any questions. I nodded vaguely. Harris pointed to one of the journalists.

'Tell us more about how you lost your hand, Vik.'

'I can't. I wish I could.'

'Who did it?'

'I can't tell you that.'

'Why not?'

'Because formally, the police didn't accuse anyone, and therefore I can't mention names.'

'Did it happen in a restaurant owned by Chef Roger Raybourne?'

I hesitated. It seemed that this journalist had done her homework. Several flashes went off at once as I considered what to say.

'I'm afraid I can't comment on that.'

Detective Harris indicated to another journalist that they could speak.

'What would you say to Aaron Stoats if he was here now?'

'I'd ask him why he thought he had to attack gay people.'

'You wouldn't tell him to rot in hell?'

The aggressive question surprised me. 'No. How would that help?'

'Do you think the dead men's family would feel the same way?'

'You'd have to ask them.' I took a sip of water.

'And will you keep a gun in the restaurant now?' another journalist chipped in. 'Just in case it happens again?'

I stared at the questioner for several seconds before answering. 'No. We won't be doing that. If anyone brings a gun into The Kosher Delhi, whether they're an employee or a customer, they'll be asked to leave.'

'But wouldn't it protect you? Your customers?'

'I think you're missing the point,' I said coldly.

Another journalist shouted out a question but I turned to Detective Harris and whispered that I wanted to finish now. Harris leaned over and switched off my mic and stood up to usher me out of the room.

The police cordoned off The Kosher Delhi for thirty-six hours while they finished their investigations and forensics, although frankly, I couldn't tell what more they could learn, or even needed; they had shot the 'perp', and dozens of witnesses had given them statements, wasn't that enough?

When they let us back in, Myra and I returned to the restaurant and met Gina and Jack there to inspect the disarray caused by Aaron Stoates. The irony of such a violent and horrific attack was that much of the damage was comparatively superficial. Broken tables and chairs, smashed plates and glass, photos knocked off the wall. But they were just things. We could easily replace things. In the kitchen, pots, racks, more dishes and the food we had been cooking at the time were strewn all over the floor. In the midst of all the madness, Gina had instructed the kitchen staff to turn off all the gas and electrics, and they had done so. They could have just run away, but they didn't; they acted with incredible bravery and then stayed to shuttle customers out of the back door. I was so proud of them.

But among the broken fixtures and fittings there was more poignant damage. The area of the ceiling where Stoats had fired his gun had been cracked, and a small part of it had crashed to the floor, and we also found the hole in the wall where Stoats had shot his pistol at me. The police had recovered all the bullets, but the hole was still there, halfway up the wall.

We would have to repair the ceiling for safety reasons, but we decided that we should keep the bullet hole as an important reminder of what had happened. We had it covered it with glass and Myra arranged for a plaque to commemorate the victims, to warn us of what could happen again if such an event was forgotten about.

Our biggest concern was how to mark the place where the two men had been killed. We had learned their identities by that time, Noah and Frank, although everyone called Frank by his nickname, Bumble. We were still discussing that when a group arrived at the restaurant entrance, carrying flowers. I recognised them instantly as the other men and women who had been eating at Noah and Bumble's table that evening. They had brought the flowers intending to leave them outside the restaurant, but seeing that we were present, they came in to meet us. After a teary exchange, one of the women insisted we should keep using the table where they had all been sitting, but suggested that we hang a photograph of their two friends on the wall beside it. We put their beautiful flowers in vases to bring some colour and life back to the shattered restaurant.

Over the next few days, more and more flowers arrived. In no time, The Kosher Delhi looked more like a florist than a restaurant. They made me smile and cry in equal measures every time I looked at them.

It took us less than a week to get the restaurant up and running again. All the staff came in to help, and I told them all that they would remain on full pay during this time and (after talking to Myra), I announced that if anyone didn't want to come back to work when we reopened then we completely understood, and we would give them two months' salary and a glowing reference. Not a single member of staff left.

I was also asked to speak at several community events over the following weeks, aimed at promoting peace and equality, and I said yes to them all. I read up more about racism in America and brutality against the LGBT community, and gun laws and similar shootings, and I learned more about inequality and violence in those few weeks than I had done in my entire life.

I still don't know if anything I said at such meetings made any difference, but if a single person who heard me speak decided themselves to do one thing to help afterwards, then it was worth every minute of my time.

We reopened on the evening of 24 July. Flowers still adorned every table and most of the bar area. It began as a sombre serving, with people speaking in hushed tones, reading our new plaque and staring at the photograph of Noah and Bumble. Our waiters brought food and drink, and people ate gravely. It must have been over an hour before I heard anyone laugh, but someone did. And then someone else proposed a toast, and suddenly there was noise in the restaurant again. It felt so much better. We only served one seating, and when it finished, no one wanted to go home and instead one of the women sitting at the table where Noah and Bumble had been shot started to sing. Everyone listened in silence and then applauded when she had finished. Before we knew it, an impromptu singalong had begun, which lasted over an hour.

It had been a terrible couple of weeks, but I was starting to feel that we could begin to move on.

Seventeen

15 September 1994

Everyone had told me that Labor Day, the first Monday in September, marks a significant moment in the New York calendar. To some, it signals the end of summer, marking a return from the beaches to the city. For The Kosher Delhi, it marked a change in our clientele, from summer tourists back to local regulars. But it was more than that. Before the attack on the restaurant we had been popular, but now we seemed to have become a magnet for celebrities as well. Diners would shake my hand as I moved through the restaurant, personally thanking me for taking a brave stand against bigotry. We were turning away hundreds of people every week, but nobody seemed to mind queuing on the sidewalk. Restaurant reviews raved about my fusion dishes, devoting column inches to their taste combinations and cultural heritage, and Myra gave us all a bonus for the extra hours we were working. It was wonderful to witness such an uplift in custom, but I would have gladly forsaken every additional cover if that could have meant the shooting had never happened.

Gina and I started to share the responsibilities of opening and closing the restaurant, a steady routine which made our personal lives that little bit easier – although the KD felt like my whole life by now. I tried not to think about Yvonne. Those memories only made me sad.

My last Wednesday in New York was a busy midweek night in the middle of September; Gina and Jack had gone home to get some sleep before returning for the early morning shift, so I was the only one still at the KD, doing my final checks before locking up and heading back to Elizabeth and Neel's apartment.

It was well after midnight, not long after Gina had left, when there was a tap on the restaurant's front door. I sighed inwardly but smiled; what had my sous chef left behind now? I put down my pen, walked to the door and slid open the bolts.

'What have you forgot—'

I stopped abruptly.

'Hello, Vik.'

I held the door open. Yvonne stood in the doorway looking as if she had stepped straight out of one of her MTV videos: burgundy floral dress over bare legs, pashmina scarf, black ankle boots, bright red lipstick, and a bowler hat reminiscent of *A Clockwork Orange*. It suited her. She grasped a clutch bag. She watched me look her over and then removed her hat and looked down at her toes. It was almost demure, although I never would have associated Yvonne with that word before. She had changed her hairstyle too; gone was the peroxide blonde, and in its place was a straight brown fringe.

She looked far more gaunt then I remembered. It had been over six months since I had walked out on our relationship, but I could have sworn that she wasn't so skinny when I had last seen her.

Yvonne gave me a half smile. 'I think we've been here before.'

For a moment I wondered what she meant, and then I remembered the first time that she had come round to my house in Leeds, after I hadn't phoned her. 'Oh. Yeah…'

'Aren't you going to invite me in this time?'

I contemplated for an instant whether I should make her stand outside, but then she smiled again, and I opened the door wider. Yvonne eased past me (did she deliberately brush my arm?) and stepped in. She headed towards the middle of the restaurant, looking around. I closed the door behind her and slid the bolts back. I watched her sidle slowly between the tables, caressing the wooden tops with her fingers, pausing to scrutinise one or two of the photos on the walls. She scratched her left forearm vigorously, then turned to face me.

'So this is the very famous Kosher Delhi. I've seen so many photos of it, and of you as head chef, Vik, read so much about it in the last few months that I feel I know it. Isn't it strange that this is the first time I've been here?'

I had thought about that too. Many times. And now here she was. In my restaurant. Alone with me in my restaurant. So what did I feel about that? I straightened some napkins while she gazed about her.

'Cat got your tongue, Vik?'

Yvonne was studying me, tugging the ends of her scarf so it slid across her shoulders. She crossed one of her legs behind the other.

I cleared my throat. 'What are you doing here, Yvonne?'

'What am I doing here?'

'Yes. What do you want?'

Yvonne clasped her hands together, all her fingers interlocked.

'Vik. There's no need to be rude. I was in the area. With… I just came to see you. It's been such a long time, and the last time we saw each other was so terrible. Despite everything that's gone on after that, I just…I just hoped that we might still be friends. You know.'

'Friends?'

'Aye. Well, at least, not enemies.'

I crossed my arms aggressively. 'Talking of enemies, how's your friend, Wilton?'

'Oh, Vik, there's no need to be like that.'

'No need to be–'

I took a step towards her, and something in that movement must have looked threatening because Yvonne stepped backwards, almost tripping over her feet.

'Vik–'

I stopped. 'What do you mean, there is no need to be like that? I have every right to be *like that*. Wilton Stratford Pine is not my friend, and in many ways, I think that I absolutely bloody well can describe him as my enemy, seeing as he stole my girlfriend from me.'

'Vik, he didn't steal me from–'

'Of course he did.'

'He didn't. He–'

'Oh. Oh, right. Well if he didn't steal you, then I guess that means that you just left me of your own accord and decided I wasn't good enough for you. Too boring or unfashionable, or I couldn't help you with your career any more, and so you looked for someone else. Oh right. Well, that's OK then. That's a much better reason.'

Even from several feet away, I recognised that flicker in Yvonne's eyes, and I saw she had gathered herself again. She pointed a finger at me.

'It wasn't anything like that, Vik Cohen, and you know it.'

'I know it? I do not.'

'You fucking do. You fucking know that I had no intention of hurting you. I never wanted to do that. But we just – started to drift apart, remember?'

'I didn't think we were drifting. That was your interpretation. Remember?'

'My interpretation?'

'Exactly.'

Yvonne pursed her lips, looked away. She scratched her arm again. 'I thought you were falling out of… I thought you were starting to like me less.'

'Why on earth did you think that?'

'The way you behaved.'

'How? How did I behave?'

'You know. You seemed more interested in spending time with your aunt and uncle, you didn't want to talk about my show, about *Boon!*–'

'I was being offered the position of Head Chef in a new restaurant and a new hand!'

'But my show. It was so important to me. And…'

Yvonne's voice trailed away. She looked down at the floor, took a deep breath and exhaled.

'Does everything have to be about you, Yvonne?'

I watched her. Was she crying? I wasn't sure. I wasn't ready to comfort her, but it made me wonder: was there any truth in what she was saying? Had I been to blame for any part of our break-up? Had I not paid her enough attention at the time? Should I have been more encouraging? I swallowed.

'Yvonne–'

'And when we had sex,' Yvonne started again. 'You…you didn't seem so interested any more. It was as if, as if you didn't want me. I mean, was it so surprising that I found comfort in someone else?'

I opened my mouth but didn't reply. I felt as if I had been cuffed across the ears. 'Oh, Yvonne. You nearly had me.'

'What?'

'You were this close to making me think that I might actually, genuinely have been to blame for what you did.'

'Sorry?'

'Yvonne. How can you ever say that I wasn't interested in you? That I made you rush into Wilton Stratford Pine's beckoning arms? That is one of the craziest, stupidest, most cruel things you have ever said to me.'

'But, Vik–'

'You clearly wanted Wilton more than me, for whatever reason, and so you fucked him and blamed me. Well, you know what, that was your choice, your decision so you can carry on fucking him and leave me alone.'

Yvonne took a step towards me and said desperately, 'I'm sorry, Vik, I'm sorry!'

'It's too late, Yvonne.' I heard a police siren in the distance. 'And it is too late. I think you had better leave.'

Yvonne didn't react for a moment and then she nodded once. She sniffed loudly, wiped the heel of her hand across her eyes, and shook her head as if to clear it. She started walking towards the door but stopped when she reached me.

'I almost came to visit you after the shooting, you know.'

I automatically glanced at the photo of Noah and Bumble, shrugged, scuffed my toes on the floor.

'I'm sorry I didn't,' she added.

'Don't worry, you probably wouldn't have got in anyway. The building was always full of policemen and builders.'

Yvonne gave me a half smile, reached out, touched my arm. I flinched slightly but didn't move it. 'I'm so sorry. I read all about it, of course. I couldn't believe it.'

'Yes, well. Trust me, it happened.'

'And he did it because you have gay staff?'

'And gay customers. And Jewish diners. And black staff. You name it, he hated it.'

'Fucking prick.'

I couldn't help it – I smiled. Then I looked away. Those two words were the first I heard her say which sounded like the old Yvonne.

'I saw the speech you made with the police, when they made the statement about the gunman.'

'It wasn't exactly a speech.'

'It was fucking brilliant, Vik. I was so proud of you.'

I couldn't think of how to respond to that. I didn't remember Yvonne ever saying she was proud of me. I shook my head, slightly embarrassed.

I sighed and massaged my forehead above my left eye. 'Yvonne, why did you really come here tonight? Did you really want to just "make up" with me?'

Yvonne hesitated and then gave a quick shake of her head. 'I was in the area, I wasn't lying about that. I was out with Wilton, at a club, and we…we had an argument. We fought.'

She paused. I waited for her to continue.

'And…he hit me.' She looked away and pulled her scarf tighter around her shoulders.

'He hit you?'

Yvonne nodded. I couldn't believe what I had heard.

'Why?'

Yvonne shrugged. 'Something I said.'

'He hit you because of something you said?'

'I think I made him angry.'

'You made him… What did you do?'

'I can't remember exactly. We were in the VIP area and–'

'No. I mean, what did you do after he hit you? I assume you, oh, stormed off after throwing a beer over him or something?' That was what the Yvonne who I had known would have done.

'No, I…' Yvonne's eyes glazed over. 'I think I sat there for a moment. He said something else. Then he struck me again.'

'He did what?' I was incredulous. 'And you didn't do anything in response? You didn't even shout at him?'

Yvonne was still standing close to me. She said very quietly, 'It wasn't the first time, Vik.'

If I had been shocked before, now I was stunned. I forgot all about my anger from earlier and now, automatically, reached out to console her, but as I did so, Yvonne flinched. I took my hand away from her right shoulder, worried. Yvonne flicked her neck muscles and pulled her scarf more tightly around her.

'Yvonne, what has Wilton been doing to you?'

She picked at her fingernails, as if deciding how to respond, then she turned around and faced away from me. Slowly, with both hands, she pulled her pashmina scarf away from her neck and down her chest, so it was bunched up in front of her. I could see her low-cut dress and the bare skin of her back. And her shoulders. I stared at them. They were covered in bruises.

'What the hell?'

Then she turned ninety degrees to me, bent over very slightly and started to gather up her dress. As she pulled up her dress, I saw more bruises and what looked like scars at the top of her thigh.

'Yvonne…'

Yvonne dropped her dress again, pulled out a chair from one of the tables and sank into it.

'Yvonne? What's going on?'

She pulled her leg away and tucked it under her chair. She was crying. Silently, but tears were streaming down her cheeks. I took a step towards her but stopped. I didn't know how to comfort her. She tried to say something, but nothing came out. She coughed and tried again.

'It's Wilton. Wilton did this to me.'

And then she told me. It took a while, as she had to pause frequently to wipe away tears, or I had to ask her to stop for a moment while I processed a particular point she had just detailed. But when she had finished, it was all clear.

She had, of course, started the affair with Wilton Stratford Pine and, naturally, during the tour of New England, all had been good with their relationship, and for the first month after that, back in Manhattan. Then Pine got drunk one night and hit her for the first time. He slapped her face and punched her hard in the forearm. Fortunately, the slap had just stung, but the punch left a bruise which Yvonne said developed into the size of a lemon. Pine had, of course, apologised profusely, swore he would never do it again, said that he felt - and apparently had shown – terrible guilt, and Yvonne decided to forgive him.

'I can't believe I did that,' Yvonne whispered. 'Me. Forgive a man for hitting me. When I was working for the women's charity in Leeds, I always told women that they should leave their husbands the first time they got knocked about, but, well, I guess I've seen it from a different perspective now. I *wanted* to believe he honestly felt remorse. And yes, I admit it, I wanted to believe him because he was doing so much for me, for my career. I was hypnotised by that. By him.

'He struck me again, of course, another time – other times. But he's not stupid. He only hit me on parts of my body which he knew we could cover up when I was out in public or making a video.' A deep sob rose from her chest. 'Why did I accept it? Why?'

I didn't have an answer.

Yvonne wiped a finger across her top lip. 'I think some of it was because of the drugs.'

'Drugs?'

'Aye. And I dinnae mean barbiturates and Xanax.'

'Then what do you mean? I didn't think you were ever into drugs.'

'I wasn't, not at first. It had happened gradually.'

'Go on.'

'When I moved in with Wilton, he always had skunk at home. I loved it. One day, when I was feeling nervous before a performance, he suggested I try cocaine. It was incredible. Within weeks, I was doing coke all the time. It gives you such a confidence hit when you're high. Before I knew it, I was addicted to it.'

'Jeez, Yvonne.'

'But that was just the start. It affected my sleep so badly that one night I tried sleeping tablets. But they only worked for a while. When Wilton's dealer offered me opium at a party, I took that, and then,' her shoulders heaved, 'it wasn't long before I was smoking heroin. It was like nothing else I'd ever experienced. I thought I could handle it, no problem, as long as I didn't inject it. I couldn't tell Wilton of course – he would have gone ballistic.'

'Why? Wasn't he supplying the drugs to you?'

'The coke, yes, but he didn't want me using heroin. You can't perform when you're smacked up on H.'

'And you have done all this while you've been singing?'

Yvonne nodded sadly. 'Weed and coke are just temporary highs, I've even sung several times in gigs when I was on E.

People don't notice. Half of the audience is probably whacked out themselves.'

'But the heroin.'

'The heroin.' Yvonne bit her bottom lip and squeezed her eyes tight shut. 'Wilton's dealer kept on about it. Subtly at first. He told me again and again how great it was, what an intense high I would get from injecting it, and how I should just try it. "Let yourself experiment," he said. So one day, I asked him how I could try heroin without the needle marks showing anywhere, such as my arm. So that no one would know. That's when he showed me how to shoot up between my toes.'

The shock must have shown on my face. 'Your toes? Is that possible?'

'Aye, trust me. It works like a dream.'

'And you can't see the needle marks?'

'Not unless you look carefully. And I only did it once or twice. I can show you if you like.' Yvonne reached down to one of her boots.

'No. No, you don't have to. I believe you.'

Yvonne sat back in her chair and bit her fingernails.

I recoiled in mine. 'Christ Almighty. What a shithead.'

'A shithead.' Yvonne nodded. 'Yes, that describes his dealer pretty accurately.'

'I meant Wilton. He was the one who started you down this road.'

'But I walked down it happily enough,' Yvonne said quietly.

I shook my head. 'So what did Wilton say when he found out about the heroin? He can't have been happy to have one of his performers losing the plot.'

She shrugged. 'That's why I've got the bruises.'

When Yvonne had finished her story, I went into the kitchen and returned with a bottle. 'I think we need a glass of something.'

I sat down opposite her, poured us each a large glass of Californian Alexander Valley, our favourite wine when we were together, and we clinked glasses. Yvonne smiled, and for a second, so did I, but then I caught myself and steeled my emotions again.

'So now what?' I asked Yvonne.

'Now?'

'Yes, what are you going to do now? I mean, I assume you're going to leave him but how are you planning to do that?'

Yvonne focused on her glass and swirled her wine around before taking a sip. 'It's not that easy, Vik,' she said hoarsely.

'What do you mean not that easy? Yvonne!'

Yvonne banged her glass on the table. 'You don't understand, Vik.'

'I think I do. You have an abusive boyfriend slash manager, and you need to get out of both relationships. What part of that do I not understand?'

'The part that...the fact that if I leave him, then I've got no career left in the States. Even if I try to leave him, he will beat me up. I know that. He's invested his time and money and energy in me, he's told me so many times. If I do take off, he will come after me. Plus, I need to get clean without him.'

This caught me completely unawares. 'You mean, you mean you are still doing the heroin now?'

'Yes. Of course. Smoking it anyway. Not frequently, but regularly enough. I can't...stop. That's what addiction is.'

'Holy shit.'

I looked at the clock on our wall. It was close to one o'clock in the morning.

'I can't believe you are still doing those drugs, Yvonne.'

Yvonne leaned forwards and clasped my hand. 'You have to understand, Vik, I need them. I want them. Sort of. They give you such a high, the best ever. I know…I know I am addicted, and I am, I think I am just this side of a complete meltdown, but I also know that I can't carry on like this. Doing this. I have to stop. I have to make it stop. But I don't know how. I…I've wondered before about asking you to help, coming to you, but I presumed you wouldn't want to see me.'

'You were probably right.'

'But then tonight, when I ran out of the club… I thought of you immediately. I knew your restaurant was close by. I guess I'm lucky you were working so late.'

I gently squeezed Yvonne's fingers in return. 'Have you tried asking for help?'

'From who? A shrink?'

'Why not?'

'It'd be a complete waste of time,' Yvonne said sharply. 'Even if I thought they could help, I barely have any cash of my own to pay for any sessions. And if I asked Wilton to take care of it, well, he'd just laugh and tell me to cut out the heroin and snort another line of coke.'

'He's that controlling?'

Yvonne nodded.

I thought for a moment. 'What about going to the police?'

'The police.' Yvonne bristled. 'The police won't help.'

'Why not? You're being beaten up and abused by your…your boyfriend.'

'Look at me. I'm some drugged-up, Scottish, pseudo-rock chick having the time of her life making videos on MTV. A nice, wealthy American manager wouldn't hurt me.'

'A women's refuge, then.'

That won't work. That won't help.'

'But why–'

'It just won't, Vik, all right?' Yvonne spat the words at me, and I pulled my hand away.

For several minutes, Yvonne sat very still, sipping her wine, staring at the table in front of her. Outside the restaurant we heard laughter coming from a nearby bar or a group on their way to another club. Another police siren echoed somewhere from the direction of Chinatown.

'There is one thing you could do,' Yvonne said tentatively.

'Go on.'

'But I'm not sure you'll like it.'

'Try me.'

She bit one of her fingernails. 'OK...'

And then my ex-girlfriend stared deep into my eyes. 'Do you remember that conversation we had in bed one night in Weston-Super-Mare, after we threw the bottle at that old man?'

'After *you* threw the bottle.'

Yvonne ignored my response. 'Well, I want you to do that now. I want you to kill Wilton.'

I rocked back in my chair. 'You fucking what?'

'I want you to kill Wilton. You said you loved me enough to kill for me, Vik. So now I'm asking you. Do what you promised, Vik. Please.'

I stared at Yvonne. I couldn't believe that she was bringing this up. Something that was said so long ago.

'Yvonne, what are you saying? Why on earth are you asking me to do that?'

'It's the only answer, Vik. The only way out for me. And I know you'll do it if you still love me.'

'You know I'll kill Wilton Stratford Pine?'

'Yes.'

'Just because you ask me to?'

'Yes.'

I thought for a moment. 'You know, when we were in... Wesson, I didn't actually say yes.'

'You said you'd make sure no one would hurt me. I remember feeling so safe when you said that.'

I looked at Yvonne's pleading face. When we had been together, she had always been able to make me feel as if I was the centre of her world. It seemed she was still able to do that, even now, even when she was with someone else.

I tapped the stalk of my wine glass. 'What I said, Yvonne – whatever I said – was when I was head over heels...about you. I was obsessed with you. I would have said anything to have impressed you.'

'You mean you didn't mean it?'

I rubbed my forehead. 'You know what – I probably did mean it at the time. After all, at that point, I still believed that you had killed that old man by throwing your bottle at him and I wanted to...be what you wanted me to be.'

'But –'

'But not any more.'

'Vik, please.'

'Yvonne, we are not having this crazy conversation.'

She looked down at her feet, I stood and began to pace around the room. I stared for a moment at the photo of Bumble and Noah, ran my fingers over the glass cover protecting the bullet hole in the wall. I peered through the door into the kitchen. Then I returned to the table and sat opposite Yvonne.

'Yvonne, I cannot believe you'd really want to kill anyone. You need a therapist, not a hitman. You don't really mean it, do you?

You just want to know that I'm still here for you. I understand that. But I don't understand why you find it so difficult to just leave Pine.'

When she finally answered me, Yvonne's voice was so quiet I could barely hear her.

'Because that would mean I have to run away yet again. And I am so tired of running away.'

'What do you mean?'

'You know what I mean, Vik. All my life I have been running away from something or other. And I don't know if I can carry on doing that.'

'But I don't understand. I didn't know that. What have you been running away from?'

'You *know*, Vik. You do. I mean, we ran away together from Wesson didn't we?'

'Well...'

'And Leeds.'

'Leeds? No, we just found jobs in Wesson. Didn't we?'

Yvonne pulled out a pack of cigarettes from her clutch bag and offered me one. I declined. 'Do you mind?' she asked. I shook my head. She lit one and sat back heavily in her chair. 'I forgot that we never discussed that.'

'Discussed what?'

'Why we left Leeds.'

That triggered a memory of a late night, half-stoned conversation from years earlier, with Gary, in Miles' flat in Wesson. He had urged me to talk to Yvonne about why she had wanted to leave Leeds. I had, as usual, chickened out.

'Go on then. Why did you want to leave Leeds?'

She looked away.

'Is there something you're not telling me?'

'I was stealing from people, and people found out.'

'Stealing? Stealing what?'

Yvonne shrugged. 'Cash mostly, the odd credit card. But that was harder because then I had to use it to buy something and sell that. It was far easier to steal money from someone in the squat. I mean, who knows where anything is in such a chaotic environment as that, right? Plus a bit of dope here and there, and once I stole a girl's jewellery. One of the squatter's.' She blew a smoke ring. 'I feel bad about that. Cash is cash, but jewellery means something to someone. It was hardly worth anything either. I wish I hadn't done that. Gary gave me some shit about it too.

'Anyhow, eventually, some of the guys in my squat realised that I never complained about having any of my own money nicked – which was stupid of me really, I should have just lied and said I was missing some too – and they confronted me. I denied it of course, but they didn't believe me. And then the girl who had thought she had just misplaced her jewellery put two and two together and threatened to go to the police to report me. The only reason she didn't was that clearly as squatters, the cops weren't exactly our best friends, or likely to care much about what they would think was a bit of missing tack.'

I was astounded. Even after all the years we had been together, it had never once occurred to me that Yvonne would do anything like that. It just didn't seem like her. Yes, we had half-inched a few already opened bottles of liquor or some beer from the Hotel Neptune, but that was just silly, minor stuff, not personal, not stealing from people who were also struggling. That didn't fit with Yvonne, the socialist warrior. But…now, when I looked back and started to think about how Yvonne did always seem to have cash when I first met her, it made some sense. I would never have guessed it – I couldn't see past her aura of perfection at the time.

Something clicked in my brain. 'So it was fortunate that you…found that copy of the *Western Gazette* on the bus – with the job ad, yes?'

Yvonne gave me a rueful smile. 'You're finally catching on. I went to the Leeds city library and looked through a whole load of regional newspapers, and when I saw the jobs page in the *Gazette*, I nicked it.'

'But why Weston-Super-Mare?'

'Vik! Don't be an arse. I wasn't specifically looking for a job in Wesson. I just wanted to get out of Leeds, preferably as far away as possible. I saw the paper, had an idea, and the Hotel Neptune job ad was just serendipitous. Plus it was by the sea, which I did like. But the jobs could have been in Wales or the Isle of Wight for all I cared.'

I let that sink in. I didn't exactly feel used, maybe a bit cheated, but it wasn't as if I had put up much of a fight when Yvonne had suggested we move down to the south-west. I could see now that Gary had been trying to warn me about Yvonne, but looking back, I think even if I had known the whole truth, I would still have followed her at that time.

'OK, so you ran away from Leeds with me, and we ran away together from Wesson. That's hardly a lifetime of fleeing.'

'And then leaving London for New York? Wasn't I running away from Jane and the band?'

I blew out my cheeks. 'I wouldn't call that running away. You had been offered a new opportunity in a new and exciting land. Admittedly by a man who turned out to be a total creep, but that's beside the point. You didn't run away.'

'I didn't exactly give Terry another chance.'

'Terry was ill. I think you're being hard on yourself.'

'Maybe. I'm not sure. Maybe there was a part of me that wanted to get away, that didn't believe that The Libertine Dolls was right for me. For my career, as you would say.'

'Jeez, Yvonne, I think you're looking for a pattern that doesn't really exist.'

Yvonne looked around for somewhere to stub out her cigarette, and I reached behind me to grab a plate from the bar.

'I haven't told you the worst of it yet,' she said.

My hand hovered in mid-air as I handed her the plate. 'What else is there? I know everything about your time since then. OK, I suppose you could say you ran away from me, but I think that was different. Worse,' I added quickly as Yvonne opened her mouth.

Yvonne pursed her lips and nodded. 'I can only say sorry again, Vik.' I didn't respond. 'But you don't know about my life before I met you.'

'You mean in Inverness? And Dougie?'

'Aye. And more than that.'

'More?' I thought for a moment. 'I know Dougie mentioned you hadn't seen your parents for a while. Is that it?'

'No, there's something else.' Yvonne was speaking very quietly again. 'I've never told you about my sister.'

'Your sister? I didn't even know you had a sister.'

Yvonne didn't answer.

'So where is she? Why don't you talk about her?'

'You mean you haven't guessed? Even after all our time together?'

'Guessed? No…'

For a few seconds, Yvonne looked as if she was about to speak and then didn't. She waved her hand at the wine bottle. 'Can I have some more wine, please?'

I poured us both two more, large glasses, draining the Californian red. When Yvonne started speaking again, she was crying and her voice cracked. 'My sister…my sister's name was Kirstine.'

'Was?'

Yvonne nodded. 'She died. Nearly…' Yvonne looked up at the ceiling, and I could see her counting silently. 'Nine years ago. My God.'

She paused again. I waited, but she said nothing more.

I cleared my throat. 'I'm really sorry.'

Yvonne nodded. 'I can't believe you didn't guess. When Dougie mentioned her, I was sure you must know. And then, of course, I named our song "K" after her. You never made the connection between the song title and Kirstine?'

I flicked my mind back again to the evening when Dougie had visited us. I thought about the song. I remembered watching Yvonne cry as she sang it on stage.

'I knew she was someone important to you. And if you remember, I did question you about her when we were in bed that night, but you said you didn't ever want me to ask you about her again. So I didn't.'

Still with damp eyes, Yvonne smiled weakly. 'You're such a good man, Vik. I should never have got you involved with all this. I should never have fucked you around so much.'

'Yes, well I agree with that bit of your assessment.'

Yvonne let out a deep breath. 'D'you know what? I haven't talked about Kirstine for so long. Not properly, I mean. For the first few years after she died, whenever I phoned Ma, we always talked about her, but then, we just stopped. It was too painful for both of us. Talking about her wasn't going to bring her back. So when Dougie mentioned her again…'

'I understand.'

Yvonne picked up her wine and took a long drink.

'Maybe. But what you cannae understand is what it made me become. This,' she thumped herself on her chest, 'this woman you see sitting here, is the way she is because of Kirstine, because of what happened to Kirstine.'

Outside it was quiet again apart from the occasional shout or dog barking. I didn't say anything else. I knew I had to let Yvonne tell me her story when she was ready. When she could speak again. She turned her head and faced the windows looking out on to the street.

'Kirstine was two years younger than me. She was such a happy child. Outgoing, lively. Everyone loved her, me included of course. We were so happy together as sisters, never jealous of each other and we rarely squabbled. But as she reached her teens, she was starting to realise that she wasn't like the other kids, or her friends. We talked about it, and I told her it didn't matter how she felt. But I think it was only when she turned fifteen that she realised she might be gay.

'She told me how she had been at a school disco and all her mates, her girlfriends were talking about the boys, but when she looked across the room to another bunch of kids, she suddenly realised that she fancied one of the girls and had no interest in any lad. It was a big moment for her. Her feelings didn't change and she knew without a doubt that she was gay.

'As soon as she understood she was a lesbian, she told everyone. Can you believe that? In, what, 1985. No one in Scotland told their friends or parents that they were gay in 1985. But she did, Kirstine did. Because she wanted them to know who she really was, and she didn't see any problem in being open. Unfortunately, other people in Inverness did have a problem with it. They didn't like what they called "poofs" or "queers", even if they might get off seeing two girls kissing on a porno. And one night, one night…'

Now Yvonne was crying properly again, and I found I couldn't help myself. Despite all she put me through in the last six months, despite how had she had made me feel and how much I had resented her for it, I got up and dragged my chair around the table and set it beside her, and pulled her into my chest with both arms. She cried for another five minutes, loud, heaving sobs interspersed by weaker tears, before she finally sat up, rubbed her eyes and carried on. And then it all came out in a rush as if she knew that if she didn't finish the story now, then she wouldn't be able to start it again.

'We went to a club, and I met a lad, and he took me home to his flat, and I let Kirstine walk home on her own. She told me she would be fine. I found out later what happened because an old woman in a cottage on the green, right by our house, was woken by a commotion, and she looked out of her window and called the police. But they didn't come for ages, and by then it was too late. The old woman said that a group of young men got hold of her just before she reached our house. Half a dozen of them, she said. They started by just wolf-whistling and shouting out – that's what woke her – and calling her a queer, so they must have known her. Then she saw them pushing Kirstine around, and then one of the boys pushed her to the ground, and then someone kicked her and then someone else, and at some point, they must have kicked her in the head.' A short pause. 'She never properly recovered. She had such severe brain damage that she needed help with nearly everything in her life from then on.

'Ma looked after her and I tried to help, but it reached a point when I just couldn't do it any more. I tried and tried, but I was too angry, with the fuckers who did it to her, with my parents, with myself. If I hadn't gone home without her…'

She took another deep breath. 'The pricks who did it were never caught. The police didn't treat it as a homophobic attack, I don't think they even had a category for such a crime in Inverness in those days. Everyone in our area knew who had been involved, but they all shut up shop and protected each other, and the police didn't care enough. Ma couldn't do anything, and Da was too weak, too traumatised.

'Kirstine survived another six months and then she had a massive haemorrhage and died. I know now that was a blessing in disguise, it was no life she had, that any of us had, but it didn't seem that way to me at the time.

'I just about scraped through my A-levels, and then I went to university. In Leeds.' Yvonne turned her head to look at me. 'I ran away from my family, Vik. I haven't seen my parents since the day I left.'

Eighteen

We carried on talking for the next few hours – about our evenings on the pier in Weston-Super-Mare, The Libertine Dolls, our lives in London. There had been many happy times, Yvonne was keen to remind me. Every now and then, she nodded off where she was sitting, and I watched her sleep for a few minutes before she jerked awake again. When she woke, she looked around wildly as if she wasn't sure where she was, scratched the back of her hand fiercely, entwined her scarf around her fingers and pulled it across her shoulders. We switched from wine to coffee.

At one point, after waking up suddenly, Yvonne shook her head and clapped her hands to her face. 'Vik, I can't believe it. I haven't even asked you how your arm is. Is it OK? How are you feeling now?'

'It's fine, thanks,' I said. 'But I'm glad I have my bionic hand now. I wouldn't be able to work here without it.'

Yvonne looked around the restaurant, at the exposed brick wall and vintage décor, as if she was seeing it for the first time. I suppose she was. 'I'm glad somebody finally gave you a break,' she said.

'I worked for it. I had to prove myself to Myra or she would have booted me out long ago, robotic hand or not. You never thought I'd make it in a proper restaurant, did you?'

Yvonne looked slightly stunned by the accusation in my voice. 'I only wanted to make sure that you didn't meet another psychopathic racist like Chef Kevin.'

I nodded. 'Sometimes I wonder if it was because you didn't want to come second. You know, in my list of priorities.'

She sighed. 'Tell me about the hand,' she said.

I explained that Neel's invention sometimes helped me forget I had even lost my real hand.

'I can show you how good it is,' I offered.

We moved to the kitchen, and I chopped up some carrots and did my party trick of picking up single strands of spaghetti. Yvonne laughed and clapped her hands, and for a few minutes, we might have been back in the flat in Holloway, trying out the lyrics of a new Libertine Dolls song or needling Terry about a comment he had made on how much better the music scene used to be when he was younger.

'You know,' Yvonne said, stroking my arm as we walked back into the restaurant, 'things might still have been all right between us after I toured with Wilton and *Boon!*'

I was taken aback. 'You're kidding, right? How could that ever have worked?'

We sat down again at our table. 'When I came back from the tour, and we were in our flat, and I told you about Wilton and me, our…affair, there was a part of me which desperately wanted you to fight for me, not to walk out, and if you had – fought for me, said you still wanted me – then I might have stayed with you and not gone off with Wilton again.'

'But you had already been unfaithful. Why would I do that?'

'People forgive people all the time.'

I thought about that. 'I don't think I could have, Yvonne. You hurt me so much.'

Yvonne bit her lip and nodded slowly. After several minutes, she whispered, 'I'm sorry.'

I didn't respond but I didn't know what to think about Yvonne's admission. I tossed her new thoughts around in my mind. My conclusion was that I had still been right to walk out.

A refuse truck rumbled down the street outside. A dog started barking. The first streaks of dawn were taking away the dark.

Yvonne got up and stretched. 'Jesus, what time is it?'

I glanced at the clock on the wall. 'Can you believe that? Nearly five in the morning.'

'Christ, I'm sorry, Vik, I didn't mean to keep you up all night. I only came to, well…'

I gave her the slightest of nods but didn't reply.

'I'd better leave soon. Wilton won't care where I've been, but if I get back to our apartment before him, it will make it easier.'

'You've moved in with him then?' She nodded. 'And he won't be home by this hour?'

Yvonne gave me a wan smile. 'He does most of his networking at night.'

'It's a long time since I've partied till dawn. At least, it feels like it.' I looked across at my ex-girlfriend. 'You know, Yvonne, I think there's only one answer to your problem. If you won't go to the police, and if you don't want to go to a charity or a refuge here in New York,' – Yvonne shook her head vehemently - 'then the only thing you can do is go away for a while.'

'Away? What do you mean away?'

'I mean home. Back to Britain. London, or Scotland maybe. Inverness. See your parents after all these years.'

Yvonne looked shocked, as if I had said her pet dog had died. 'I cannae do that, Vik. It wouldn't work.'

'Why not? You'd be safe, and you could get your head sorted out.'

'But where would I get ma fix?'

'Your fix?' I shook my head. 'You can get a fix anywhere. What you need is to get away from the trigger for the fix, which is Wilton Stratford Pine. You'd have to give it up. That would be the point of going away.'

'You mean…go cold turkey?'

'There is no other way. Maybe a methadone programme back home could help.'

Yvonne started scratching the back of her hand. 'Oh, Vik, I couldn't do that. I wouldn't last. If I were in London, I'd fall off the wagon in two seconds, and if I were in Inverness then, well, I'd either go mad or end up in a drug den. I know I would. I'm not strong enough.'

'Not strong enough…the Yvonne I used to know, the one I followed everywhere and anywhere would never have said that.'

I watched her intertwining her fingers, gripping her hands so tightly that her knuckles glowed white, and forced myself to recall again that night in Wesson when she had asked me if I would kill for her. It may have been another chapter, but it was still a key part of my lifetime. An important time. I looked around the restaurant and came to a rapid conclusion. Surely this place could cope without me for a few weeks? I thought of the creative menus I drew up every week that were intended to showcase my innovative ideas. That was part of the restaurant's marketing strategy. Maybe Gina could rotate some of the menus from earlier in the year – nobody would notice. I took a deep breath.

'I'll help you, Yvonne.'

'Vik… I don't think you can. What about Wilton?'

'Fuck Pine.'

Yvonne swallowed. 'I'm not asking for your help. You know that.'

'Then why did you come here tonight? You could have just gone home after you left Pine in the club.'

Yvonne opened her mouth to reply but didn't say anything. She let her shoulders drop.

'I'll help you kick your habit,' I said firmly. 'I meant that I'll come back to England with you for a while. I'll help you sort yourself out. You need a friend to straighten you up, get you clean.'

Yvonne sat upright and stared straight at me. 'You'd do that for me? Now? After all we've been through? After everything you learned about me last night?'

'Of course.'

'Oh, Vik, I don't know what to say.' She looked close to tears.

I shrugged. 'It'll be good for me too. I can visit my parents, see Ajay. We can check how Terry is. I'm not your boyfriend, Yvonne, but I do want to remain your friend.'

Yvonne smiled weakly. She leaned towards me and raised the back of her hand to within a millimetre of my cheek. I found I was holding my breath. At the last moment, she withdrew and looked down.

'When would we go?' Yvonne asked.

'As soon as I can speak to Myra and get some time off. It'll also depend on the flights, when tickets are available, which ones we can afford.'

'So...'

'It all depends on Myra. Next week?'

'Oh, but, Vik.' Yvonne sounded scared. 'That would mean I would need to go back to our apartment, mine and Wilton's.

And if I had to do that, then I don't know if I could manage. He might beat me if I tell him I'm leaving, and I don't think I could lie convincingly, and –'

'Yvonne.' I interrupted her. 'You don't have to go back there.'

'But all my stuff's still at his place. Where else would I go?'

I took a deep breath. 'Come and stay with me. I'll be fine on the sofa for a few days.'

'Oh, Vik... Really? You'd let me stay with you?'

'Only if you promise not to shoot up in the bathroom.'

Yvonne looked taken aback.

'Just joking,' I added quickly, hoping I was.

Yvonne nodded eagerly. 'OK, great. Thank you. But...but I will have to go back to Wilton's apartment one more time, at least to get my passport.'

I thought about this. 'I need to call Myra to tell her that I've got to take some time off. I have to work the lunchtime shift, but Gina can manage this evening without me. You can crash at my place during the day and then we'll go to your apartment after I've finished this afternoon.'

Yvonne stood up and walked around the table, opened her arms and hugged me tightly. I let my arms rest lightly on her shoulder blades.

Then she said quietly, 'You know, Vik. I... I didn't really mean it. I didn't really want you to kill Wilton for me. I just, I just said that because I was, I am so desperate I didn't know what else to do. You know? It was a way out,' she finished, 'but I didn't really mean it.'

She looked at me desperately and I knew what I had to say.

'I know.'

Although I didn't. After all the years I had known Yvonne, I couldn't recognise this needy, desperate addict, scratching her arms, and who had only hours earlier asked me to kill someone. How was this the same woman who made The Libertine Dolls so magnetic onstage, whose social and political principles had always been part of the attraction?

She smiled softly and pushed a strand of hair back behind her ear. 'Are you sure you wouldn't have killed him if I had asked one more time?'

I thought about it. 'When you first came in here tonight, of course I wouldn't have killed him. I'm not a violent person. I didn't think you were.'

'And now? Now that we've talked?'

We went back to my apartment. I had a quick shower and got ready to go straight back to the restaurant, while Yvonne made herself a cup of tea before crashing on my bed fully clothed. I left her asleep and left an urgent message with Myra.

When I arrived at the KD, she was already there, leafing through her Filofax.

'Vik. I've cancelled a meeting to see you so there better be a good reason for you dragging me down here.' She beckoned to one of the waiters to bring her a coffee. 'Now. What's this you're saying about needing to go away? You realise this place is on every celebrity's to-do list right now, and you're talking about taking time off?'

I suppose I thought that Myra would understand, but my account of Yvonne's plight didn't change her expression.

'People come here every week just to eat your food, to see what you've come up with next. You're at the zenith of your career. Why would you risk all that for a woman who has only ever let you down?'

I thought of Yvonne's pleas, her scratched arms, the track marks between her toes. 'Because I think I can make a difference in her life,' I said.

Myra checked her watch. 'So what you're saying is she'd be lost without you, is that it? Well, you need to work out how you can support her without jeopardising the fortunes of my restaurant.'

I looked at Gina who was stocking the bar. She flashed me a sympathetic grimace, but there was something in her eyes that made me think Myra's view was shared.

'You're not between a rock and a hard place. Yvonne needs to sort this out herself,' said Myra in a gentler tone.

I touched my right arm nervously. 'Myra, you know how much I appreciate all you've done for me. And I love this restaurant. But ironically, Yvonne is the reason I'm sitting here today with you. If I hadn't met her, I wouldn't have come to New York. Now she needs my help.'

Myra tapped her pen on the table. 'You can have a week off with Yvonne, but that is all. Remember, Vik, there are plenty of other great chefs in New York.'

At five o'clock, Yvonne turned up at The Kosher Delhi and sat patiently at a corner table in the restaurant, causing plenty of whispers and furtive glances from my chefs and waiting staff, most of whom knew the story of our relationship, and all of whom had seen her on MTV. She was wearing the same clothes as she had been the previous night, but despite that, she still somehow managed to make herself seem fresh and alluring. Gina glared at me for an instant as I went out to see my ex-girlfriend, but her scowl was accompanied by a gentle touch on my shoulder when we left.

We hailed a cab and Yvonne told the driver where to go. The cabbie looked at me nervously in his rear-view mirror before pulling away. Yvonne glanced across at me.

'Vik! You've still got your robot hand on!'

I looked down at my right wrist. 'I often wear it when I'm not working now. It's such a part of me these days that sometimes I forget I'm wearing it.'

For some reason, we both laughed, which eased some of the tension. Forty minutes later, we pulled up at Yvonne/Pine's apartment on the Upper West Side. Yvonne led me confidently past the building's front desk, the concierge cordially greeting Yvonne and perusing me discreetly, and we went up in the elevator to the twentieth floor.

Pine's apartment was everything one would expect from a perfidious, stinking rich, self-proclaimed Svengali: large, ostentatious in its furnishings, huge abstract paintings on the walls, and delicate glass and marble statuettes on bookshelves and coffee tables, mostly effigies of naked women. It was so far from what the old Yvonne would have valued that it made me realise just how much control Pine must have had over her. Yvonne disappeared into one of the bedrooms, calling out that she was 'just going to get a few things'. I stayed in the open-plan lounge/kitchen and wondered why anyone needed a TV the size of a small elephant.

We hadn't been there five minutes when I heard a key in the front door. I didn't have time to call out before Wilton Stratford Pine walked in. He was wearing a smart suit over a black T-shirt. He dropped his keys on a table by the door, glanced up, saw me and stood stock still. He looked me up and down, did a slight double-take as he noticed my robot hand and quickly recovered his composure. His lips curled into a thin smile.

'Vik. How…nice to see you.'

'Wilton.'

'I presume if you are here then Yvonne is too?' He looked towards the bedrooms. 'In which case, I should thank you for bringing her home. I assume that is what you have done, yes?'

I gave a non-committal grunt. He gave a light laugh and waved at the enormous L-shaped sofa that dominated one corner of the room.

'Please, have a seat.'

I took a step towards it.

'Don't bother, Vik, we're leaving immediately.'

Yvonne was framed in the doorway of one bedroom, now wearing jeans and a red sweater, gripping a large shoulder bag. She crossed the room to stand beside me. Pine looked confused, then amused and then, as Yvonne took hold of my arm, angry. He took a step forwards.

'Yvonne? What's going on?'

Yvonne stood her ground and glared at him. We could have been standing in the Anchor in Weston-Super-Mare, with Yvonne facing down Spike and the London lads. I felt a twitch of pride.

'Ah'm leaving, Wilton, that's what's happening. And Vik here is helping me.'

'You're…leaving?'

'Aye, that's what I said. You going deaf in your old age?'

I touched Yvonne's fingers. They were trembling. 'Yvonne.'

'It's OK, Vik,' Yvonne replied, 'let's just go.'

She took a step towards the door of the apartment, but Pine moved sideways to intercept her.

'Actually, Vik, it's not OK,' Wilton said. 'I don't know what you've said to your ex-girlfriend, but whatever it is, she is clearly confused and in no right mind to make any career decisions. And what you need, Von,' he slipped a hand in his jacket pocket, 'is a quick boost to sort yourself out.' He pulled out a small cellophane bag with what looked like cocaine in it.

For a moment, Yvonne paused and looked at the package dangling from Pine's fingers, but then she shook her head and marched forwards.

'It's too late, Wilton. I'm not going there any more. Vik is going to help me kick my habit.'

'He's going to what?'

'Help me stop using.'

'Stop…using?' Pine threw back his head and laughed. 'You're kidding yourself, sweetheart. You can't just stop when you want to. You've no idea. And you are not going to just walk out on me when you feel like it. Do you understand? You signed a contract.'

'What I understand, Wilton,' Yvonne spat, tightening her grip on my arm and her bag, 'is that you are a nasty piece of shit who I should never have got involved with in the first place. But now I can see that, I am no longer staying another minute. Now get the fuck out of our way.'

So saying, Yvonne pulled me another few steps towards the front door but Pine was too quick for her. With a couple of large strides, he was beside us, and before I realised what he was doing, he had yanked her out of my grasp. He pulled her into his body.

'I think not,' he snarled. 'You are staying right here with me, and you –' he pointed a finger at me, '– you can get the fuck out of my apartment or I'll call security and tell them you threatened me. Now.'

Yvonne struggled to break his hold on her. 'Get yer hands off me, Wilton, before I wrench them off.'

Pine laughed at her bravado, but even to my eyes she seemed weak and very vulnerable. Yvonne tried to stamp on his foot, but Pine dodged her easily. She was a slip of a thing compared to six months ago, thin and pale. Yvonne looked furious, but I could also see the first inklings of something else in her eyes: numbness? acceptance?

I looked down at the glass coffee table next to me. A sandstone figure of a kneeling woman, about ten inches high, stood on the table top. I bent down and picked it up with my left hand before transferring it to my right, robot hand. I held it up and paused while I caught Pine's eye; he just sneered at me, and in that moment I knew he had no idea what my hand could do. I hurled it downwards through the glass surface. The table top shattered into a multitude of pieces. Pine and Yvonne both flinched.

'I suggest,' I said in a far calmer voice than I felt, 'that you let Yvonne leave. Unless you want me to give you another demonstration of what this hand can do.' I glanced down at his arm. 'I've never tried to grip a human wrist with it before, but I am quite interested to find out what would happen if I squeezed one. Maybe my mechanics might malfunction out of my control.'

I held Pine's gaze as confidently as I could, while my heart was beating rapidly against my chest. I couldn't crush a human with my robot hand – the smart sensor pads on the finger tips weren't designed that way. If I clutched Pine's hand with mine, then all that would happen is that we would exchange a firm handshake. But Pine wasn't to know that. I hoped.

For a moment, I thought Pine was going to call my bluff, but then he sneered and pushed Yvonne away from him. She immediately spun on her heels. 'Wilton, if ye ever touch me again, I swear I will shove ma guitar so far up yer arse, you won't be able to sit down for a week.'

Part of my inside glowed. That was the Yvonne I remembered. She grabbed her bag.

'Come on, Vik.'

As we left, Yvonne took my left hand and squeezed it. Emotions shot right up my arm and down my other side, and I swear the fingers on my robot hand twitched of their own accord.

That evening, I bought our plane tickets for London. They were eye-wateringly expensive, but by now I didn't care. I bought Yvonne a single, myself a return, with my flight coming back a week later to satisfy Myra.

It was thirteen months since we had arrived together in New York. We departed simultaneously too, just no longer together.

Part 4

London to Inverness

Nineteen

London, Autumn 1994

We arrived back in London after a hellish flight, during which Yvonne suffered both diarrhoea and vomiting, and got a taxi direct to Ajay and Ritika's flat. I had phoned my brother the day before we left New York and pleaded with him to let us stay in their spare room again, just for the week. I had considered not telling him about Yvonne's condition and her aim of quitting drugs, but I knew they would find out soon enough once she was going cold turkey. So I decided to divulge the truth. I could hear the shock in Ajay's voice, but it was Ritika we were more concerned about. Ajay passed me over to speak to her direct, and I promised her that if Yvonne was ever too much for her to handle then we would leave. She agreed, and I thought I heard a tiny bit of satisfaction in her voice, bordering on schadenfreude, as if she had predicted where Yvonne was heading. She even offered to let me use their blow-up mattress so I could sleep in their spare room with Yvonne, and not have to crash on their sofa in the living room. I was sure that was more for their benefit than mine, but I couldn't argue.

We knew how difficult it was going to be for Yvonne, so as soon as we were installed at Ajay's, she immediately contacted a London drugs charity to get their help and advice. She also called Terry.

Yvonne knew she could trust Terry with his experience of bands going off the rails, and he would know just how to talk to her. We were both delighted when he took Yvonne's call, as we weren't sure how his health was, or if he would want to see us again. Terry admitted he had been sad when The Libertine Dolls had gone their separate ways, but he didn't hold any grudges.

'Besides,' he added when we met, gently tapping his heart, 'I can't afford to get upset any more about something as trivial as a few guitarists having a spat.'

Yvonne hugged him until June told her to let go or he might stop breathing again.

With Terry's and my support, Yvonne kept her word and went cold turkey, but there were times when I could see her suffering, or when she woke up crying.

Terry and June also updated us on what had happened to the other women from The Libertine Dolls. Keisha had gone off on her own and Terry had heard that she had joined a new band. Jane and Steph had auditioned for Louis Vance's manufactured girl band, but were rejected. I felt sorry for our two friends, and it seemed as if The Libertine Dolls had broken up for no reason. Terry said Jane was still singing in pubs, but he hadn't heard from Steph for months.

While Yvonne was recovering in the flat, I wandered around London, visiting some of my old haunts, bringing her back anything she requested. The day of my return flight to New York seemed impossibly soon. Yvonne was suffering from terrible pains and nausea, and for the first few days, hardly left her bed. The evening before my flight back to New York, Ajay and Ritika were out and I sat with Yvonne in front of their TV and we watched some vintage comedy together. I made some soup and we laughed for a long time at the familiar sketches.

'I can't go back to New York yet,' I said, as the credits rolled.

Yvonne reached out to stroke my hair. I thought of the restaurant and what would be happening there. I was sure that Gina would be managing it fine. It was far more important that I continued to help Yvonne.

When I explained this to Myra from the payphone opposite the flat, there was a palpable silence.

'So I guess you've made your decision,' she said. 'Is this open-ended, Vik? Because I'll have to get some cover in.'

'I understand, but I have to do this. I promise I will be back in a few weeks and I'll work double-shifts to make up the time.'

There was a long silence.

'We'll talk when you're back,' Myra said bluntly.

'I told Myra I'd be back in a few weeks,' I said when Yvonne opened the front door to me.

She nodded as if nothing important had happened, and waved me back inside the flat. 'There's a great film on, it's just starting. Did you get the stuff I asked for from the corner shop?'

I managed to change my airline ticket to a later date, and while Yvonne's health gradually improved with the help of the charity and Terry's regular visits, I took the opportunity to visit my parents in Yorkshire.

Mum cried when she saw my arm again, and then sobbed even more when I showed her my photos of Uncle Neel and Aunt Elizabeth.

'They've done so much for me,' I said to my parents. 'They're good people.'

My mother nodded and stroked the photograph. 'He looks so happy.'

'He is. Well, he's happy he's married to Elizabeth. But I know he still hurts that he hasn't seen you or your sisters for so long.'

'You have to understand, Vikram, it was so difficult. We had only just arrived in England and we needed to support each other as a family, and when he said he wouldn't marry the bride who had been chosen for him, well, it hurt everyone. Our parents were devastated.'

'It hasn't been easy for your mother either,' Dad chipped in.

I nodded and gave Mum a hug.

'I have been thinking about this since you wrote to us. And I do regret it,' my mother said sadly. 'But it's too late now. What can I do?'

'I don't think it is too late,' I said. 'I know Uncle Neel would love to hear from you. Maybe it's time to move on.'

She nodded. 'I will write to him. It will be the first time he has heard from any of us in over twenty years.'

I didn't mention Aunt Prisha, that would have to wait for another day.

My mother closed her eyes, and for a moment, I thought she was just tired, but then I saw her bottom lip tremble and tears started to flow down her cheeks again. My father and I wrapped our arms around her. We stood like that for several minutes before Mum wiped her eyes and went into the kitchen to make dinner. Dad poured the two of us more tea.

'One question, Vikram,' he said. 'How did you find out where Uncle Neel was living?'

'I, ah, looked in the New York phonebook,' I said quickly. 'I remembered someone in the family had said he was last heard of living on the East Coast, and I guess I struck lucky.'

Dad tilted his head on one side. Then I brought out my robot hand out of my bag and my father choked on his tea.

Ajay and I spent as much time together as we could. Although we had exchanged letters while I had been in New York, I hadn't gone into detail about my experiences there. Consequently, we spent many evenings together, my brother listening in awe as I filled him in about Neel and Elizabeth and our uncle's success in America, and we discussed with some dismay how sad it was that we had been given such a different spin on the story by our parents. It wasn't long before Ajay was making plans to visit New York.

I showed him and Ritika photos of The Kosher Delhi. They were horrified by my account of Aaron Stoats' attack, and amazed at my robot hand. Ajay insisted on trying it, even though it worked erratically for him as it had been specifically moulded for my arm. I also cooked for them whenever they asked – that was my deal for letting Yvonne and me stay longer than our original one week plan.

I rang Gina a few times and during every conversation she sounded busier. She told me that the interim head chef Myra had employed had made her own mark on the menu and was settling in well, although it wasn't the same without me. It made me realise how much I missed the restaurant.

Twenty

Inverness, November 1994

Five days after I visited my parents, I disembarked from a plane and walked through the arrival doors at Inverness airport. Yvonne was in the arrivals lounge to meet me. She waved as I came through the doors and I noticed immediately that her hair was back to the short, spiky, peroxide style it used to be. She was wearing a short, tartan dress and black leggings underneath a heavy Army style coat. A pair of sunglasses were propped on her forehead, despite it being November. She put her arms around my neck to pull me in, but we didn't kiss.

I nodded at her overcoat. 'New style?'

Yvonne pulled it open and did a quick twirl. 'You like it? It's my da's but I borrowed it cos it's so pigging cold today.'

'So how did it go? The big reunion, I mean.'

It was hard to believe that when Yvonne had arrived again in Inverness a few days prior, it was the first time she had seen her parents since she had left to go to Leeds University. That was eight years previously.

'Better than I had thought it might,' she said cautiously. 'There were a lot of tears at first, and it was all a bit awkward. They'd seen photos of me in New York, of course, and I tried to explain how the media overdramatise everything, but I showed them the better reviews I had of *Boon!* and that made them happy. And then Ma cooked a big meal and we didn't stop gassing all evening.'

Her eyes were damp and moments later, she slipped her shades over them.

'I'm sorry, Yvonne, it must have been tough.'

'It's OK, Vik, I needed to do all this. I want to do it.'

I gave her an awkward hug and patted her sleeves. 'This is heavy material. I didn't think you felt the cold.'

'I told you before. Scotland has proper cold, not your namby-pamby Somerset temperatures. Now, are you ready to go?'

I held out a small package, wrapped in red and white wrapping paper, tied with a blue ribbon.

'Happy birthday for last month, Yvonne. It's just a small memento.'

Yvonne grabbed it with both hands and shook it. 'I wonder what it is?' For some reason, she held it up to her ear. 'Nah, I think I'll open it later. Thanks, Vik.' She placed a kiss on my cheek. 'Come on, I want to show you where I grew up. I'll take you on a mini-tour of my childhood haunts.'

'Are we not getting a taxi to your house first?'

We left the terminal building and headed for a small car park. Yvonne was right, it was bloody cold. Inverness airport is on the edge of the Moray Firth, and as I only had a lightweight fleece which Ajay had lent me, I felt the wind whip right through my bones. I also had to squint because the sun was bright and low in the sky.

Yvonne pulled out a car key from her pocket and twiddled it around her forefinger. 'Nope. Today, you get chauffeured around by me.'

We reached an old Ford with a dent in the passenger door, and empty crisp packets and squashed cans of Irn-Bru lying in the footwell.

'This is my da's as well, in case you're wondering. Sorry about the mess, we…haven't had much time to clear it up. I've been out walking with them most days. Imagine that! Me, hiking!'

'How did you find that?'

'It was tough, but it was really good for me. Helped me blow away some final cobwebs from my habit.'

I reached over my shoulder for the seat belt. 'Do you realise this is the first time I've been in a car just with you? I didn't even know you could drive.'

Yvonne tutted. 'I learned when I lived here. Most of my gang learned as soon as we could, so we could get to pubs and raves out of town. Can you not drive?'

'I never learned. Never needed to.'

We pulled out of the airport, and I studied Yvonne again as she manoeuvred between two slower cars. Her dress was riding high on her thighs, and although she had thick leggings on, I couldn't help but glance down.

Staring straight ahead, Yvonne said, 'I can see you checking me out. Don't try to deny it.'

I half-smiled. 'Actually, I was thinking how well you look. But more importantly, how are you feeling? Are you…coming along?'

Yvonne shifted into fourth gear. 'You mean, am I still coping having gone cold turkey on the heroin? Aye, I'm managing. It's no easy some of the time, but I'm keeping my mind on other things. But I won't lie to you, Vik, there are times when I could still do with a fix. But I don't do it. I won't.'

'I'm glad. Do your parents know about your addiction?'

'Not yet. I just told them I'd been ill. Ma isn't so well herself. But I will tell them, I just need a bit of time. Find the right moment.'

'I'm sure it'll be fine.'

Yvonne gave a small nod.

We drove on in silence, passing flat, expansive, wind-driven fields, sometimes inhabited with flocks of grazing sheep, the Cairngorms in the distance. Finally, we entered a suburb of Inverness. The weather had changed, the sun replaced by clouds. Yvonne turned down a side street, and stopped by a pair of high, wrought iron gates. She switched the engine off and sat still for a moment staring ahead. Then she turned and looked out of the car, through the gates.

'This is where we buried Kirstine.' She opened the door. 'Come on, I'll show you.'

We pushed open the gates. There was no one else in the cemetery. We wrapped our coats around us, and Yvonne led the way down gravel paths, past many Victorian gravestones and untended plots until we came to the end of a row. There she stopped, looking down at a grave with fresh flowers laid by it. I stood beside her and read the words on the headstone: 'Kirstine Anderson, 1970–1986. Missed for ever by her parents and sister.' For the first time since we had returned from the US, Yvonne slipped her hand into mine and rested her head on my shoulder. I didn't resist. We stayed like that until a crow landed on a nearby gravestone and its caw startled us both.

'As much as I don't believe in God, this place does somehow give me comfort,' Yvonne said quietly. 'I can see why people want to believe. Ma and Da chose to bury her here. They felt it was right and who was I to argue?'

We fell silent again. There was some irony in Yvonne's last statement, but I wasn't about to mention that. I watched her bend down and rearrange the flowers.

'Do you think about her much now?'

Yvonne's voice cracked as she replied. 'If I didn't stop myself, I would think about her every day. But you can't live that way for ever.'

'I…guess not.'

'Alcohol helps, and drugs. And the rush you get from music. And even the odd Away Day. That adrenalin hit you get.' She paused. 'Distractions are what you need, so you don't have to think about the person you've lost.'

'Makes sense.'

'The trouble was, I carried on drinking and smoking way past when they were merely diversion techniques. Made myself go for months, years without properly thinking about Kirstine, without letting myself work through what happened. That was stupid of me, I know that now. But, well, you don't worry about it at the time.'

Yvonne stood up again and wrapped her arms around her body. 'I've talked to Ma about Kirstine every day since I've been home. I realised it was the first time I'd done that since we moved to Wesson. That's too long, isn't it.' She shook her head. 'We've cried constantly, but it's been so good talking about her again. Last night, Da got out some photos of all of us and we shared some stories that we remembered about her. I think it helped. Nothing we can say or do can change what happened, but that doesn't mean Kirstine didn't exist. She was, is still so important to us.'

'I wish you had let me help you by talking about her when we were living together.'

'I know, but I couldn't, Vik. I still wasn't ready.' She shook her head. 'It only seems like yesterday when we were living in the Hotel Neptune, drinking with Miles and Gary.'

I thought for a moment. 'That was nearly four years ago.'

'No!' Yvonne pulled away from me for a moment. 'It can't have been. Really?'

I nodded. 'And even longer since we met in Leeds.'

Yvonne squashed herself into the crook of my arm. 'You were so innocent then, weren't you! And I corrupted you with all my vices. Was that bad of me?'

'Part of me loved it.'

Yvonne laughed. 'And now look at you. A famous chef at one of New York's hippest restaurants. Who'd have thought.'

'You had your own fame.'

'Notoriety maybe.' Yvonne didn't speak for a minute. 'It's such a cliché to say that the exposure I had in New York went to my head. It wasn't the lifestyle so much, although as you know, the drugs got to me. And when you've just shot up, man, everything is worth it, everything is fan fucking tastic.

'No, it was more some inner hope that people would listen to me, to hear what I really cared about, what I wanted to say. Turns out they couldn't give a shit about what I thought as long as I flashed some skin. But it also turns out that I didn't have as much to say as I thought I did. Not when I was in that state anyway.' She kicked some gravel under her feet. 'I reckon I wasn't the only woman Wilton has exploited over the years. Looks like you were right about him.'

'Hmm.'

'Don't worry, Vik. I don't need New York any more. Not now that I've got you again.' Yvonne squeezed my arm. 'I'm going to stay here for a while. Stay home and stop running away. I need to look after Ma, she's not doing too well at the moment. Dougie's back here too so I know he'll help me. He's still a twat, but he knows what I went through with Kirstine, so he's a twat I can talk to.

'But, well, after that I thought that we, you and I, could find a little place together in London. I could start over with another band, an even better one this time. After all, there's nothing for me in the States now.'

'There is for me.' I stared at her. 'Yvonne… I wasn't expecting anything like this.'

'Come on, Vik.'

'I wasn't.' I tried to ease myself gently away from her, but Yvonne held me tight. 'Are you saying you want us to get back together?'

She traced her thumb over my arm.

'Of course. Don't you? Isn't that why you're still hanging around?'

I didn't respond. I thought about the KD, how much I'd missed it over the last few weeks. I thought about Yvonne and Wilton Stratford Pine, and all they had done to me. But I could also remember how I had loved being with her in Leeds and Wesson. Part of me wanted to believe what she was saying, that she was ready to turn over a new leaf. But I wasn't sure she could do so yet. And even if she could, did I really want her back? I ran my fingers over the top of Kirstine's gravestone and shivered.

Yvonne noticed. 'Did you feel something spiritual from the gravestone? Or are you cold?'

'I'm not warm… But, well, like you said, this place does make me think. It's not just Kirstine, is it, who has been on the wrong end of bigoted idiots. Poor Noah and Bumble got shot, even if it was by a man with a mental illness.'

'He was a racist, homophobic prick,' Yvonne agreed, 'but other people should be held accountable for how he felt.' She looked up at my face. 'You didn't answer my question, Vik. Do you think we could make it? What do you really want?'

'I know I want to cook,' I answered instantly. 'That's so clear to me now. That's what I want to do more than anything else. Although Myra has got an interim head chef, who Gina says is excelling.' Now it was my turn to scuff my toes in the dirt.

Yvonne seemed unconcerned. 'Well, in that case, couldn't you go back to being a chef in London instead? There must be all sorts of opportunities there for you now.'

I tried not to sound too exasperated. 'Do you not understand what the Kosher Delhi means to me, Yvonne?' Then I sighed. 'You know, I dropped in to see Chef Michel at Le Jardin when I was in London, and even he had heard about the food I was cooking in the KD. That means something.'

Yvonne scratched her arm. 'Aren't you scared of those bampots with guns, though?'

'You mean, am I frightened that some other madman will shoot more gay men or black people in other restaurants? More of my friends or staff?' I blew out my cheeks. 'I hadn't thought of it like that. Yes, I guess there is a part of me which is nervous, but what can I do? I have to go back. To do what I want to do, to stand up for what I believe in. You taught me that, Yvonne.'

We walked back to the car in silence, slowly at first and then more quickly as the first spots of rain began to fall. We yanked open the car doors and jumped in, brushing raindrops off our coats. The rain started to fall even heavier, and we sat there silently, watching it bounce off the windscreen.

Yvonne swivelled in her seat to face me. 'What happened to us, Vik?'

'What do you mean, what happened?'

'We had such a strong relationship.'

'I thought so too. At the time.'

'So what went wrong?'

'You cheated on me with Wilton Stratford Pine. I couldn't accept that.'

'But we were together for so long. One fuck ruined all that?'

'You know it was more than one fuck,' I spat. 'You'd been seeing Pine behind my back. That hurt.' I sighed, and my shoulders sagged. I said more quietly, 'I idolised you, Yvonne. For four years, you showed me what I had been missing in my life, you gave me a new zest for life. I loved being with you and being around you. But I was always worried that you might leave me, and I was constantly on edge. And…too often it was all about you. That was hard to live with sometimes. I mean, we were quite different people, weren't we?'

'That didn't matter.'

'I know that. And…and I thought you liked being with me.'

Yvonne reached out and hovered her fingers over the end of my right arm. 'You were so good for me. We had some wonderful times.'

'Then why did you go off with Wilton fucking Pine?'

My outburst came from nowhere. Suddenly, I did want to know why she had ruined our relationship, drained my self-belief. It wasn't fair, wasn't right. I banged my left fist on the car door. Beside me, I heard Yvonne catch her breath, and when I looked up, she had pushed herself back into her seat and, to my surprise, she seemed nervous. I had never seen her look afraid before just because someone raised their voice to her.

I sighed again, sat back in my seat and closed my eyes. 'I'm sorry, I didn't mean to shout. You just…touched a nerve. You know, I've risked my job at the KD to come back with you, and I don't even know if Myra will keep me on.'

Yvonne seemed to relax. 'It's OK. I shouted at you enough during our time together. It's just, well, since Wilton hit me, now when someone yells at me, I tense up. It's an automatic reaction.' She took a deep breath. 'God, listen to me, it's pathetic, isn't it. Look at what I've become. A recovering addict, fearful of the smallest thing.'

She shook her head. 'Wilton was so manipulative, Vik, I can't believe I couldn't see that. I thought I was so mature, so life-savvy, fully in control of my own destiny. Surely I would see through someone like him.' A long pause. 'Apparently not.'

The rain continued to hammer down on the glass, and now I could only see a few yards into the cemetery past its gates.

'Is it too late?' Yvonne's voice was a whisper, and she said it without looking at me.

We watched a couple fleeing to their car with bags over their heads.

'For us, I mean?' she said. 'For you and me?'

Was it too late? I looked down at the footwell. 'You captivated me when we first met, Yvonne. I adored and worshipped you for years.'

Yvonne's voice cracked. 'So we could start again?'

The couple had now reached their car but the man couldn't find his keys, and the woman was shouting at him across the bonnet.

I thought about the time after I left Yvonne: the first few weeks of waking up with a hollow feeling in my chest, the growing bitterness, the constant dejection and misery I had felt. Until one day, I had woken up and that pain was gone; and for a short while, I even missed that. At least that meant I was feeling something.

But then I realised I didn't want that anguish and sadness any more, and I could get on with – commit to – the rest of my life. I saw what I could do with my cooking aspirations, what I wanted from The Kosher Delhi. That was what had begun to inspire me again and was driving me now. And as much as I had loved Yvonne, still cared for her…

'I'm sorry, Yvonne. I can't go through all that again with you. It's not what I want any more. After everything I've witnessed in the last few years… I want to make a success of The Kosher Delhi. That's where my life is now, that's where I'm going. And you know you need to sort yourself out.'

I stared straight ahead through the car windscreen. Out of the corner of my eye, I could see Yvonne was crestfallen, but was trying not to show it. She said nothing for several minutes, before she nodded and examined her reflection in the rear-view mirror. Then she looked over her shoulder.

'Your present,' she said brightly, reaching into the back seat. 'I forgot.' She picked it up and shook it again. 'Should I open it now?'

I shrugged. 'Good as time as any. Don't be expecting anything expensive, though.'

Yvonne tore off the wrapping paper and held up the framed photograph inside. It was a photo taken by June after The Libertine Dolls supported Tabitha's Secret at the Town and Country club. All the women in The Libertine Dolls were grinning insanely, Terry was standing behind them holding up a bottle of Moët, and Yvonne had her arm around my shoulder. For once, I was smiling, and I didn't have my right hand tucked away in my pocket.

Yvonne sat in the driver's seat and stared at the photo for two minutes without moving, without saying a word. She didn't need to, I knew what she was thinking. Then she gave me a sad smile, turned on the ignition, and we drove off in silence.

We didn't talk any further about our relationship. I stayed with Yvonne's family that night. Met her ma and da, went to the pub, met Dougie again. Yvonne was right, he was still a twat, but somehow he seemed a milder twat than I remembered. I knew he would look out for Yvonne – if she needed someone to look out for her.

I flew back to London the next day, and twenty-four hours later I was on a Boeing 747 bound for JFK airport in New York.

Epilogue

New York, two years later

It's the height of another busy lunch serving at The Kosher Delhi. The kitchen is raucous, the volume is turned up high in the restaurant, plates are flying out of the door.

I am at my station, preparing my special gefilte fish curry. I start to gut a bluefish. My robot hand is showing a few knife scars, but it's so much a part of me now that I can't imagine life without it. Neel says he has a 'new generation' hand he wants me to try when I'm ready. I'm excited by that, but I'm perfectly happy with my old one.

The sweat is pouring off me.

Jan, one of my commis chefs, calls across: 'Chef, phone call for you.'

I shout back, 'It's the middle of serving! Tell them to call back later.'

A pause while Jan listens to the caller. 'The woman on the line wants me to tell you that you should, er, get your arse over to the phone, um, pronto...'

Around me, voices lower as they hear what Jan says. They wait for my response.

I shout back, 'What?! Who the hell is it?'

Jan says, 'I don't know, chef, sorry. She's got a Scottish accent. Says she totally gets it now and that you're gonna want to speak to her.'

I put my knife down instantly. I walk across to the phone, quicker than I mean to, nod at Jan that he is dismissed, pause and then snatch up the receiver.

'Hello?'

Acknowledgements

First, I want to thank everyone at RedDoor for believing in *The Kosher Delhi*. You've made me very happy.

My thanks to everyone who read my early drafts and gave me encouragement; in particular, my brother, Max, who made me think for the first time that this might be *the* book; and to Sarah Clarke, Ruth Buller, Dawn Varley and Jacqui Dunne who all gave me feedback and occasionally hard but deserved and very helpful criticism.

And to my editor, Sadie Mayne, who challenged and helped me on so much of the structure of the manuscript (right down to the recipe at the end of the book!). It would not have ended up as the novel it is without her input.

My thanks to Frank Turner for letting me use his lyrics; I think I was almost as excited when he said yes to that as I was when RedDoor offered me a publishing contract!

I want to thank my parents for bringing me up to believe in what's right.

And finally: I also promised myself that if I ever did get a novel published then I would thank my A-level examiners, because if they hadn't given me the crap marks which they did bestow on me, and which meant I had to subsequently change my whole plans for the following years, then my life would never have turned out the way it has. And I'm eternally grateful for that. So thank you – whoever you were.

Book Club Questions

If you would like some questions to consider for your book club, you can download a document from the author's website:

www.ivanwainewright.com/KDQuestions

About the Author

© Laura Ward lauraward.co.uk

Ivan Wainewright lives in Kent with his partner, Sarah, and their slightly neurotic rescue dog, Remi. Before moving to Kent, he lived in North London, Leeds and Singapore.

When not writing, he can be found watching (and occasionally playing) football, running, listening to music from Chumbawamba to Led Zeppelin, arguing over politics and trying to cook. He has been an independent IT consultant for many years, working solely with charities and not-for-profit organisations.

The Kosher Delhi is his first novel, and he is currently working on his second book.

www.ivanwainewright.com

Vik's Gefilte Fish Curry Recipe

Serves 4-6

Ingredients

For the gefilte fish

- 800g white fish fillets, ground
- 2 large onions, finely chopped
- 4 extra large eggs
- ½ – 1 tsp salt
- 175g sugar
- Black pepper
- 600g matzo meal
- Cabbage leaves (for steaming)

For the curry

- 1 tsp cumin seeds
- 2 tsp coriander seeds
- 9 black peppercorns
- ¾ tsp mustard seeds
- ¾ tsp turmeric powder
- Red chilli powder (qb)
- 15g garlic
- 1 large onion, one half finely diced, one half more roughly chopped
- 600ml water
- Vegetable oil

Method

First, prepare the gefilte fish.

- Grind the onions into the fish.
- Mix together the fish/onions, eggs, salt, sugar, pepper until well blended.
- Adjust seasonings to taste.
- Add matzo meal slowly, mixing very well, until it is almost thick enough to shape into balls.

- Cover the bowl and refrigerate for at least one hour, or even overnight.
- When the mixture is ready, remove from the refrigerator and form the fish mixture into balls.

Steam the fish balls
- Take a large, wide pan or heavy casserole dish, with a tight-fitting lid. Put a rack that stands at least 5cm high inside it. (A cake rack is one option). Fill the pot with water to a depth of 2½ cm.
- Line the rack with a layer of cabbage leaves. Bring the water in the pot to a boil.
- Gently place as many fish balls on top of the cabbage leaves as will fit comfortably in a single layer without touching. (You may need to do this in batches.) Place another layer of cabbage leaves over the fish balls and cover the pot tightly.
- Turn the heat down to medium and steam for 20 to 25 minutes, until the fish balls are completely cooked through.
- Remove and put on one side.

For the curry
- Place all the spices, garlic, the roughly chopped onion and 200ml of water in a blender and blend until smooth.
- Fry the remaining onion in a pan with vegetable oil until light brown.
- Add the spice paste and cook over a medium heat until the water has dried up, then continue cooking the paste for 6–7 minutes, stirring regularly.
- Add more water, season and bring to a boil.
- Cook over a moderate heat for 10-12 minutes.
- Add the cooked gefilte fish balls and simmer over a low heat for 1–2 minutes until they are warmed through.

Find out more about RedDoor Publishing and sign up to our newsletter to hear about our **latest releases, author events**, exciting **competitions** and more at

reddoorpublishing.com

YOU CAN ALSO FOLLOW US:

   @RedDoorBooks

   RedDoorPublishing

   @RedDoorBooks